King Henry VI
Parts 1,
William Sh

Dramatis Personae

King Henry VI
Duke of Gloucester, *uncle to the King, and Protector*
Duke of Bedford, *uncle to the King, and Regent of France*
Thomas Beaufort, *Duke of Exeter, great-uncle to the King*
Henry Beaufort, *great-uncle to the King, Bishop of Winchester, and afterwards Cardinal*
John Beaufort, *Earl, afterwards Duke, of Somerset*
Richard Plantagenet, *son of Richard late Earl of Cambridge, afterwards Duke of York*
Earl of Warwick
Earl of Salisbury
Earl of Suffolk
Lord Talbot *afterwards Earl of Shrewsbury*
John Talbot, *his son*
Edmund Mortimer, *Earl of March*
Sir John Fastolfe
Sir William Lucy
Sir William Glansdale
Sir Thomas Gargrave
Mayor of London
Woodvile, *Lieutenant of the Tower*
Vernon, *of the White-Rose or York faction*
Basset, *of the Red-Rose or Lancaster faction*
A Lawyer
Mortimer's Keepers
Charles, *Dauphin, and afterwards King of France*
Reignier, *Duke of Anjou, and titular King of Naples*
Duke of Burgundy
Duke of Alencon
Bastard of Orleans
Governor of Paris
Master-Gunner of Orleans, and his Son
General of the French forces in Bourdeaux
A French Sergeant
A Porter
An old Shepherd, *father to Joan la Pucelle*
Margaret, *daughter to Reignier, afterwards married to King Henry*
Countess of Auvergne
Joan la Pucelle, *commonly called Joan of Arc*
Lords, Warders of the Tower, Heralds, Officers, Soldiers, Messengers, and Attendants
Fiends appearing to La Pucelle

ACT I
SCENE I. Westminster Abbey.
Dead March. Enter the Funeral of KING HENRY the Fifth, attended on by Dukes of BEDFORD, Regent of France; GLOUCESTER, Protector; and EXETER, Earl of WARWICK, the BISHOP OF WINCHESTER, Heralds, & c

BEDFORD
Hung be the heavens with black, yield day to night!
Comets, importing change of times and states,
Brandish your crystal tresses in the sky,
And with them scourge the bad revolting stars
That have consented unto Henry's death!
King Henry the Fifth, too famous to live long!
England ne'er lost a king of so much worth.
GLOUCESTER
England ne'er had a king until his time.
Virtue he had, deserving to command:
His brandish'd sword did blind men with his beams:
His arms spread wider than a dragon's wings;
His sparking eyes, replete with wrathful fire,
More dazzled and drove back his enemies
Than mid-day sun fierce bent against their faces.
What should I say? his deeds exceed all speech:
He ne'er lift up his hand but conquered.
EXETER

We mourn in black: why mourn we not in blood?
Henry is dead and never shall revive:
Upon a wooden coffin we attend,
And death's dishonourable victory
We with our stately presence glorify,
Like captives bound to a triumphant car.
What! shall we curse the planets of mishap
That plotted thus our glory's overthrow?
Or shall we think the subtle-witted French
Conjurers and sorcerers, that afraid of him
By magic verses have contrived his end?
BISHOP OF WINCHESTER
He was a king bless'd of the King of kings.
Unto the French the dreadful judgement-day
So dreadful will not be as was his sight.
The battles of the Lord of hosts he fought:
The church's prayers made him so prosperous.
GLOUCESTER
The church! where is it? Had not churchmen pray'd,
His thread of life had not so soon decay'd:
None do you like but an effeminate prince,
Whom, like a school-boy, you may over-awe.
BISHOP OF WINCHESTER
Gloucester, whate'er we like, thou art protector
And lookest to command the prince and realm.
Thy wife is proud; she holdeth thee in awe,
More than God or religious churchmen may.
GLOUCESTER
Name not religion, for thou lovest the flesh,
And ne'er throughout the year to church thou go'st
Except it be to pray against thy foes.
BEDFORD
Cease, cease these jars and rest your minds in peace:
Let's to the altar: heralds, wait on us:
Instead of gold, we'll offer up our arms:
Since arms avail not now that Henry's dead.
Posterity, await for wretched years,
When at their mothers' moist eyes babes shall suck,
Our isle be made a nourish of salt tears,
And none but women left to wail the dead.
Henry the Fifth, thy ghost I invocate:
Prosper this realm, keep it from civil broils,
Combat with adverse planets in the heavens!
A far more glorious star thy soul will make
Than Julius Caesar or bright--
Enter a Messenger
Messenger
My honourable lords, health to you all!
Sad tidings bring I to you out of France,
Of loss, of slaughter and discomfiture:
Guienne, Champagne, Rheims, Orleans,
Paris, Guysors, Poictiers, are all quite lost.
BEDFORD
What say'st thou, man, before dead Henry's corse?
Speak softly, or the loss of those great towns
Will make him burst his lead and rise from death.
GLOUCESTER
Is Paris lost? is Rouen yielded up?
If Henry were recall'd to life again,
These news would cause him once more yield the ghost.
EXETER

How were they lost? what treachery was used?
Messenger
No treachery; but want of men and money.
Amongst the soldiers this is muttered,
That here you maintain several factions,
And whilst a field should be dispatch'd and fought,
You are disputing of your generals:
One would have lingering wars with little cost;
Another would fly swift, but wanteth wings;
A third thinks, without expense at all,
By guileful fair words peace may be obtain'd.
Awake, awake, English nobility!
Let not sloth dim your horrors new-begot:
Cropp'd are the flower-de-luces in your arms;
Of England's coat one half is cut away.
EXETER
Were our tears wanting to this funeral,
These tidings would call forth their flowing tides.
BEDFORD
Me they concern; Regent I am of France.
Give me my steeled coat. I'll fight for France.
Away with these disgraceful wailing robes!
Wounds will I lend the French instead of eyes,
To weep their intermissive miseries.
Enter to them another Messenger
Messenger
Lords, view these letters full of bad mischance.
France is revolted from the English quite,
Except some petty towns of no import:
The Dauphin Charles is crowned king of Rheims;
The Bastard of Orleans with him is join'd;
Reignier, Duke of Anjou, doth take his part;
The Duke of Alencon flieth to his side.
EXETER
The Dauphin crowned king! all fly to him!
O, whither shall we fly from this reproach?
GLOUCESTER
We will not fly, but to our enemies' throats.
Bedford, if thou be slack, I'll fight it out.
BEDFORD
Gloucester, why doubt'st thou of my forwardness?
An army have I muster'd in my thoughts,
Wherewith already France is overrun.
Enter another Messenger
Messenger
My gracious lords, to add to your laments,
Wherewith you now bedew King Henry's hearse,
I must inform you of a dismal fight
Betwixt the stout Lord Talbot and the French.
BISHOP
OF WINCHESTER
What! wherein Talbot overcame? is't so?
Messenger
O, no; wherein Lord Talbot was o'erthrown:
The circumstance I'll tell you more at large.
The tenth of August last this dreadful lord,
Retiring from the siege of Orleans,
Having full scarce six thousand in his troop.
By three and twenty thousand of the French
Was round encompassed and set upon.
No leisure had he to enrank his men;
He wanted pikes to set before his archers;
Instead whereof sharp stakes pluck'd out of hedges

They pitched in the ground confusedly,
To keep the horsemen off from breaking in.
More than three hours the fight continued;
Where valiant Talbot above human thought
Enacted wonders with his sword and lance:
Hundreds he sent to hell, and none durst stand him;
Here, there, and every where, enraged he flew:
The French exclaim'd, the devil was in arms;
All the whole army stood agazed on him:
His soldiers spying his undaunted spirit
A Talbot! a Talbot! cried out amain
And rush'd into the bowels of the battle.
Here had the conquest fully been seal'd up,
If Sir John Fastolfe had not play'd the coward:
He, being in the vaward, placed behind
With purpose to relieve and follow them,
Cowardly fled, not having struck one stroke.
Hence grew the general wreck and massacre;
Enclosed were they with their enemies:
A base Walloon, to win the Dauphin's grace,
Thrust Talbot with a spear into the back,
Whom all France with their chief assembled strength
Durst not presume to look once in the face.
BEDFORD
Is Talbot slain? then I will slay myself,
For living idly here in pomp and ease,
Whilst such a worthy leader, wanting aid,
Unto his dastard foemen is betray'd.
Messenger
O no, he lives; but is took prisoner,
And Lord Scales with him and Lord Hungerford:
Most of the rest slaughter'd or took likewise.
BEDFORD
His ransom there is none but I shall pay:
I'll hale the Dauphin headlong from his throne:
His crown shall be the ransom of my friend;
Four of their lords I'll change for one of ours.
Farewell, my masters; to my task will I;
Bonfires in France forthwith I am to make,
To keep our great Saint George's feast withal:
Ten thousand soldiers with me I will take,
Whose bloody deeds shall make all Europe quake.
Messenger
So you had need; for Orleans is besieged;
The English army is grown weak and faint:
The Earl of Salisbury craveth supply,
And hardly keeps his men from mutiny,
Since they, so few, watch such a multitude.
EXETER
Remember, lords, your oaths to Henry sworn,
Either to quell the Dauphin utterly,
Or bring him in obedience to your yoke.
BEDFORD
I do remember it; and here take my leave,
To go about my preparation.
Exit
GLOUCESTER
I'll to the Tower with all the haste I can,
To view the artillery and munition;
And then I will proclaim young Henry king.
Exit
EXETER

To Eltham will I, where the young king is,
Being ordain'd his special governor,
And for his safety there I'll best devise.
Exit
BISHOP
OF WINCHESTER
Each hath his place and function to attend:
I am left out; for me nothing remains.
But long I will not be Jack out of office:
The king from Eltham I intend to steal
And sit at chiefest stern of public weal.
Exeunt

SCENE II. France. Before Orleans.
Sound a flourish. Enter CHARLES, ALENCON, and REIGNIER, marching with drum and Soldiers
CHARLES
Mars his true moving, even as in the heavens
So in the earth, to this day is not known:
Late did he shine upon the English side;
Now we are victors; upon us he smiles.
What towns of any moment but we have?
At pleasure here we lie near Orleans;
Otherwhiles the famish'd English, like pale ghosts,
Faintly besiege us one hour in a month.
ALENCON
They want their porridge and their fat bull-beeves:
Either they must be dieted like mules
And have their provender tied to their mouths
Or piteous they will look, like drowned mice.
REIGNIER
Let's raise the siege: why live we idly here?
Talbot is taken, whom we wont to fear:
Remaineth none but mad-brain'd Salisbury;
And he may well in fretting spend his gall,
Nor men nor money hath he to make war.
CHARLES
Sound, sound alarum! we will rush on them.
Now for the honour of the forlorn French!
Him I forgive my death that killeth me
When he sees me go back one foot or fly.
Exeunt
Here alarum; they are beaten back by the English with great loss. Re-enter CHARLES, ALENCON, and REIGNIER
CHARLES
Who ever saw the like? what men have I!
Dogs! cowards! dastards! I would ne'er have fled,
But that they left me 'midst my enemies.
REIGNIER
Salisbury is a desperate homicide;
He fighteth as one weary of his life.
The other lords, like lions wanting food,
Do rush upon us as their hungry prey.
ALENCON
Froissart, a countryman of ours, records,
England all Olivers and Rowlands bred,
During the time Edward the Third did reign.
More truly now may this be verified;
For none but Samsons and Goliases
It sendeth forth to skirmish. One to ten!
Lean, raw-boned rascals! who would e'er suppose
They had such courage and audacity?
CHARLES
Let's leave this town; for they are hare-brain'd slaves,
And hunger will enforce them to be more eager:

Of old I know them; rather with their teeth
The walls they'll tear down than forsake the siege.
REIGNIER
I think, by some odd gimmors or device
Their arms are set like clocks, stiff to strike on;
Else ne'er could they hold out so as they do.
By my consent, we'll even let them alone.
ALENCON
Be it so.
Enter the BASTARD OF ORLEANS
BASTARD OF ORLEANS
Where's the Prince Dauphin? I have news for him.
CHARLES
Bastard of Orleans, thrice welcome to us.
BASTARD OF ORLEANS
Methinks your looks are sad, your cheer appall'd:
Hath the late overthrow wrought this offence?
Be not dismay'd, for succor is at hand:
A holy maid hither with me I bring,
Which by a vision sent to her from heaven
Ordained is to raise this tedious siege
And drive the English forth the bounds of France.
The spirit of deep prophecy she hath,
Exceeding the nine sibyls of old Rome:
What's past and what's to come she can descry.
Speak, shall I call her in? Believe my words,
For they are certain and unfallible.
CHARLES
Go, call her in.
Exit BASTARD OF ORLEANS
But first, to try her skill,
Reignier, stand thou as Dauphin in my place:
Question her proudly; let thy looks be stern:
By this means shall we sound what skill she hath.
Re-enter the BASTARD OF ORLEANS, with JOAN LA PUCELLE
REIGNIER
Fair maid, is't thou wilt do these wondrous feats?
JOAN LA PUCELLE
Reignier, is't thou that thinkest to beguile me?
Where is the Dauphin? Come, come from behind;
I know thee well, though never seen before.
Be not amazed, there's nothing hid from me:
In private will I talk with thee apart.
Stand back, you lords, and give us leave awhile.
REIGNIER
She takes upon her bravely at first dash.
JOAN LA PUCELLE
Dauphin, I am by birth a shepherd's daughter,
My wit untrain'd in any kind of art.
Heaven and our Lady gracious hath it pleased
To shine on my contemptible estate:
Lo, whilst I waited on my tender lambs,
And to sun's parching heat display'd my cheeks,
God's mother deigned to appear to me
And in a vision full of majesty
Will'd me to leave my base vocation
And free my country from calamity:
Her aid she promised and assured success:
In complete glory she reveal'd herself;
And, whereas I was black and swart before,
With those clear rays which she infused on me
That beauty am I bless'd with which you see.
Ask me what question thou canst possible,

And I will answer unpremeditated:
My courage try by combat, if thou darest,
And thou shalt find that I exceed my sex.
Resolve on this, thou shalt be fortunate,
If thou receive me for thy warlike mate.
CHARLES
Thou hast astonish'd me with thy high terms:
Only this proof I'll of thy valour make,
In single combat thou shalt buckle with me,
And if thou vanquishest, thy words are true;
Otherwise I renounce all confidence.
JOAN LA PUCELLE
I am prepared: here is my keen-edged sword,
Deck'd with five flower-de-luces on each side;
The which at Touraine, in Saint Katharine's churchyard,
Out of a great deal of old iron I chose forth.
CHARLES
Then come, o' God's name; I fear no woman.
JOAN LA PUCELLE
And while I live, I'll ne'er fly from a man.
Here they fight, and JOAN LA PUCELLE overcomes
CHARLES
Stay, stay thy hands! thou art an Amazon
And fightest with the sword of Deborah.
JOAN LA PUCELLE
Christ's mother helps me, else I were too weak.
CHARLES
Whoe'er helps thee, 'tis thou that must help me:
Impatiently I burn with thy desire;
My heart and hands thou hast at once subdued.
Excellent Pucelle, if thy name be so,
Let me thy servant and not sovereign be:
'Tis the French Dauphin sueth to thee thus.
JOAN LA PUCELLE
I must not yield to any rites of love,
For my profession's sacred from above:
When I have chased all thy foes from hence,
Then will I think upon a recompense.
CHARLES
Meantime look gracious on thy prostrate thrall.
REIGNIER
My lord, methinks, is very long in talk.
ALENCON
Doubtless he shrives this woman to her smock;
Else ne'er could he so long protract his speech.
REIGNIER
Shall we disturb him, since he keeps no mean?
ALENCON
He may mean more than we poor men do know:
These women are shrewd tempters with their tongues.
REIGNIER
My lord, where are you? what devise you on?
Shall we give over Orleans, or no?
JOAN LA PUCELLE
Why, no, I say, distrustful recreants!
Fight till the last gasp; I will be your guard.
CHARLES
What she says I'll confirm: we'll fight it out.
JOAN LA PUCELLE
Assign'd am I to be the English scourge.
This night the siege assuredly I'll raise:
Expect Saint Martin's summer, halcyon days,

Since I have entered into these wars.
Glory is like a circle in the water,
Which never ceaseth to enlarge itself
Till by broad spreading it disperse to nought.
With Henry's death the English circle ends;
Dispersed are the glories it included.
Now am I like that proud insulting ship
Which Caesar and his fortune bare at once.
CHARLES
Was Mahomet inspired with a dove?
Thou with an eagle art inspired then.
Helen, the mother of great Constantine,
Nor yet Saint Philip's daughters, were like thee.
Bright star of Venus, fall'n down on the earth,
How may I reverently worship thee enough?
ALENCON
Leave off delays, and let us raise the siege.
REIGNIER
Woman, do what thou canst to save our honours;
Drive them from Orleans and be immortalized.
CHARLES
Presently we'll try: come, let's away about it:
No prophet will I trust, if she prove false.
Exeunt
SCENE III. London. Before the Tower.
Enter GLOUCESTER, with his Serving-men in blue coats
GLOUCESTER
I am come to survey the Tower this day:
Since Henry's death, I fear, there is conveyance.
Where be these warders, that they wait not here?
Open the gates; 'tis Gloucester that calls.
First Warder
[Within] Who's there that knocks so imperiously?
First Serving-Man It is the noble Duke of Gloucester.
Second Warder
[Within] Whoe'er he be, you may not be let in.
First Serving-Man Villains, answer you so the lord protector?
First Warder
[Within] The Lord protect him! so we answer him:
We do no otherwise than we are will'd.
GLOUCESTER
Who willed you? or whose will stands but mine?
There's none protector of the realm but I.
Break up the gates, I'll be your warrantize.
Shall I be flouted thus by dunghill grooms?
Gloucester's men rush at the Tower Gates, and WOODVILE the Lieutenant speaks within
WOODVILE
What noise is this? what traitors have we here?
GLOUCESTER
Lieutenant, is it you whose voice I hear?
Open the gates; here's Gloucester that would enter.
WOODVILE
Have patience, noble duke; I may not open;
The Cardinal of Winchester forbids:
From him I have express commandment
That thou nor none of thine shall be let in.
GLOUCESTER
Faint-hearted Woodvile, prizest him 'fore me?
Arrogant Winchester, that haughty prelate,
Whom Henry, our late sovereign, ne'er could brook?
Thou art no friend to God or to the king:
Open the gates, or I'll shut thee out shortly.

Serving-Men Open the gates unto the lord protector,
Or we'll burst them open, if that you come not quickly.
Enter to the Protector at the Tower Gates BISHOP OF WINCHESTER and his men in tawny coats

BISHOP OF WINCHESTER
How now, ambitious Humphry! what means this?

GLOUCESTER
Peel'd priest, dost thou command me to be shut out?

BISHOP OF WINCHESTER
I do, thou most usurping proditor,
And not protector, of the king or realm.

GLOUCESTER
Stand back, thou manifest conspirator,
Thou that contrivedst to murder our dead lord;
Thou that givest whores indulgences to sin:
I'll canvass thee in thy broad cardinal's hat,
If thou proceed in this thy insolence.

BISHOP OF WINCHESTER
Nay, stand thou back, I will not budge a foot:
This be Damascus, be thou cursed Cain,
To slay thy brother Abel, if thou wilt.

GLOUCESTER
I will not slay thee, but I'll drive thee back:
Thy scarlet robes as a child's bearing-cloth
I'll use to carry thee out of this place.

BISHOP OF WINCHESTER
Do what thou darest; I beard thee to thy face.

GLOUCESTER
What! am I dared and bearded to my face?
Draw, men, for all this privileged place;
Blue coats to tawny coats. Priest, beware your beard,
I mean to tug it and to cuff you soundly:
Under my feet I stamp thy cardinal's hat:
In spite of pope or dignities of church,
Here by the cheeks I'll drag thee up and down.

BISHOP OF WINCHESTER
Gloucester, thou wilt answer this before the pope.

GLOUCESTER
Winchester goose, I cry, a rope! a rope!
Now beat them hence; why do you let them stay?
Thee I'll chase hence, thou wolf in sheep's array.
Out, tawny coats! out, scarlet hypocrite!
Here GLOUCESTER's men beat out BISHOP OF WINCHESTER's men, and enter in the hurly- burly the Mayor of London and his Officers

Mayor
Fie, lords! that you, being supreme magistrates,
Thus contumeliously should break the peace!

GLOUCESTER
Peace, mayor! thou know'st little of my wrongs:
Here's Beaufort, that regards nor God nor king,
Hath here distrain'd the Tower to his use.

BISHOP OF WINCHESTER
Here's Gloucester, a foe to citizens,
One that still motions war and never peace,
O'ercharging your free purses with large fines,
That seeks to overthrow religion,
Because he is protector of the realm,

And would have armour here out of the Tower,
To crown himself king and suppress the prince.
GLOUCESTER
I will not answer thee with words, but blows.
Here they skirmish again
Mayor
Naught rests for me in this tumultuous strife
But to make open proclamation:
Come, officer; as loud as e'er thou canst,
Cry.
Officer
All manner of men assembled here in arms this day
against God's peace and the king's, we charge and
command you, in his highness' name, to repair to
your several dwelling-places; and not to wear,
handle, or use any sword, weapon, or dagger,
henceforward, upon pain of death.
GLOUCESTER
Cardinal, I'll be no breaker of the law:
But we shall meet, and break our minds at large.
BISHOP OF WINCHESTER
Gloucester, we will meet; to thy cost, be sure:
Thy heart-blood I will have for this day's work.
Mayor
I'll call for clubs, if you will not away.
This cardinal's more haughty than the devil.
GLOUCESTER
Mayor, farewell: thou dost but what thou mayst.
BISHOP OF WINCHESTER
Abominable Gloucester, guard thy head;
For I intend to have it ere long.
Exeunt, severally, GLOUCESTER and BISHOP OF WINCHESTER with their Serving-men
Mayor
See the coast clear'd, and then we will depart.
Good God, these nobles should such stomachs bear!
I myself fight not once in forty year.
Exeunt

SCENE IV. Orleans.
Enter, on the walls, a Master Gunner and his Boy
Master-Gunner Sirrah, thou know'st how Orleans is besieged,
And how the English have the suburbs won.
Boy
Father, I know; and oft have shot at them,
Howe'er unfortunate I miss'd my aim.
Master-Gunner But now thou shalt not. Be thou ruled by me:
Chief master-gunner am I of this town;
Something I must do to procure me grace.
The prince's espials have informed me
How the English, in the suburbs close intrench'd,
Wont, through a secret grate of iron bars
In yonder tower, to overpeer the city,
And thence discover how with most advantage
They may vex us with shot, or with assault.
To intercept this inconvenience,
A piece of ordnance 'gainst it I have placed;
And even these three days have I watch'd,
If I could see them.
Now do thou watch, for I can stay no longer.
If thou spy'st any, run and bring me word;
And thou shalt find me at the governor's.
Exit

Boy
Father, I warrant you; take you no care;
I'll never trouble you, if I may spy them.
Exit
Enter, on the turrets, SALISBURY and TALBOT, GLANSDALE, GARGRAVE, and others
SALISBURY
Talbot, my life, my joy, again return'd!
How wert thou handled being prisoner?
Or by what means got'st thou to be released?
Discourse, I prithee, on this turret's top.
TALBOT
The Duke of Bedford had a prisoner
Call'd the brave Lord Ponton de Santrailles;
For him was I exchanged and ransomed.
But with a baser man of arms by far
Once in contempt they would have barter'd me:
Which I, disdaining, scorn'd; and craved death,
Rather than I would be so vile esteem'd.
In fine, redeem'd I was as I desired.
But, O! the treacherous Fastolfe wounds my heart,
Whom with my bare fists I would execute,
If I now had him brought into my power.
SALISBURY
Yet tell'st thou not how thou wert entertain'd.
TALBOT
With scoffs and scorns and contumelious taunts.
In open market-place produced they me,
To be a public spectacle to all:
Here, said they, is the terror of the French,
The scarecrow that affrights our children so.
Then broke I from the officers that led me,
And with my nails digg'd stones out of the ground,
To hurl at the beholders of my shame:
My grisly countenance made others fly;
None durst come near for fear of sudden death.
In iron walls they deem'd me not secure;
So great fear of my name 'mongst them was spread,
That they supposed I could rend bars of steel,
And spurn in pieces posts of adamant:
Wherefore a guard of chosen shot I had,
That walked about me every minute-while;
And if I did but stir out of my bed,
Ready they were to shoot me to the heart.
Enter the Boy with a linstock
SALISBURY
I grieve to hear what torments you endured,
But we will be revenged sufficiently
Now it is supper-time in Orleans:
Here, through this grate, I count each one
and view the Frenchmen how they fortify:
Let us look in; the sight will much delight thee.
Sir Thomas Gargrave, and Sir William Glansdale,
Let me have your express opinions
Where is best place to make our battery next.
GARGRAVE
I think, at the north gate; for there stand lords.
GLANSDALE
And I, here, at the bulwark of the bridge.
TALBOT
For aught I see, this city must be famish'd,
Or with light skirmishes enfeebled.
Here they shoot. SALISBURY and GARGRAVE fall
SALISBURY

O Lord, have mercy on us, wretched sinners!
GARGRAVE
O Lord, have mercy on me, woful man!
TALBOT
What chance is this that suddenly hath cross'd us?
Speak, Salisbury; at least, if thou canst speak:
How farest thou, mirror of all martial men?
One of thy eyes and thy cheek's side struck off!
Accursed tower! accursed fatal hand
That hath contrived this woful tragedy!
In thirteen battles Salisbury o'ercame;
Henry the Fifth he first train'd to the wars;
Whilst any trump did sound, or drum struck up,
His sword did ne'er leave striking in the field.
Yet livest thou, Salisbury? though thy speech doth fail,
One eye thou hast, to look to heaven for grace:
The sun with one eye vieweth all the world.
Heaven, be thou gracious to none alive,
If Salisbury wants mercy at thy hands!
Bear hence his body; I will help to bury it.
Sir Thomas Gargrave, hast thou any life?
Speak unto Talbot; nay, look up to him.
Salisbury, cheer thy spirit with this comfort;
Thou shalt not die whiles--
He beckons with his hand and smiles on me.
As who should say 'When I am dead and gone,
Remember to avenge me on the French.'
Plantagenet, I will; and like thee, Nero,
Play on the lute, beholding the towns burn:
Wretched shall France be only in my name.
Here an alarum, and it thunders and lightens
What stir is this? what tumult's in the heavens?
Whence cometh this alarum and the noise?
Enter a Messenger
Messenger
My lord, my lord, the French have gathered head:
The Dauphin, with one Joan la Pucelle join'd,
A holy prophetess new risen up,
Is come with a great power to raise the siege.
Here SALISBURY lifteth himself up and groans
TALBOT
Hear, hear how dying Salisbury doth groan!
It irks his heart he cannot be revenged.
Frenchmen, I'll be a Salisbury to you:
Pucelle or puzzel, dolphin or dogfish,
Your hearts I'll stamp out with my horse's heels,
And make a quagmire of your mingled brains.
Convey me Salisbury into his tent,
And then we'll try what these dastard Frenchmen dare.
Alarum. Exeunt
SCENE V. The same.
Here an alarum again: and TALBOT pursueth the DAUPHIN, and driveth him: then enter JOAN LA PUCELLE, driving Englishmen before her, and exit after them then re-enter TALBOT
TALBOT
Where is my strength, my valour, and my force?
Our English troops retire, I cannot stay them:
A woman clad in armour chaseth them.
Re-enter JOAN LA PUCELLE
Here, here she comes. I'll have a bout with thee;
Devil or devil's dam, I'll conjure thee:
Blood will I draw on thee, thou art a witch,
And straightway give thy soul to him thou servest.
JOAN LA PUCELLE

Come, come, 'tis only I that must disgrace thee.
Here they fight
TALBOT
Heavens, can you suffer hell so to prevail?
My breast I'll burst with straining of my courage
And from my shoulders crack my arms asunder.
But I will chastise this high-minded strumpet.
They fight again
JOAN LA PUCELLE
Talbot, farewell; thy hour is not yet come:
I must go victual Orleans forthwith.
A short alarum; then enter the town with soldiers
O'ertake me, if thou canst; I scorn thy strength.
Go, go, cheer up thy hungry-starved men;
Help Salisbury to make his testament:
This day is ours, as many more shall be.
Exit
TALBOT
My thoughts are whirled like a potter's wheel;
I know not where I am, nor what I do;
A witch, by fear, not force, like Hannibal,
Drives back our troops and conquers as she lists:
So bees with smoke and doves with noisome stench
Are from their hives and houses driven away.
They call'd us for our fierceness English dogs;
Now, like to whelps, we crying run away.
A short alarum
Hark, countrymen! either renew the fight,
Or tear the lions out of England's coat;
Renounce your soil, give sheep in lions' stead:
Sheep run not half so treacherous from the wolf,
Or horse or oxen from the leopard,
As you fly from your oft-subdued slaves.
Alarum. Here another skirmish
It will not be: retire into your trenches:
You all consented unto Salisbury's death,
For none would strike a stroke in his revenge.
Pucelle is enter'd into Orleans,
In spite of us or aught that we could do.
O, would I were to die with Salisbury!
The shame hereof will make me hide my head.
Exit TALBOT. Alarum; retreat; flourish
SCENE VI. The same.
Enter, on the walls, JOAN LA PUCELLE, CHARLES, REIGNIER, ALENCON, and Soldiers
JOAN LA PUCELLE
Advance our waving colours on the walls;
Rescued is Orleans from the English
Thus Joan la Pucelle hath perform'd her word.
CHARLES
Divinest creature, Astraea's daughter,
How shall I honour thee for this success?
Thy promises are like Adonis' gardens
That one day bloom'd and fruitful were the next.
France, triumph in thy glorious prophetess!
Recover'd is the town of Orleans:
More blessed hap did ne'er befall our state.
REIGNIER
Why ring not out the bells aloud throughout the town?
Dauphin, command the citizens make bonfires
And feast and banquet in the open streets,
To celebrate the joy that God hath given us.
ALENCON

All France will be replete with mirth and joy,
When they shall hear how we have play'd the men.
CHARLES
'Tis Joan, not we, by whom the day is won;
For which I will divide my crown with her,
And all the priests and friars in my realm
Shall in procession sing her endless praise.
A statelier pyramis to her I'll rear
Than Rhodope's or Memphis' ever was:
In memory of her when she is dead,
Her ashes, in an urn more precious
Than the rich-jewel'd of Darius,
Transported shall be at high festivals
Before the kings and queens of France.
No longer on Saint Denis will we cry,
But Joan la Pucelle shall be France's saint.
Come in, and let us banquet royally,
After this golden day of victory.
Flourish. Exeunt
ACT II
SCENE I. Before Orleans.
Enter a Sergeant of a band with two Sentinels
Sergeant
Sirs, take your places and be vigilant:
If any noise or soldier you perceive
Near to the walls, by some apparent sign
Let us have knowledge at the court of guard.
First Sentinel
Sergeant, you shall.
Exit Sergeant
Thus are poor servitors,
When others sleep upon their quiet beds,
Constrain'd to watch in darkness, rain and cold.
Enter TALBOT, BEDFORD, BURGUNDY, and Forces, with scaling-ladders, their drums beating a dead march
TALBOT
Lord Regent, and redoubted Burgundy,
By whose approach the regions of Artois,
Wallon and Picardy are friends to us,
This happy night the Frenchmen are secure,
Having all day carousing and banqueted:
Embrace we then this opportunity
As fitting best to quittance their deceit
Contrived by art and baleful sorcery.
BEDFORD
Coward of France! how much he wrongs his fame,
Despairing of his own arm's fortitude,
To join with witches and the help of hell!
BURGUNDY
Traitors have never other company.
But what's that Pucelle whom they term so pure?
TALBOT
A maid, they say.
BEDFORD
A maid! and be so martial!
BURGUNDY
Pray God she prove not masculine ere long,
If underneath the standard of the French
She carry armour as she hath begun.
TALBOT
Well, let them practise and converse with spirits:
God is our fortress, in whose conquering name
Let us resolve to scale their flinty bulwarks.
BEDFORD

Ascend, brave Talbot; we will follow thee.
TALBOT
Not all together: better far, I guess,
That we do make our entrance several ways;
That, if it chance the one of us do fail,
The other yet may rise against their force.
BEDFORD
Agreed: I'll to yond corner.
BURGUNDY
And I to this.
TALBOT
And here will Talbot mount, or make his grave.
Now, Salisbury, for thee, and for the right
Of English Henry, shall this night appear
How much in duty I am bound to both.
Sentinels
Arm! arm! the enemy doth make assault!
Cry: 'St. George,' 'A Talbot.'
The French leap over the walls in their shirts. Enter, several ways, the BASTARD OF ORLEANS, ALENCON, and REIGNIER, half ready, and half unready
ALENCON
How now, my lords! what, all unready so?
BASTARD OF ORLEANS
Unready! ay, and glad we 'scaped so well.
REIGNIER
'Twas time, I trow, to wake and leave our beds,
Hearing alarums at our chamber-doors.
ALENCON
Of all exploits since first I follow'd arms,
Ne'er heard I of a warlike enterprise
More venturous or desperate than this.
BASTARD OF ORLEANS
I think this Talbot be a fiend of hell.
REIGNIER
If not of hell, the heavens, sure, favour him.
ALENCON
Here cometh Charles: I marvel how he sped.
BASTARD OF ORLEANS
Tut, holy Joan was his defensive guard.
Enter CHARLES and JOAN LA PUCELLE
CHARLES
Is this thy cunning, thou deceitful dame?
Didst thou at first, to flatter us withal,
Make us partakers of a little gain,
That now our loss might be ten times so much?
JOAN LA PUCELLE
Wherefore is Charles impatient with his friend!
At all times will you have my power alike?
Sleeping or waking must I still prevail,
Or will you blame and lay the fault on me?
Improvident soldiers! had your watch been good,
This sudden mischief never could have fall'n.
CHARLES
Duke of Alencon, this was your default,
That, being captain of the watch to-night,
Did look no better to that weighty charge.
ALENCON
Had all your quarters been as safely kept
As that whereof I had the government,
We had not been thus shamefully surprised.
BASTARD OF ORLEANS
Mine was secure.
REIGNIER

And so was mine, my lord.
CHARLES
And, for myself, most part of all this night,
Within her quarter and mine own precinct
I was employ'd in passing to and fro,
About relieving of the sentinels:
Then how or which way should they first break in?
JOAN LA PUCELLE
Question, my lords, no further of the case,
How or which way: 'tis sure they found some place
But weakly guarded, where the breach was made.
And now there rests no other shift but this;
To gather our soldiers, scatter'd and dispersed,
And lay new platforms to endamage them.
Alarum. Enter an English Soldier, crying 'A Talbot! a Talbot!' They fly, leaving their clothes behind
Soldier
I'll be so bold to take what they have left.
The cry of Talbot serves me for a sword;
For I have loaden me with many spoils,
Using no other weapon but his name.
Exit

SCENE II. Orleans. Within the town.
Enter TALBOT, BEDFORD, BURGUNDY, a Captain, and others
BEDFORD
The day begins to break, and night is fled,
Whose pitchy mantle over-veil'd the earth.
Here sound retreat, and cease our hot pursuit.
Retreat sounded
TALBOT
Bring forth the body of old Salisbury,
And here advance it in the market-place,
The middle centre of this cursed town.
Now have I paid my vow unto his soul;
For every drop of blood was drawn from him,
There hath at least five Frenchmen died tonight.
And that hereafter ages may behold
What ruin happen'd in revenge of him,
Within their chiefest temple I'll erect
A tomb, wherein his corpse shall be interr'd:
Upon the which, that every one may read,
Shall be engraved the sack of Orleans,
The treacherous manner of his mournful death
And what a terror he had been to France.
But, lords, in all our bloody massacre,
I muse we met not with the Dauphin's grace,
His new-come champion, virtuous Joan of Arc,
Nor any of his false confederates.
BEDFORD
'Tis thought, Lord Talbot, when the fight began,
Roused on the sudden from their drowsy beds,
They did amongst the troops of armed men
Leap o'er the walls for refuge in the field.
BURGUNDY
Myself, as far as I could well discern
For smoke and dusky vapours of the night,
Am sure I scared the Dauphin and his trull,
When arm in arm they both came swiftly running,
Like to a pair of loving turtle-doves
That could not live asunder day or night.
After that things are set in order here,
We'll follow them with all the power we have.
Enter a Messenger
Messenger

All hail, my lords! which of this princely train
Call ye the warlike Talbot, for his acts
So much applauded through the realm of France?
TALBOT
Here is the Talbot: who would speak with him?
Messenger
The virtuous lady, Countess of Auvergne,
With modesty admiring thy renown,
By me entreats, great lord, thou wouldst vouchsafe
To visit her poor castle where she lies,
That she may boast she hath beheld the man
Whose glory fills the world with loud report.
BURGUNDY
Is it even so? Nay, then, I see our wars
Will turn unto a peaceful comic sport,
When ladies crave to be encounter'd with.
You may not, my lord, despise her gentle suit.
TALBOT
Ne'er trust me then; for when a world of men
Could not prevail with all their oratory,
Yet hath a woman's kindness over-ruled:
And therefore tell her I return great thanks,
And in submission will attend on her.
Will not your honours bear me company?
BEDFORD
No, truly; it is more than manners will:
And I have heard it said, unbidden guests
Are often welcomest when they are gone.
TALBOT
Well then, alone, since there's no remedy,
I mean to prove this lady's courtesy.
Come hither, captain.
Whispers
You perceive my mind?
Captain
I do, my lord, and mean accordingly.
Exeunt

SCENE III. Auvergne. The COUNTESS's castle.
Enter the COUNTESS and her Porter
COUNTESS OF AUVERGNE
Porter, remember what I gave in charge;
And when you have done so, bring the keys to me.
Porter
Madam, I will.
Exit
COUNTESS OF AUVERGNE
The plot is laid: if all things fall out right,
I shall as famous be by this exploit
As Scythian Tomyris by Cyrus' death.
Great is the rumor of this dreadful knight,
And his achievements of no less account:
Fain would mine eyes be witness with mine ears,
To give their censure of these rare reports.
Enter Messenger and TALBOT
Messenger
Madam,
According as your ladyship desired,
By message craved, so is Lord Talbot come.
COUNTESS OF AUVERGNE
And he is welcome. What! is this the man?

Messenger
Madam, it is.
COUNTESS OF AUVERGNE
Is this the scourge of France?
Is this the Talbot, so much fear'd abroad
That with his name the mothers still their babes?
I see report is fabulous and false:
I thought I should have seen some Hercules,
A second Hector, for his grim aspect,
And large proportion of his strong-knit limbs.
Alas, this is a child, a silly dwarf!
It cannot be this weak and writhled shrimp
Should strike such terror to his enemies.
TALBOT
Madam, I have been bold to trouble you;
But since your ladyship is not at leisure,
I'll sort some other time to visit you.
COUNTESS OF AUVERGNE
What means he now? Go ask him whither he goes.
Messenger
Stay, my Lord Talbot; for my lady craves
To know the cause of your abrupt departure.
TALBOT
Marry, for that she's in a wrong belief,
I go to certify her Talbot's here.
Re-enter Porter with keys
COUNTESS OF AUVERGNE
If thou be he, then art thou prisoner.
TALBOT
Prisoner! to whom?
COUNTESS OF AUVERGNE
To me, blood-thirsty lord;
And for that cause I trained thee to my house.
Long time thy shadow hath been thrall to me,
For in my gallery thy picture hangs:
But now the substance shall endure the like,
And I will chain these legs and arms of thine,
That hast by tyranny these many years
Wasted our country, slain our citizens
And sent our sons and husbands captivate.
TALBOT
Ha, ha, ha!
COUNTESS OF AUVERGNE
Laughest thou, wretch? thy mirth shall turn to moan.
TALBOT
I laugh to see your ladyship so fond
To think that you have aught but Talbot's shadow
Whereon to practise your severity.
COUNTESS OF AUVERGNE
Why, art not thou the man?
TALBOT
I am indeed.
COUNTESS OF AUVERGNE
Then have I substance too.
TALBOT

No, no, I am but shadow of myself:
You are deceived, my substance is not here;
For what you see is but the smallest part
And least proportion of humanity:
I tell you, madam, were the whole frame here,
It is of such a spacious lofty pitch,
Your roof were not sufficient to contain't.
COUNTESS OF AUVERGNE
This is a riddling merchant for the nonce;
He will be here, and yet he is not here:
How can these contrarieties agree?
TALBOT
That will I show you presently.
Winds his horn. Drums strike up: a peal of ordnance. Enter soldiers
How say you, madam? are you now persuaded
That Talbot is but shadow of himself?
These are his substance, sinews, arms and strength,
With which he yoketh your rebellious necks,
Razeth your cities and subverts your towns
And in a moment makes them desolate.
COUNTESS OF AUVERGNE
Victorious Talbot! pardon my abuse:
I find thou art no less than fame hath bruited
And more than may be gather'd by thy shape.
Let my presumption not provoke thy wrath;
For I am sorry that with reverence
I did not entertain thee as thou art.
TALBOT
Be not dismay'd, fair lady; nor misconstrue
The mind of Talbot, as you did mistake
The outward composition of his body.
What you have done hath not offended me;
Nor other satisfaction do I crave,
But only, with your patience, that we may
Taste of your wine and see what cates you have;
For soldiers' stomachs always serve them well.
COUNTESS OF AUVERGNE
With all my heart, and think me honoured
To feast so great a warrior in my house.
Exeunt

SCENE IV. London. The Temple-garden.
Enter the Earls of SOMERSET, SUFFOLK, and WARWICK; RICHARD PLANTAGENET, VERNON, and another Lawyer
RICHARD PLANTAGENET
Great lords and gentlemen, what means this silence?
Dare no man answer in a case of truth?
SUFFOLK
Within the Temple-hall we were too loud;
The garden here is more convenient.
RICHARD PLANTAGENET
Then say at once if I maintain'd the truth;
Or else was wrangling Somerset in the error?
SUFFOLK
Faith, I have been a truant in the law,
And never yet could frame my will to it;
And therefore frame the law unto my will.
SOMERSET
Judge you, my Lord of Warwick, then, between us.

WARWICK
Between two hawks, which flies the higher pitch;
Between two dogs, which hath the deeper mouth;
Between two blades, which bears the better temper:
Between two horses, which doth bear him best;
Between two girls, which hath the merriest eye;
I have perhaps some shallow spirit of judgement;
But in these nice sharp quillets of the law,
Good faith, I am no wiser than a daw.
RICHARD PLANTAGENET
Tut, tut, here is a mannerly forbearance:
The truth appears so naked on my side
That any purblind eye may find it out.
SOMERSET
And on my side it is so well apparell'd,
So clear, so shining and so evident
That it will glimmer through a blind man's eye.
RICHARD PLANTAGENET
Since you are tongue-tied and so loath to speak,
In dumb significants proclaim your thoughts:
Let him that is a true-born gentleman
And stands upon the honour of his birth,
If he suppose that I have pleaded truth,
From off this brier pluck a white rose with me.
SOMERSET
Let him that is no coward nor no flatterer,
But dare maintain the party of the truth,
Pluck a red rose from off this thorn with me.
WARWICK
I love no colours, and without all colour
Of base insinuating flattery
I pluck this white rose with Plantagenet.
SUFFOLK
I pluck this red rose with young Somerset
And say withal I think he held the right.
VERNON
Stay, lords and gentlemen, and pluck no more,
Till you conclude that he upon whose side
The fewest roses are cropp'd from the tree
Shall yield the other in the right opinion.
SOMERSET
Good Master Vernon, it is well objected:
If I have fewest, I subscribe in silence.
RICHARD PLANTAGENET
And I.
VERNON
Then for the truth and plainness of the case.
I pluck this pale and maiden blossom here,
Giving my verdict on the white rose side.
SOMERSET
Prick not your finger as you pluck it off,
Lest bleeding you do paint the white rose red
And fall on my side so, against your will.
VERNON
If I my lord, for my opinion bleed,
Opinion shall be surgeon to my hurt
And keep me on the side where still I am.
SOMERSET
Well, well, come on: who else?
Lawyer

Unless my study and my books be false,
The argument you held was wrong in you:
To SOMERSET
In sign whereof I pluck a white rose too.
RICHARD PLANTAGENET
Now, Somerset, where is your argument?
SOMERSET
Here in my scabbard, meditating that
Shall dye your white rose in a bloody red.
RICHARD PLANTAGENET
Meantime your cheeks do counterfeit our roses;
For pale they look with fear, as witnessing
The truth on our side.
SOMERSET
No, Plantagenet,
'Tis not for fear but anger that thy cheeks
Blush for pure shame to counterfeit our roses,
And yet thy tongue will not confess thy error.
RICHARD PLANTAGENET
Hath not thy rose a canker, Somerset?
SOMERSET
Hath not thy rose a thorn, Plantagenet?
RICHARD PLANTAGENET
Ay, sharp and piercing, to maintain his truth;
Whiles thy consuming canker eats his falsehood.
SOMERSET
Well, I'll find friends to wear my bleeding roses,
That shall maintain what I have said is true,
Where false Plantagenet dare not be seen.
RICHARD PLANTAGENET
Now, by this maiden blossom in my hand,
I scorn thee and thy fashion, peevish boy.
SUFFOLK
Turn not thy scorns this way, Plantagenet.
RICHARD PLANTAGENET
Proud Pole, I will, and scorn both him and thee.
SUFFOLK
I'll turn my part thereof into thy throat.
SOMERSET
Away, away, good William de la Pole!
We grace the yeoman by conversing with him.
WARWICK
Now, by God's will, thou wrong'st him, Somerset;
His grandfather was Lionel Duke of Clarence,
Third son to the third Edward King of England:
Spring crestless yeomen from so deep a root?
RICHARD PLANTAGENET
He bears him on the place's privilege,
Or durst not, for his craven heart, say thus.
SOMERSET
By him that made me, I'll maintain my words
On any plot of ground in Christendom.
Was not thy father, Richard Earl of Cambridge,
For treason executed in our late king's days?
And, by his treason, stand'st not thou attainted,
Corrupted, and exempt from ancient gentry?

His trespass yet lives guilty in thy blood;
And, till thou be restored, thou art a yeoman.
RICHARD
PLANTAGENET
My father was attached, not attainted,
Condemn'd to die for treason, but no traitor;
And that I'll prove on better men than Somerset,
Were growing time once ripen'd to my will.
For your partaker Pole and you yourself,
I'll note you in my book of memory,
To scourge you for this apprehension:
Look to it well and say you are well warn'd.
SOMERSET
Ah, thou shalt find us ready for thee still;
And know us by these colours for thy foes,
For these my friends in spite of thee shall wear.
RICHARD
PLANTAGENET
And, by my soul, this pale and angry rose,
As cognizance of my blood-drinking hate,
Will I for ever and my faction wear,
Until it wither with me to my grave
Or flourish to the height of my degree.
SUFFOLK
Go forward and be choked with thy ambition!
And so farewell until I meet thee next.
Exit
SOMERSET
Have with thee, Pole. Farewell, ambitious Richard.
Exit
RICHARD
PLANTAGENET
How I am braved and must perforce endure it!
WARWICK
This blot that they object against your house
Shall be wiped out in the next parliament
Call'd for the truce of Winchester and Gloucester;
And if thou be not then created York,
I will not live to be accounted Warwick.
Meantime, in signal of my love to thee,
Against proud Somerset and William Pole,
Will I upon thy party wear this rose:
And here I prophesy: this brawl to-day,
Grown to this faction in the Temple-garden,
Shall send between the red rose and the white
A thousand souls to death and deadly night.
RICHARD
PLANTAGENET
Good Master Vernon, I am bound to you,
That you on my behalf would pluck a flower.
VERNON
In your behalf still will I wear the same.
Lawyer
And so will I.
RICHARD
PLANTAGENET
Thanks, gentle sir.
Come, let us four to dinner: I dare say
This quarrel will drink blood another day.
Exeunt
SCENE V. The Tower of London.
Enter MORTIMER, brought in a chair, and Gaolers
MORTIMER

Kind keepers of my weak decaying age,
Let dying Mortimer here rest himself.
Even like a man new haled from the rack,
So fare my limbs with long imprisonment.
And these grey locks, the pursuivants of death,
Nestor-like aged in an age of care,
Argue the end of Edmund Mortimer.
These eyes, like lamps whose wasting oil is spent,
Wax dim, as drawing to their exigent;
Weak shoulders, overborne with burthening grief,
And pithless arms, like to a wither'd vine
That droops his sapless branches to the ground;
Yet are these feet, whose strengthless stay is numb,
Unable to support this lump of clay,
Swift-winged with desire to get a grave,
As witting I no other comfort have.
But tell me, keeper, will my nephew come?
First Gaoler
Richard Plantagenet, my lord, will come:
We sent unto the Temple, unto his chamber;
And answer was return'd that he will come.
MORTIMER
Enough: my soul shall then be satisfied.
Poor gentleman! his wrong doth equal mine.
Since Henry Monmouth first began to reign,
Before whose glory I was great in arms,
This loathsome sequestration have I had:
And even since then hath Richard been obscured,
Deprived of honour and inheritance.
But now the arbitrator of despairs,
Just death, kind umpire of men's miseries,
With sweet enlargement doth dismiss me hence:
I would his troubles likewise were expired,
That so he might recover what was lost.
Enter RICHARD PLANTAGENET
First Gaoler
My lord, your loving nephew now is come.
MORTIMER
Richard Plantagenet, my friend, is he come?
RICHARD
PLANTAGENET
Ay, noble uncle, thus ignobly used,
Your nephew, late despised Richard, comes.
MORTIMER
Direct mine arms I may embrace his neck,
And in his bosom spend my latter gasp:
O, tell me when my lips do touch his cheeks,
That I may kindly give one fainting kiss.
And now declare, sweet stem from York's great stock,
Why didst thou say, of late thou wert despised?
RICHARD
PLANTAGENET
First, lean thine aged back against mine arm;
And, in that ease, I'll tell thee my disease.
This day, in argument upon a case,
Some words there grew 'twixt Somerset and me;
Among which terms he used his lavish tongue
And did upbraid me with my father's death:
Which obloquy set bars before my tongue,
Else with the like I had requited him.
Therefore, good uncle, for my father's sake,
In honour of a true Plantagenet

And for alliance sake, declare the cause
My father, Earl of Cambridge, lost his head.
MORTIMER
That cause, fair nephew, that imprison'd me
And hath detain'd me all my flowering youth
Within a loathsome dungeon, there to pine,
Was cursed instrument of his decease.
RICHARD
PLANTAGENET
Discover more at large what cause that was,
For I am ignorant and cannot guess.
MORTIMER
I will, if that my fading breath permit
And death approach not ere my tale be done.
Henry the Fourth, grandfather to this king,
Deposed his nephew Richard, Edward's son,
The first-begotten and the lawful heir,
Of Edward king, the third of that descent:
During whose reign the Percies of the north,
Finding his usurpation most unjust,
Endeavor'd my advancement to the throne:
The reason moved these warlike lords to this
Was, for that--young King Richard thus removed,
Leaving no heir begotten of his body--
I was the next by birth and parentage;
For by my mother I derived am
From Lionel Duke of Clarence, the third son
To King Edward the Third; whereas he
From John of Gaunt doth bring his pedigree,
Being but fourth of that heroic line.
But mark: as in this haughty attempt
They laboured to plant the rightful heir,
I lost my liberty and they their lives.
Long after this, when Henry the Fifth,
Succeeding his father Bolingbroke, did reign,
Thy father, Earl of Cambridge, then derived
From famous Edmund Langley, Duke of York,
Marrying my sister that thy mother was,
Again in pity of my hard distress
Levied an army, weening to redeem
And have install'd me in the diadem:
But, as the rest, so fell that noble earl
And was beheaded. Thus the Mortimers,
In whom the tide rested, were suppress'd.
RICHARD
PLANTAGENET
Of which, my lord, your honour is the last.
MORTIMER
True; and thou seest that I no issue have
And that my fainting words do warrant death;
Thou art my heir; the rest I wish thee gather:
But yet be wary in thy studious care.
RICHARD
PLANTAGENET
Thy grave admonishments prevail with me:
But yet, methinks, my father's execution
Was nothing less than bloody tyranny.
MORTIMER
With silence, nephew, be thou politic:
Strong-fixed is the house of Lancaster,
And like a mountain, not to be removed.
But now thy uncle is removing hence:
As princes do their courts, when they are cloy'd

With long continuance in a settled place.
RICHARD
PLANTAGENET
O, uncle, would some part of my young years
Might but redeem the passage of your age!
MORTIMER
Thou dost then wrong me, as that slaughterer doth
Which giveth many wounds when one will kill.
Mourn not, except thou sorrow for my good;
Only give order for my funeral:
And so farewell, and fair be all thy hopes
And prosperous be thy life in peace and war!
Dies
RICHARD
PLANTAGENET
And peace, no war, befall thy parting soul!
In prison hast thou spent a pilgrimage
And like a hermit overpass'd thy days.
Well, I will lock his counsel in my breast;
And what I do imagine let that rest.
Keepers, convey him hence, and I myself
Will see his burial better than his life.
Exeunt Gaolers, bearing out the body of MORTIMER
Here dies the dusky torch of Mortimer,
Choked with ambition of the meaner sort:
And for those wrongs, those bitter injuries,
Which Somerset hath offer'd to my house:
I doubt not but with honour to redress;
And therefore haste I to the parliament,
Either to be restored to my blood,
Or make my ill the advantage of my good.
Exit
ACT III
SCENE I. London. The Parliament-house.
Flourish. Enter KING HENRY VI, EXETER, GLOUCESTER, WARWICK, SOMERSET, and SUFFOLK; the BISHOP OF WINCHESTER, RICHARD PLANTAGENET, and others. GLOUCESTER offers to put up a bill; BISHOP OF WINCHESTER snatches it, and tears it
BISHOP
OF WINCHESTER
Comest thou with deep premeditated lines,
With written pamphlets studiously devised,
Humphrey of Gloucester? If thou canst accuse,
Or aught intend'st to lay unto my charge,
Do it without invention, suddenly;
As I with sudden and extemporal speech
Purpose to answer what thou canst object.
GLOUCESTER
Presumptuous priest! this place commands my patience,
Or thou shouldst find thou hast dishonour'd me.
Think not, although in writing I preferr'd
The manner of thy vile outrageous crimes,
That therefore I have forged, or am not able
Verbatim to rehearse the method of my pen:
No, prelate; such is thy audacious wickedness,
Thy lewd, pestiferous and dissentious pranks,
As very infants prattle of thy pride.
Thou art a most pernicious usurer,
Forward by nature, enemy to peace;
Lascivious, wanton, more than well beseems
A man of thy profession and degree;
And for thy treachery, what's more manifest?
In that thou laid'st a trap to take my life,
As well at London bridge as at the Tower.

Beside, I fear me, if thy thoughts were sifted,
The king, thy sovereign, is not quite exempt
From envious malice of thy swelling heart.
BISHOP OF WINCHESTER
Gloucester, I do defy thee. Lords, vouchsafe
To give me hearing what I shall reply.
If I were covetous, ambitious or perverse,
As he will have me, how am I so poor?
Or how haps it I seek not to advance
Or raise myself, but keep my wonted calling?
And for dissension, who preferreth peace
More than I do?--except I be provoked.
No, my good lords, it is not that offends;
It is not that that hath incensed the duke:
It is, because no one should sway but he;
No one but he should be about the king;
And that engenders thunder in his breast
And makes him roar these accusations forth.
But he shall know I am as good--
GLOUCESTER
As good!
Thou bastard of my grandfather!
BISHOP OF WINCHESTER
Ay, lordly sir; for what are you, I pray,
But one imperious in another's throne?
GLOUCESTER
Am I not protector, saucy priest?
BISHOP OF WINCHESTER
And am not I a prelate of the church?
GLOUCESTER
Yes, as an outlaw in a castle keeps
And useth it to patronage his theft.
BISHOP OF WINCHESTER
Unreverent Gloster!
GLOUCESTER
Thou art reverent
Touching thy spiritual function, not thy life.
BISHOP OF WINCHESTER
Rome shall remedy this.
WARWICK
Roam thither, then.
SOMERSET
My lord, it were your duty to forbear.
WARWICK
Ay, see the bishop be not overborne.
SOMERSET
Methinks my lord should be religious
And know the office that belongs to such.
WARWICK
Methinks his lordship should be humbler;
it fitteth not a prelate so to plead.
SOMERSET
Yes, when his holy state is touch'd so near.
WARWICK
State holy or unhallow'd, what of that?
Is not his grace protector to the king?
RICHARD PLANTAGENET

[Aside] Plantagenet, I see, must hold his tongue,
Lest it be said 'Speak, sirrah, when you should;
Must your bold verdict enter talk with lords?'
Else would I have a fling at Winchester.

KING HENRY VI
Uncles of Gloucester and of Winchester,
The special watchmen of our English weal,
I would prevail, if prayers might prevail,
To join your hearts in love and amity.
O, what a scandal is it to our crown,
That two such noble peers as ye should jar!
Believe me, lords, my tender years can tell
Civil dissension is a viperous worm
That gnaws the bowels of the commonwealth.
A noise within, 'Down with the tawny-coats!'
What tumult's this?

WARWICK
An uproar, I dare warrant,
Begun through malice of the bishop's men.
A noise again, 'Stones! stones!' Enter Mayor

Mayor
O, my good lords, and virtuous Henry,
Pity the city of London, pity us!
The bishop and the Duke of Gloucester's men,
Forbidden late to carry any weapon,
Have fill'd their pockets full of pebble stones
And banding themselves in contrary parts
Do pelt so fast at one another's pate
That many have their giddy brains knock'd out:
Our windows are broke down in every street
And we for fear compell'd to shut our shops.
Enter Serving-men, in skirmish, with bloody pates

KING HENRY VI
We charge you, on allegiance to ourself,
To hold your slaughtering hands and keep the peace.
Pray, uncle Gloucester, mitigate this strife.
First Serving-man Nay, if we be forbidden stones,
We'll fall to it with our teeth.
Second Serving-man Do what ye dare, we are as resolute.
Skirmish again

GLOUCESTER
You of my household, leave this peevish broil
And set this unaccustom'd fight aside.
Third Serving-man My lord, we know your grace to be a man
Just and upright; and, for your royal birth,
Inferior to none but to his majesty:
And ere that we will suffer such a prince,
So kind a father of the commonweal,
To be disgraced by an inkhorn mate,
We and our wives and children all will fight
And have our bodies slaughtered by thy foes.
First Serving-man Ay, and the very parings of our nails
Shall pitch a field when we are dead.
Begin again

GLOUCESTER
Stay, stay, I say!
And if you love me, as you say you do,
Let me persuade you to forbear awhile.

KING HENRY VI
O, how this discord doth afflict my soul!
Can you, my Lord of Winchester, behold
My sighs and tears and will not once relent?
Who should be pitiful, if you be not?

Or who should study to prefer a peace.
If holy churchmen take delight in broils?
WARWICK
Yield, my lord protector; yield, Winchester;
Except you mean with obstinate repulse
To slay your sovereign and destroy the realm.
You see what mischief and what murder too
Hath been enacted through your enmity;
Then be at peace except ye thirst for blood.
BISHOP OF WINCHESTER
He shall submit, or I will never yield.
GLOUCESTER
Compassion on the king commands me stoop;
Or I would see his heart out, ere the priest
Should ever get that privilege of me.
WARWICK
Behold, my Lord of Winchester, the duke
Hath banish'd moody discontented fury,
As by his smoothed brows it doth appear:
Why look you still so stern and tragical?
GLOUCESTER
Here, Winchester, I offer thee my hand.
KING HENRY VI
Fie, uncle Beaufort! I have heard you preach
That malice was a great and grievous sin;
And will not you maintain the thing you teach,
But prove a chief offender in the same?
WARWICK
Sweet king! the bishop hath a kindly gird.
For shame, my lord of Winchester, relent!
What, shall a child instruct you what to do?
BISHOP OF WINCHESTER
Well, Duke of Gloucester, I will yield to thee;
Love for thy love and hand for hand I give.
GLOUCESTER
[Aside] Ay, but, I fear me, with a hollow heart.--
See here, my friends and loving countrymen,
This token serveth for a flag of truce
Betwixt ourselves and all our followers:
So help me God, as I dissemble not!
BISHOP OF WINCHESTER
[Aside] So help me God, as I intend it not!
KING HENRY VI
O, loving uncle, kind Duke of Gloucester,
How joyful am I made by this contract!
Away, my masters! trouble us no more;
But join in friendship, as your lords have done.
First Serving-man Content: I'll to the surgeon's.
Second Serving-man And so will I.
Third Serving-man And I will see what physic the tavern affords.
Exeunt Serving-men, Mayor, &c
WARWICK
Accept this scroll, most gracious sovereign,
Which in the right of Richard Plantagenet
We do exhibit to your majesty.
GLOUCESTER
Well urged, my Lord of Warwick: or sweet prince,
And if your grace mark every circumstance,
You have great reason to do Richard right;

Especially for those occasions
At Eltham Place I told your majesty.
KING HENRY VI
And those occasions, uncle, were of force:
Therefore, my loving lords, our pleasure is
That Richard be restored to his blood.
WARWICK
Let Richard be restored to his blood;
So shall his father's wrongs be recompensed.
BISHOP OF WINCHESTER
As will the rest, so willeth Winchester.
KING HENRY VI
If Richard will be true, not that alone
But all the whole inheritance I give
That doth belong unto the house of York,
From whence you spring by lineal descent.
RICHARD PLANTAGENET
Thy humble servant vows obedience
And humble service till the point of death.
KING HENRY VI
Stoop then and set your knee against my foot;
And, in reguerdon of that duty done,
I gird thee with the valiant sword of York:
Rise Richard, like a true Plantagenet,
And rise created princely Duke of York.
RICHARD PLANTAGENET
And so thrive Richard as thy foes may fall!
And as my duty springs, so perish they
That grudge one thought against your majesty!
ALL
Welcome, high prince, the mighty Duke of York!
SOMERSET
[Aside] Perish, base prince, ignoble Duke of York!
GLOUCESTER
Now will it best avail your majesty
To cross the seas and to be crown'd in France:
The presence of a king engenders love
Amongst his subjects and his loyal friends,
As it disanimates his enemies.
KING HENRY VI
When Gloucester says the word, King Henry goes;
For friendly counsel cuts off many foes.
GLOUCESTER
Your ships already are in readiness.
Sennet. Flourish. Exeunt all but EXETER
EXETER
Ay, we may march in England or in France,
Not seeing what is likely to ensue.
This late dissension grown betwixt the peers
Burns under feigned ashes of forged love
And will at last break out into a flame:
As fester'd members rot but by degree,
Till bones and flesh and sinews fall away,
So will this base and envious discord breed.
And now I fear that fatal prophecy
Which in the time of Henry named the Fifth
Was in the mouth of every sucking babe;
That Henry born at Monmouth should win all
And Henry born at Windsor lose all:

Which is so plain that Exeter doth wish
His days may finish ere that hapless time.
Exit

SCENE II. France. Before Rouen.
Enter JOAN LA PUCELLE disguised, with four Soldiers with sacks upon their backs
JOAN LA PUCELLE
These are the city gates, the gates of Rouen,
Through which our policy must make a breach:
Take heed, be wary how you place your words;
Talk like the vulgar sort of market men
That come to gather money for their corn.
If we have entrance, as I hope we shall,
And that we find the slothful watch but weak,
I'll by a sign give notice to our friends,
That Charles the Dauphin may encounter them.
First Soldier
Our sacks shall be a mean to sack the city,
And we be lords and rulers over Rouen;
Therefore we'll knock.
Knocks
Watch
[Within] Qui est la?
JOAN LA PUCELLE
Paysans, pauvres gens de France;
Poor market folks that come to sell their corn.
Watch
Enter, go in; the market bell is rung.
JOAN LA PUCELLE
Now, Rouen, I'll shake thy bulwarks to the ground.
Exeunt
Enter CHARLES, the BASTARD OF ORLEANS, ALENCON, REIGNIER, and forces
CHARLES
Saint Denis bless this happy stratagem!
And once again we'll sleep secure in Rouen.
BASTARD OF ORLEANS
Here enter'd Pucelle and her practisants;
Now she is there, how will she specify
Where is the best and safest passage in?
REIGNIER
By thrusting out a torch from yonder tower;
Which, once discern'd, shows that her meaning is,
No way to that, for weakness, which she enter'd.
Enter JOAN LA PUCELLE on the top, thrusting out a torch burning
JOAN LA PUCELLE
Behold, this is the happy wedding torch
That joineth Rouen unto her countrymen,
But burning fatal to the Talbotites!
Exit
BASTARD OF ORLEANS
See, noble Charles, the beacon of our friend;
The burning torch in yonder turret stands.
CHARLES
Now shine it like a comet of revenge,
A prophet to the fall of all our foes!
REIGNIER
Defer no time, delays have dangerous ends;
Enter, and cry 'The Dauphin!' presently,
And then do execution on the watch.
Alarum. Exeunt
An alarum. Enter TALBOT in an excursion
TALBOT
France, thou shalt rue this treason with thy tears,
If Talbot but survive thy treachery.

Pucelle, that witch, that damned sorceress,
Hath wrought this hellish mischief unawares,
That hardly we escaped the pride of France.
Exit
An alarum: excursions. BEDFORD, brought in sick in a chair. Enter TALBOT and BURGUNDY without: within JOAN LA PUCELLE, CHARLES, BASTARD OF ORLEANS, ALENCON, and REIGNIER, on the walls
JOAN LA PUCELLE
Good morrow, gallants! want ye corn for bread?
I think the Duke of Burgundy will fast
Before he'll buy again at such a rate:
'Twas full of darnel; do you like the taste?
BURGUNDY
Scoff on, vile fiend and shameless courtezan!
I trust ere long to choke thee with thine own
And make thee curse the harvest of that corn.
CHARLES
Your grace may starve perhaps before that time.
BEDFORD
O, let no words, but deeds, revenge this treason!
JOAN LA PUCELLE
What will you do, good grey-beard? break a lance,
And run a tilt at death within a chair?
TALBOT
Foul fiend of France, and hag of all despite,
Encompass'd with thy lustful paramours!
Becomes it thee to taunt his valiant age
And twit with cowardice a man half dead?
Damsel, I'll have a bout with you again,
Or else let Talbot perish with this shame.
JOAN LA PUCELLE
Are ye so hot, sir? yet, Pucelle, hold thy peace;
If Talbot do but thunder, rain will follow.
The English whisper together in council
God speed the parliament! who shall be the speaker?
TALBOT
Dare ye come forth and meet us in the field?
JOAN LA PUCELLE
Belike your lordship takes us then for fools,
To try if that our own be ours or no.
TALBOT
I speak not to that railing Hecate,
But unto thee, Alencon, and the rest;
Will ye, like soldiers, come and fight it out?
ALENCON
Signior, no.
TALBOT
Signior, hang! base muleters of France!
Like peasant foot-boys do they keep the walls
And dare not take up arms like gentlemen.
JOAN LA PUCELLE
Away, captains! let's get us from the walls;
For Talbot means no goodness by his looks.
God be wi' you, my lord! we came but to tell you
That we are here.
Exeunt from the walls
TALBOT
And there will we be too, ere it be long,
Or else reproach be Talbot's greatest fame!
Vow, Burgundy, by honour of thy house,
Prick'd on by public wrongs sustain'd in France,
Either to get the town again or die:
And I, as sure as English Henry lives
And as his father here was conqueror,

As sure as in this late-betrayed town
Great Coeur-de-lion's heart was buried,
So sure I swear to get the town or die.
BURGUNDY
My vows are equal partners with thy vows.
TALBOT
But, ere we go, regard this dying prince,
The valiant Duke of Bedford. Come, my lord,
We will bestow you in some better place,
Fitter for sickness and for crazy age.
BEDFORD
Lord Talbot, do not so dishonour me:
Here will I sit before the walls of Rouen
And will be partner of your weal or woe.
BURGUNDY
Courageous Bedford, let us now persuade you.
BEDFORD
Not to be gone from hence; for once I read
That stout Pendragon in his litter sick
Came to the field and vanquished his foes:
Methinks I should revive the soldiers' hearts,
Because I ever found them as myself.
TALBOT
Undaunted spirit in a dying breast!
Then be it so: heavens keep old Bedford safe!
And now no more ado, brave Burgundy,
But gather we our forces out of hand
And set upon our boasting enemy.
Exeunt all but BEDFORD and Attendants
An alarum: excursions. Enter FASTOLFE and a Captain
Captain
Whither away, Sir John Fastolfe, in such haste?
FASTOLFE
Whither away! to save myself by flight:
We are like to have the overthrow again.
Captain
What! will you fly, and leave Lord Talbot?
FASTOLFE
Ay,
All the Talbots in the world, to save my life!
Exit
Captain
Cowardly knight! ill fortune follow thee!
Exit
Retreat: excursions. JOAN LA PUCELLE, ALENCON, and CHARLES fly
BEDFORD
Now, quiet soul, depart when heaven please,
For I have seen our enemies' overthrow.
What is the trust or strength of foolish man?
They that of late were daring with their scoffs
Are glad and fain by flight to save themselves.
BEDFORD dies, and is carried in by two in his chair
An alarum. Re-enter TALBOT, BURGUNDY, and the rest
TALBOT
Lost, and recover'd in a day again!
This is a double honour, Burgundy:
Yet heavens have glory for this victory!
BURGUNDY
Warlike and martial Talbot, Burgundy
Enshrines thee in his heart and there erects
Thy noble deeds as valour's monuments.
TALBOT

Thanks, gentle duke. But where is Pucelle now?
I think her old familiar is asleep:
Now where's the Bastard's braves, and Charles his gleeks?
What, all amort? Rouen hangs her head for grief
That such a valiant company are fled.
Now will we take some order in the town,
Placing therein some expert officers,
And then depart to Paris to the king,
For there young Henry with his nobles lie.
BURGUNDY
What wills Lord Talbot pleaseth Burgundy.
TALBOT
But yet, before we go, let's not forget
The noble Duke of Bedford late deceased,
But see his exequies fulfill'd in Rouen:
A braver soldier never couched lance,
A gentler heart did never sway in court;
But kings and mightiest potentates must die,
For that's the end of human misery.
Exeunt
SCENE III. The plains near Rouen.
Enter CHARLES, the BASTARD OF ORLEANS, ALENCON, JOAN LA PUCELLE, and forces
JOAN LA PUCELLE
Dismay not, princes, at this accident,
Nor grieve that Rouen is so recovered:
Care is no cure, but rather corrosive,
For things that are not to be remedied.
Let frantic Talbot triumph for a while
And like a peacock sweep along his tail;
We'll pull his plumes and take away his train,
If Dauphin and the rest will be but ruled.
CHARLES
We have been guided by thee hitherto,
And of thy cunning had no diffidence:
One sudden foil shall never breed distrust.
BASTARD OF ORLEANS
Search out thy wit for secret policies,
And we will make thee famous through the world.
ALENCON
We'll set thy statue in some holy place,
And have thee reverenced like a blessed saint:
Employ thee then, sweet virgin, for our good.
JOAN LA PUCELLE
Then thus it must be; this doth Joan devise:
By fair persuasions mix'd with sugar'd words
We will entice the Duke of Burgundy
To leave the Talbot and to follow us.
CHARLES
Ay, marry, sweeting, if we could do that,
France were no place for Henry's warriors;
Nor should that nation boast it so with us,
But be extirped from our provinces.
ALENCON
For ever should they be expulsed from France
And not have title of an earldom here.
JOAN LA PUCELLE
Your honours shall perceive how I will work
To bring this matter to the wished end.
Drum sounds afar off
Hark! by the sound of drum you may perceive
Their powers are marching unto Paris-ward.
Here sound an English march. Enter, and pass over at a distance, TALBOT and his forces

There goes the Talbot, with his colours spread,
And all the troops of English after him.
French march. Enter BURGUNDY and forces
Now in the rearward comes the duke and his:
Fortune in favour makes him lag behind.
Summon a parley; we will talk with him.
Trumpets sound a parley
CHARLES
A parley with the Duke of Burgundy!
BURGUNDY
Who craves a parley with the Burgundy?
JOAN LA PUCELLE
The princely Charles of France, thy countryman.
BURGUNDY
What say'st thou, Charles? for I am marching hence.
CHARLES
Speak, Pucelle, and enchant him with thy words.
JOAN LA PUCELLE
Brave Burgundy, undoubted hope of France!
Stay, let thy humble handmaid speak to thee.
BURGUNDY
Speak on; but be not over-tedious.
JOAN LA PUCELLE
Look on thy country, look on fertile France,
And see the cities and the towns defaced
By wasting ruin of the cruel foe.
As looks the mother on her lowly babe
When death doth close his tender dying eyes,
See, see the pining malady of France;
Behold the wounds, the most unnatural wounds,
Which thou thyself hast given her woful breast.
O, turn thy edged sword another way;
Strike those that hurt, and hurt not those that help.
One drop of blood drawn from thy country's bosom
Should grieve thee more than streams of foreign gore:
Return thee therefore with a flood of tears,
And wash away thy country's stained spots.
BURGUNDY
Either she hath bewitch'd me with her words,
Or nature makes me suddenly relent.
JOAN LA PUCELLE
Besides, all French and France exclaims on thee,
Doubting thy birth and lawful progeny.
Who joint'st thou with but with a lordly nation
That will not trust thee but for profit's sake?
When Talbot hath set footing once in France
And fashion'd thee that instrument of ill,
Who then but English Henry will be lord
And thou be thrust out like a fugitive?
Call we to mind, and mark but this for proof,
Was not the Duke of Orleans thy foe?
And was he not in England prisoner?
But when they heard he was thine enemy,
They set him free without his ransom paid,
In spite of Burgundy and all his friends.
See, then, thou fight'st against thy countrymen
And joint'st with them will be thy slaughtermen.
Come, come, return; return, thou wandering lord:
Charles and the rest will take thee in their arms.
BURGUNDY
I am vanquished; these haughty words of hers
Have batter'd me like roaring cannon-shot,
And made me almost yield upon my knees.

34

Forgive me, country, and sweet countrymen,
And, lords, accept this hearty kind embrace:
My forces and my power of men are yours:
So farewell, Talbot; I'll no longer trust thee.
JOAN LA PUCELLE
[Aside] Done like a Frenchman: turn, and turn again!
CHARLES
Welcome, brave duke! thy friendship makes us fresh.
BASTARD OF ORLEANS
And doth beget new courage in our breasts.
ALENCON
Pucelle hath bravely play'd her part in this,
And doth deserve a coronet of gold.
CHARLES
Now let us on, my lords, and join our powers,
And seek how we may prejudice the foe.
Exeunt
SCENE IV. Paris. The palace.
Enter KING HENRY VI, GLOUCESTER, BISHOP OF WINCHESTER, YORK, SUFFOLK, SOMERSET, WARWICK, EXETER, VERNON BASSET, and others. To them with his Soldiers, TALBOT
TALBOT
My gracious prince, and honourable peers,
Hearing of your arrival in this realm,
I have awhile given truce unto my wars,
To do my duty to my sovereign:
In sign, whereof, this arm, that hath reclaim'd
To your obedience fifty fortresses,
Twelve cities and seven walled towns of strength,
Beside five hundred prisoners of esteem,
Lets fall his sword before your highness' feet,
And with submissive loyalty of heart
Ascribes the glory of his conquest got
First to my God and next unto your grace.
Kneels
KING HENRY VI
Is this the Lord Talbot, uncle Gloucester,
That hath so long been resident in France?
GLOUCESTER
Yes, if it please your majesty, my liege.
KING HENRY VI
Welcome, brave captain and victorious lord!
When I was young, as yet I am not old,
I do remember how my father said
A stouter champion never handled sword.
Long since we were resolved of your truth,
Your faithful service and your toil in war;
Yet never have you tasted our reward,
Or been reguerdon'd with so much as thanks,
Because till now we never saw your face:
Therefore, stand up; and, for these good deserts,
We here create you Earl of Shrewsbury;
And in our coronation take your place.
Sennet. Flourish. Exeunt all but VERNON and BASSET
VERNON
Now, sir, to you, that were so hot at sea,
Disgracing of these colours that I wear
In honour of my noble Lord of York:
Darest thou maintain the former words thou spakest?
BASSET
Yes, sir; as well as you dare patronage
The envious barking of your saucy tongue
Against my lord the Duke of Somerset.
VERNON

35

Sirrah, thy lord I honour as he is.
BASSET
Why, what is he? as good a man as York.
VERNON
Hark ye; not so: in witness, take ye that.
Strikes him
BASSET
Villain, thou know'st the law of arms is such
That whoso draws a sword, 'tis present death,
Or else this blow should broach thy dearest blood.
But I'll unto his majesty, and crave
I may have liberty to venge this wrong;
When thou shalt see I'll meet thee to thy cost.
VERNON
Well, miscreant, I'll be there as soon as you;
And, after, meet you sooner than you would.
Exeunt

ACT IV
SCENE I. Paris. A hall of state.
Enter KING HENRY VI, GLOUCESTER, BISHOP OF WINCHESTER, YORK, SUFFOLK, SOMERSET, WARWICK, TALBOT, EXETER, the Governor, of Paris, and others
GLOUCESTER
Lord bishop, set the crown upon his head.
BISHOP OF WINCHESTER
God save King Henry, of that name the sixth!
GLOUCESTER
Now, governor of Paris, take your oath,
That you elect no other king but him;
Esteem none friends but such as are his friends,
And none your foes but such as shall pretend
Malicious practises against his state:
This shall ye do, so help you righteous God!
Enter FASTOLFE
FASTOLFE
My gracious sovereign, as I rode from Calais,
To haste unto your coronation,
A letter was deliver'd to my hands,
Writ to your grace from the Duke of Burgundy.
TALBOT
Shame to the Duke of Burgundy and thee!
I vow'd, base knight, when I did meet thee next,
To tear the garter from thy craven's leg,
Plucking it off
Which I have done, because unworthily
Thou wast installed in that high degree.
Pardon me, princely Henry, and the rest
This dastard, at the battle of Patay,
When but in all I was six thousand strong
And that the French were almost ten to one,
Before we met or that a stroke was given,
Like to a trusty squire did run away:
In which assault we lost twelve hundred men;
Myself and divers gentlemen beside
Were there surprised and taken prisoners.
Then judge, great lords, if I have done amiss;
Or whether that such cowards ought to wear
This ornament of knighthood, yea or no.
GLOUCESTER
To say the truth, this fact was infamous
And ill beseeming any common man,
Much more a knight, a captain and a leader.
TALBOT

When first this order was ordain'd, my lords,
Knights of the garter were of noble birth,
Valiant and virtuous, full of haughty courage,
Such as were grown to credit by the wars;
Not fearing death, nor shrinking for distress,
But always resolute in most extremes.
He then that is not furnish'd in this sort
Doth but usurp the sacred name of knight,
Profaning this most honourable order,
And should, if I were worthy to be judge,
Be quite degraded, like a hedge-born swain
That doth presume to boast of gentle blood.
KING HENRY VI
Stain to thy countrymen, thou hear'st thy doom!
Be packing, therefore, thou that wast a knight:
Henceforth we banish thee, on pain of death.
Exit FASTOLFE
And now, my lord protector, view the letter
Sent from our uncle Duke of Burgundy.
GLOUCESTER
What means his grace, that he hath changed his style?
No more but, plain and bluntly, 'To the king!'
Hath he forgot he is his sovereign?
Or doth this churlish superscription
Pretend some alteration in good will?
What's here?
Reads
'I have, upon especial cause,
Moved with compassion of my country's wreck,
Together with the pitiful complaints
Of such as your oppression feeds upon,
Forsaken your pernicious faction
And join'd with Charles, the rightful King of France.'
O monstrous treachery! can this be so,
That in alliance, amity and oaths,
There should be found such false dissembling guile?
KING HENRY VI
What! doth my uncle Burgundy revolt?
GLOUCESTER
He doth, my lord, and is become your foe.
KING HENRY VI
Is that the worst this letter doth contain?
GLOUCESTER
It is the worst, and all, my lord, he writes.
KING HENRY VI
Why, then, Lord Talbot there shall talk with him
And give him chastisement for this abuse.
How say you, my lord? are you not content?
TALBOT
Content, my liege! yes, but that I am prevented,
I should have begg'd I might have been employ'd.
KING HENRY VI
Then gather strength and march unto him straight:
Let him perceive how ill we brook his treason
And what offence it is to flout his friends.
TALBOT
I go, my lord, in heart desiring still
You may behold confusion of your foes.
Exit
Enter VERNON and BASSET
VERNON
Grant me the combat, gracious sovereign.
BASSET

And me, my lord, grant me the combat too.
YORK
This is my servant: hear him, noble prince.
SOMERSET
And this is mine: sweet Henry, favour him.
KING HENRY VI
Be patient, lords; and give them leave to speak.
Say, gentlemen, what makes you thus exclaim?
And wherefore crave you combat? or with whom?
VERNON
With him, my lord; for he hath done me wrong.
BASSET
And I with him; for he hath done me wrong.
KING HENRY VI
What is that wrong whereof you both complain?
First let me know, and then I'll answer you.
BASSET
Crossing the sea from England into France,
This fellow here, with envious carping tongue,
Upbraided me about the rose I wear;
Saying, the sanguine colour of the leaves
Did represent my master's blushing cheeks,
When stubbornly he did repugn the truth
About a certain question in the law
Argued betwixt the Duke of York and him;
With other vile and ignominious terms:
In confutation of which rude reproach
And in defence of my lord's worthiness,
I crave the benefit of law of arms.
VERNON
And that is my petition, noble lord:
For though he seem with forged quaint conceit
To set a gloss upon his bold intent,
Yet know, my lord, I was provoked by him;
And he first took exceptions at this badge,
Pronouncing that the paleness of this flower
Bewray'd the faintness of my master's heart.
YORK
Will not this malice, Somerset, be left?
SOMERSET
Your private grudge, my Lord of York, will out,
Though ne'er so cunningly you smother it.
KING HENRY VI
Good Lord, what madness rules in brainsick men,
When for so slight and frivolous a cause
Such factious emulations shall arise!
Good cousins both, of York and Somerset,
Quiet yourselves, I pray, and be at peace.
YORK
Let this dissension first be tried by fight,
And then your highness shall command a peace.
SOMERSET
The quarrel toucheth none but us alone;
Betwixt ourselves let us decide it then.
YORK
There is my pledge; accept it, Somerset.
VERNON
Nay, let it rest where it began at first.
BASSET
Confirm it so, mine honourable lord.
GLOUCESTER
Confirm it so! Confounded be your strife!
And perish ye, with your audacious prate!

Presumptuous vassals, are you not ashamed
With this immodest clamorous outrage
To trouble and disturb the king and us?
And you, my lords, methinks you do not well
To bear with their perverse objections;
Much less to take occasion from their mouths
To raise a mutiny betwixt yourselves:
Let me persuade you take a better course.
EXETER
It grieves his highness: good my lords, be friends.
KING HENRY VI
Come hither, you that would be combatants:
Henceforth I charge you, as you love our favour,
Quite to forget this quarrel and the cause.
And you, my lords, remember where we are,
In France, amongst a fickle wavering nation:
If they perceive dissension in our looks
And that within ourselves we disagree,
How will their grudging stomachs be provoked
To wilful disobedience, and rebel!
Beside, what infamy will there arise,
When foreign princes shall be certified
That for a toy, a thing of no regard,
King Henry's peers and chief nobility
Destroy'd themselves, and lost the realm of France!
O, think upon the conquest of my father,
My tender years, and let us not forego
That for a trifle that was bought with blood
Let me be umpire in this doubtful strife.
I see no reason, if I wear this rose,
Putting on a red rose
That any one should therefore be suspicious
I more incline to Somerset than York:
Both are my kinsmen, and I love them both:
As well they may upbraid me with my crown,
Because, forsooth, the king of Scots is crown'd.
But your discretions better can persuade
Than I am able to instruct or teach:
And therefore, as we hither came in peace,
So let us still continue peace and love.
Cousin of York, we institute your grace
To be our regent in these parts of France:
And, good my Lord of Somerset, unite
Your troops of horsemen with his bands of foot;
And, like true subjects, sons of your progenitors,
Go cheerfully together and digest.
Your angry choler on your enemies.
Ourself, my lord protector and the rest
After some respite will return to Calais;
From thence to England; where I hope ere long
To be presented, by your victories,
With Charles, Alencon and that traitorous rout.
Flourish. Exeunt all but YORK, WARWICK, EXETER and VERNON
WARWICK
My Lord of York, I promise you, the king
Prettily, methought, did play the orator.
YORK
And so he did; but yet I like it not,
In that he wears the badge of Somerset.
WARWICK
Tush, that was but his fancy, blame him not;
I dare presume, sweet prince, he thought no harm.
YORK

An if I wist he did,--but let it rest;
Other affairs must now be managed.
Exeunt all but EXETER
EXETER
Well didst thou, Richard, to suppress thy voice;
For, had the passions of thy heart burst out,
I fear we should have seen decipher'd there
More rancorous spite, more furious raging broils,
Than yet can be imagined or supposed.
But howsoe'er, no simple man that sees
This jarring discord of nobility,
This shouldering of each other in the court,
This factious bandying of their favourites,
But that it doth presage some ill event.
'Tis much when sceptres are in children's hands;
But more when envy breeds unkind division;
There comes the rain, there begins confusion.
Exit
SCENE II. Before Bourdeaux.
Enter TALBOT, with trump and drum
TALBOT
Go to the gates of Bourdeaux, trumpeter:
Summon their general unto the wall.
Trumpet sounds. Enter General and others, aloft
English John Talbot, captains, calls you forth,
Servant in arms to Harry King of England;
And thus he would: Open your city gates;
Be humble to us; call my sovereign yours,
And do him homage as obedient subjects;
And I'll withdraw me and my bloody power:
But, if you frown upon this proffer'd peace,
You tempt the fury of my three attendants,
Lean famine, quartering steel, and climbing fire;
Who in a moment even with the earth
Shall lay your stately and air-braving towers,
If you forsake the offer of their love.
General
Thou ominous and fearful owl of death,
Our nation's terror and their bloody scourge!
The period of thy tyranny approacheth.
On us thou canst not enter but by death;
For, I protest, we are well fortified
And strong enough to issue out and fight:
If thou retire, the Dauphin, well appointed,
Stands with the snares of war to tangle thee:
On either hand thee there are squadrons pitch'd,
To wall thee from the liberty of flight;
And no way canst thou turn thee for redress,
But death doth front thee with apparent spoil
And pale destruction meets thee in the face.
Ten thousand French have ta'en the sacrament
To rive their dangerous artillery
Upon no Christian soul but English Talbot.
Lo, there thou stand'st, a breathing valiant man,
Of an invincible unconquer'd spirit!
This is the latest glory of thy praise
That I, thy enemy, due thee withal;
For ere the glass, that now begins to run,
Finish the process of his sandy hour,
These eyes, that see thee now well coloured,
Shall see thee wither'd, bloody, pale and dead.
Drum afar off

Hark! hark! the Dauphin's drum, a warning bell,
Sings heavy music to thy timorous soul;
And mine shall ring thy dire departure out.
Exeunt General, & c
TALBOT
He fables not; I hear the enemy:
Out, some light horsemen, and peruse their wings.
O, negligent and heedless discipline!
How are we park'd and bounded in a pale,
A little herd of England's timorous deer,
Mazed with a yelping kennel of French curs!
If we be English deer, be then in blood;
Not rascal-like, to fall down with a pinch,
But rather, moody-mad and desperate stags,
Turn on the bloody hounds with heads of steel
And make the cowards stand aloof at bay:
Sell every man his life as dear as mine,
And they shall find dear deer of us, my friends.
God and Saint George, Talbot and England's right,
Prosper our colours in this dangerous fight!
Exeunt

SCENE III. Plains in Gascony.
Enter a Messenger that meets YORK. Enter YORK with trumpet and many Soldiers
YORK
Are not the speedy scouts return'd again,
That dogg'd the mighty army of the Dauphin?
Messenger
They are return'd, my lord, and give it out
That he is march'd to Bourdeaux with his power,
To fight with Talbot: as he march'd along,
By your espials were discovered
Two mightier troops than that the Dauphin led,
Which join'd with him and made their march for Bourdeaux.
YORK
A plague upon that villain Somerset,
That thus delays my promised supply
Of horsemen, that were levied for this siege!
Renowned Talbot doth expect my aid,
And I am lowted by a traitor villain
And cannot help the noble chevalier:
God comfort him in this necessity!
If he miscarry, farewell wars in France.
Enter Sir William LUCY
LUCY
END PART 1

Dramatis Personae

KING HENRY THE SIXTH
HUMPHREY, DUKE OF GLOUCESTER, his uncle
CARDINAL BEAUFORT, BISHOP OF WINCHESTER, great-uncle to the King
RICHARD PLANTAGENET, DUKE OF YORK
EDWARD and RICHARD, his sons
DUKE OF SOMERSET
DUKE OF SUFFOLK
DUKE OF BUCKINGHAM
LORD CLIFFORD
YOUNG CLIFFORD, his son
EARL OF SALISBURY
EARL OF WARWICK
LORD SCALES
LORD SAY
SIR HUMPHREY STAFFORD
WILLIAM STAFFORD, his brother
SIR JOHN STANLEY
VAUX
MATTHEW GOFFE
A LIEUTENANT, a SHIPMASTER, a MASTER'S MATE, and WALTER WHITMORE
TWO GENTLEMEN, prisoners with Suffolk
JOHN HUME and JOHN SOUTHWELL, two priests
ROGER BOLINGBROKE, a conjurer
A SPIRIT raised by him
THOMAS HORNER, an armourer
PETER, his man
CLERK OF CHATHAM
MAYOR OF SAINT ALBANS
SAUNDER SIMPCOX, an impostor
ALEXANDER IDEN, a Kentish gentleman
JACK CADE, a rebel
GEORGE BEVIS, JOHN HOLLAND, DICK THE BUTCHER, SMITH THE WEAVER,
MICHAEL, &c., followers of Cade
TWO MURDERERS
MARGARET, Queen to King Henry
ELEANOR, Duchess of Gloucester
MARGERY JOURDAIN, a witch
WIFE to SIMPCOX
Lords, Ladies, and Attendants; Petitioners, Aldermen, a Herald,
a Beadle, a Sheriff, Officers, Citizens, Prentices, Falconers,
Guards, Soldiers, Messengers, &c.

ACT I

SCENE I. London. The palace.
Flourish of trumpets: then hautboys. Enter KING HENRY VI, GLOUCESTER, SALISBURY, WARWICK, and CARDINAL, on the one side; QUEEN MARGARET, SUFFOLK, YORK, SOMERSET, and BUCKINGHAM, on the other

SUFFOLK
As by your high imperial majesty
I had in charge at my depart for France,
As procurator to your excellence,
To marry Princess Margaret for your grace,
So, in the famous ancient city, Tours,
In presence of the Kings of France and Sicil,
The Dukes of Orleans, Calaber, Bretagne and Alencon,
Seven earls, twelve barons and twenty reverend bishops,
I have perform'd my task and was espoused:
And humbly now upon my bended knee,
In sight of England and her lordly peers,
Deliver up my title in the queen
To your most gracious hands, that are the substance

Of that great shadow I did represent;
The happiest gift that ever marquess gave,
The fairest queen that ever king received.
KING HENRY VI
Suffolk, arise. Welcome, Queen Margaret:
I can express no kinder sign of love
Than this kind kiss. O Lord, that lends me life,
Lend me a heart replete with thankfulness!
For thou hast given me in this beauteous face
A world of earthly blessings to my soul,
If sympathy of love unite our thoughts.
QUEEN MARGARET
Great King of England and my gracious lord,
The mutual conference that my mind hath had,
By day, by night, waking and in my dreams,
In courtly company or at my beads,
With you, mine alder-liefest sovereign,
Makes me the bolder to salute my king
With ruder terms, such as my wit affords
And over-joy of heart doth minister.
KING HENRY VI
Her sight did ravish; but her grace in speech,
Her words y-clad with wisdom's majesty,
Makes me from wondering fall to weeping joys;
Such is the fulness of my heart's content.
Lords, with one cheerful voice welcome my love.
ALL
[Kneeling] Long live Queen Margaret, England's
happiness!
QUEEN MARGARET
We thank you all.
Flourish
SUFFOLK
My lord protector, so it please your grace,
Here are the articles of contracted peace
Between our sovereign and the French king Charles,
For eighteen months concluded by consent.
GLOUCESTER
[Reads] 'Imprimis, it is agreed between the French
king Charles, and William de la Pole, Marquess of
Suffolk, ambassador for Henry King of England, that
the said Henry shall espouse the Lady Margaret,
daughter unto Reignier King of Naples, Sicilia and
Jerusalem, and crown her Queen of England ere the
thirtieth of May next ensuing. Item, that the duchy
of Anjou and the county of Maine shall be released
and delivered to the king her father'--
Lets the paper fall
KING HENRY VI
Uncle, how now!
GLOUCESTER
Pardon me, gracious lord;
Some sudden qualm hath struck me at the heart
And dimm'd mine eyes, that I can read no further.
KING HENRY VI
Uncle of Winchester, I pray, read on.
CARDINAL
[Reads] 'Item, It is further agreed between them,
that the duchies of Anjou and Maine shall be
released and delivered over to the king her father,
and she sent over of the King of England's own
proper cost and charges, without having any dowry.'
KING HENRY VI

They please us well. Lord marquess, kneel down:
We here create thee the first duke of Suffolk,
And gird thee with the sword. Cousin of York,
We here discharge your grace from being regent
I' the parts of France, till term of eighteen months
Be full expired. Thanks, uncle Winchester,
Gloucester, York, Buckingham, Somerset,
Salisbury, and Warwick;
We thank you all for the great favour done,
In entertainment to my princely queen.
Come, let us in, and with all speed provide
To see her coronation be perform'd.
Exeunt KING HENRY VI, QUEEN MARGARET, and SUFFOLK

GLOUCESTER
Brave peers of England, pillars of the state,
To you Duke Humphrey must unload his grief,
Your grief, the common grief of all the land.
What! did my brother Henry spend his youth,
His valour, coin and people, in the wars?
Did he so often lodge in open field,
In winter's cold and summer's parching heat,
To conquer France, his true inheritance?
And did my brother Bedford toil his wits,
To keep by policy what Henry got?
Have you yourselves, Somerset, Buckingham,
Brave York, Salisbury, and victorious Warwick,
Received deep scars in France and Normandy?
Or hath mine uncle Beaufort and myself,
With all the learned council of the realm,
Studied so long, sat in the council-house
Early and late, debating to and fro
How France and Frenchmen might be kept in awe,
And had his highness in his infancy
Crowned in Paris in despite of foes?
And shall these labours and these honours die?
Shall Henry's conquest, Bedford's vigilance,
Your deeds of war and all our counsel die?
O peers of England, shameful is this league!
Fatal this marriage, cancelling your fame,
Blotting your names from books of memory,
Razing the characters of your renown,
Defacing monuments of conquer'd France,
Undoing all, as all had never been!

CARDINAL
Nephew, what means this passionate discourse,
This peroration with such circumstance?
For France, 'tis ours; and we will keep it still.

GLOUCESTER
Ay, uncle, we will keep it, if we can;
But now it is impossible we should:
Suffolk, the new-made duke that rules the roast,
Hath given the duchy of Anjou and Maine
Unto the poor King Reignier, whose large style
Agrees not with the leanness of his purse.

SALISBURY
Now, by the death of Him that died for all,
These counties were the keys of Normandy.
But wherefore weeps Warwick, my valiant son?

WARWICK
For grief that they are past recovery:
For, were there hope to conquer them again,
My sword should shed hot blood, mine eyes no tears.
Anjou and Maine! myself did win them both;

Those provinces these arms of mine did conquer:
And are the cities, that I got with wounds,
Delivered up again with peaceful words?
Mort Dieu!
YORK
For Suffolk's duke, may he be suffocate,
That dims the honour of this warlike isle!
France should have torn and rent my very heart,
Before I would have yielded to this league.
I never read but England's kings have had
Large sums of gold and dowries with their wives:
And our King Henry gives away his own,
To match with her that brings no vantages.
GLOUCESTER
A proper jest, and never heard before,
That Suffolk should demand a whole fifteenth
For costs and charges in transporting her!
She should have stayed in France and starved
in France, Before--
CARDINAL
My Lord of Gloucester, now ye grow too hot:
It was the pleasure of my lord the King.
GLOUCESTER
My Lord of Winchester, I know your mind;
'Tis not my speeches that you do mislike,
But 'tis my presence that doth trouble ye.
Rancour will out: proud prelate, in thy face
I see thy fury: if I longer stay,
We shall begin our ancient bickerings.
Lordings, farewell; and say, when I am gone,
I prophesied France will be lost ere long.
Exit
CARDINAL
So, there goes our protector in a rage.
'Tis known to you he is mine enemy,
Nay, more, an enemy unto you all,
And no great friend, I fear me, to the king.
Consider, lords, he is the next of blood,
And heir apparent to the English crown:
Had Henry got an empire by his marriage,
And all the wealthy kingdoms of the west,
There's reason he should be displeased at it.
Look to it, lords! let not his smoothing words
Bewitch your hearts; be wise and circumspect.
What though the common people favour him,
Calling him 'Humphrey, the good Duke of
Gloucester,'
Clapping their hands, and crying with loud voice,
'Jesu maintain your royal excellence!'
With 'God preserve the good Duke Humphrey!'
I fear me, lords, for all this flattering gloss,
He will be found a dangerous protector.
BUCKINGHAM
Why should he, then, protect our sovereign,
He being of age to govern of himself?
Cousin of Somerset, join you with me,
And all together, with the Duke of Suffolk,
We'll quickly hoise Duke Humphrey from his seat.
CARDINAL
This weighty business will not brook delay:
I'll to the Duke of Suffolk presently.
Exit
SOMERSET

Cousin of Buckingham, though Humphrey's pride
And greatness of his place be grief to us,
Yet let us watch the haughty cardinal:
His insolence is more intolerable
Than all the princes in the land beside:
If Gloucester be displaced, he'll be protector.
BUCKINGHAM
Or thou or I, Somerset, will be protector,
Despite Duke Humphrey or the cardinal.
Exeunt BUCKINGHAM and SOMERSET
SALISBURY
Pride went before, ambition follows him.
While these do labour for their own preferment,
Behoves it us to labour for the realm.
I never saw but Humphrey Duke of Gloucester
Did bear him like a noble gentleman.
Oft have I seen the haughty cardinal,
More like a soldier than a man o' the church,
As stout and proud as he were lord of all,
Swear like a ruffian and demean himself
Unlike the ruler of a commonweal.
Warwick, my son, the comfort of my age,
Thy deeds, thy plainness and thy housekeeping,
Hath won the greatest favour of the commons,
Excepting none but good Duke Humphrey:
And, brother York, thy acts in Ireland,
In bringing them to civil discipline,
Thy late exploits done in the heart of France,
When thou wert regent for our sovereign,
Have made thee fear'd and honour'd of the people:
Join we together, for the public good,
In what we can, to bridle and suppress
The pride of Suffolk and the cardinal,
With Somerset's and Buckingham's ambition;
And, as we may, cherish Duke Humphrey's deeds,
While they do tend the profit of the land.
WARWICK
So God help Warwick, as he loves the land,
And common profit of his country!
YORK
[Aside] And so says York, for he hath greatest cause.
SALISBURY
Then let's make haste away, and look unto the main.
WARWICK
Unto the main! O father, Maine is lost;
That Maine which by main force Warwick did win,
And would have kept so long as breath did last!
Main chance, father, you meant; but I meant Maine,
Which I will win from France, or else be slain,
Exeunt WARWICK and SALISBURY
YORK
Anjou and Maine are given to the French;
Paris is lost; the state of Normandy
Stands on a tickle point, now they are gone:
Suffolk concluded on the articles,
The peers agreed, and Henry was well pleased
To change two dukedoms for a duke's fair daughter.
I cannot blame them all: what is't to them?
'Tis thine they give away, and not their own.
Pirates may make cheap pennyworths of their pillage
And purchase friends and give to courtezans,
Still revelling like lords till all be gone;
While as the silly owner of the goods

Weeps over them and wrings his hapless hands
And shakes his head and trembling stands aloof,
While all is shared and all is borne away,
Ready to starve and dare not touch his own:
So York must sit and fret and bite his tongue,
While his own lands are bargain'd for and sold.
Methinks the realms of England, France and Ireland
Bear that proportion to my flesh and blood
As did the fatal brand Althaea burn'd
Unto the prince's heart of Calydon.
Anjou and Maine both given unto the French!
Cold news for me, for I had hope of France,
Even as I have of fertile England's soil.
A day will come when York shall claim his own;
And therefore I will take the Nevils' parts
And make a show of love to proud Duke Humphrey,
And, when I spy advantage, claim the crown,
For that's the golden mark I seek to hit:
Nor shall proud Lancaster usurp my right,
Nor hold the sceptre in his childish fist,
Nor wear the diadem upon his head,
Whose church-like humours fits not for a crown.
Then, York, be still awhile, till time do serve:
Watch thou and wake when others be asleep,
To pry into the secrets of the state;
Till Henry, surfeiting in joys of love,
With his new bride and England's dear-bought queen,
And Humphrey with the peers be fall'n at jars:
Then will I raise aloft the milk-white rose,
With whose sweet smell the air shall be perfumed;
And in my standard bear the arms of York
To grapple with the house of Lancaster;
And, force perforce, I'll make him yield the crown,
Whose bookish rule hath pull'd fair England down.
Exit

SCENE II. GLOUCESTER'S house.
Enter GLOUCESTER and his DUCHESS
DUCHESS
Why droops my lord, like over-ripen'd corn,
Hanging the head at Ceres' plenteous load?
Why doth the great Duke Humphrey knit his brows,
As frowning at the favours of the world?
Why are thine eyes fixed to the sullen earth,
Gazing on that which seems to dim thy sight?
What seest thou there? King Henry's diadem,
Enchased with all the honours of the world?
If so, gaze on, and grovel on thy face,
Until thy head be circled with the same.
Put forth thy hand, reach at the glorious gold.
What, is't too short? I'll lengthen it with mine:
And, having both together heaved it up,
We'll both together lift our heads to heaven,
And never more abase our sight so low
As to vouchsafe one glance unto the ground.
GLOUCESTER
O Nell, sweet Nell, if thou dost love thy lord,
Banish the canker of ambitious thoughts.
And may that thought, when I imagine ill
Against my king and nephew, virtuous Henry,
Be my last breathing in this mortal world!
My troublous dream this night doth make me sad.
DUCHESS

What dream'd my lord? tell me, and I'll requite it
With sweet rehearsal of my morning's dream.
GLOUCESTER
Methought this staff, mine office-badge in court,
Was broke in twain; by whom I have forgot,
But, as I think, it was by the cardinal;
And on the pieces of the broken wand
Were placed the heads of Edmund Duke of Somerset,
And William de la Pole, first duke of Suffolk.
This was my dream: what it doth bode, God knows.
DUCHESS
Tut, this was nothing but an argument
That he that breaks a stick of Gloucester's grove
Shall lose his head for his presumption.
But list to me, my Humphrey, my sweet duke:
Methought I sat in seat of majesty
In the cathedral church of Westminster,
And in that chair where kings and queens are crown'd;
Where Henry and dame Margaret kneel'd to me
And on my head did set the diadem.
GLOUCESTER
Nay, Eleanor, then must I chide outright:
Presumptuous dame, ill-nurtured Eleanor,
Art thou not second woman in the realm,
And the protector's wife, beloved of him?
Hast thou not worldly pleasure at command,
Above the reach or compass of thy thought?
And wilt thou still be hammering treachery,
To tumble down thy husband and thyself
From top of honour to disgrace's feet?
Away from me, and let me hear no more!
DUCHESS
What, what, my lord! are you so choleric
With Eleanor, for telling but her dream?
Next time I'll keep my dreams unto myself,
And not be cheque'd.
GLOUCESTER
Nay, be not angry; I am pleased again.
Enter Messenger
Messenger
My lord protector, 'tis his highness' pleasure
You do prepare to ride unto Saint Alban's,
Where as the king and queen do mean to hawk.
GLOUCESTER
I go. Come, Nell, thou wilt ride with us?
DUCHESS
Yes, my good lord, I'll follow presently.
Exeunt GLOUCESTER and Messenger
Follow I must; I cannot go before,
While Gloucester bears this base and humble mind.
Were I a man, a duke, and next of blood,
I would remove these tedious stumbling-blocks
And smooth my way upon their headless necks;
And, being a woman, I will not be slack
To play my part in Fortune's pageant.
Where are you there? Sir John! nay, fear not, man,
We are alone; here's none but thee and I.
Enter HUME
HUME
Jesus preserve your royal majesty!
DUCHESS
What say'st thou? majesty! I am but grace.
HUME

But, by the grace of God, and Hume's advice,
Your grace's title shall be multiplied.
DUCHESS
What say'st thou, man? hast thou as yet conferr'd
With Margery Jourdain, the cunning witch,
With Roger Bolingbroke, the conjurer?
And will they undertake to do me good?
HUME
This they have promised, to show your highness
A spirit raised from depth of under-ground,
That shall make answer to such questions
As by your grace shall be propounded him.
DUCHESS
It is enough; I'll think upon the questions:
When from St. Alban's we do make return,
We'll see these things effected to the full.
Here, Hume, take this reward; make merry, man,
With thy confederates in this weighty cause.
Exit
HUME
Hume must make merry with the duchess' gold;
Marry, and shall. But how now, Sir John Hume!
Seal up your lips, and give no words but mum:
The business asketh silent secrecy.
Dame Eleanor gives gold to bring the witch:
Gold cannot come amiss, were she a devil.
Yet have I gold flies from another coast;
I dare not say, from the rich cardinal
And from the great and new-made Duke of Suffolk,
Yet I do find it so; for to be plain,
They, knowing Dame Eleanor's aspiring humour,
Have hired me to undermine the duchess
And buz these conjurations in her brain.
They say 'A crafty knave does need no broker;'
Yet am I Suffolk and the cardinal's broker.
Hume, if you take not heed, you shall go near
To call them both a pair of crafty knaves.
Well, so it stands; and thus, I fear, at last
Hume's knavery will be the duchess' wreck,
And her attainture will be Humphrey's fall:
Sort how it will, I shall have gold for all.
Exit
SCENE III. The palace.
Enter three or four Petitioners, PETER, the Armourer's man, being one
First Petitioner
My masters, let's stand close: my lord protector
will come this way by and by, and then we may deliver
our supplications in the quill.
Second Petitioner
Marry, the Lord protect him, for he's a good man!
Jesu bless him!
Enter SUFFOLK and QUEEN MARGARET
PETER
Here a' comes, methinks, and the queen with him.
I'll be the first, sure.
Second Petitioner
Come back, fool; this is the Duke of Suffolk, and
not my lord protector.
SUFFOLK
How now, fellow! would'st anything with me?
First Petitioner
I pray, my lord, pardon me; I took ye for my lord
protector.

QUEEN MARGARET
[Reading] 'To my Lord Protector!' Are your
supplications to his lordship? Let me see them:
what is thine?
First Petitioner
Mine is, an't please your grace, against John
Goodman, my lord cardinal's man, for keeping my
house, and lands, and wife and all, from me.
SUFFOLK
Thy wife, too! that's some wrong, indeed. What's
yours? What's here!
Reads
'Against the Duke of Suffolk, for enclosing the
commons of Melford.' How now, sir knave!
Second Petitioner
Alas, sir, I am but a poor petitioner of our whole township.
PETER
[Giving his petition] Against my master, Thomas
Horner, for saying that the Duke of York was rightful
heir to the crown.
QUEEN MARGARET
What sayst thou? did the Duke of York say he was
rightful heir to the crown?
PETER
That my master was? no, forsooth: my master said
that he was, and that the king was an usurper.
SUFFOLK
Who is there?
Enter Servant
Take this fellow in, and send for
his master with a pursuivant presently: we'll hear
more of your matter before the King.
Exit Servant with PETER
QUEEN MARGARET
And as for you, that love to be protected
Under the wings of our protector's grace,
Begin your suits anew, and sue to him.
Tears the supplication
Away, base cullions! Suffolk, let them go.
ALL
Come, let's be gone.
Exeunt
QUEEN MARGARET
My Lord of Suffolk, say, is this the guise,
Is this the fashion in the court of England?
Is this the government of Britain's isle,
And this the royalty of Albion's king?
What shall King Henry be a pupil still
Under the surly Gloucester's governance?
Am I a queen in title and in style,
And must be made a subject to a duke?
I tell thee, Pole, when in the city Tours
Thou ran'st a tilt in honour of my love
And stolest away the ladies' hearts of France,
I thought King Henry had resembled thee
In courage, courtship and proportion:
But all his mind is bent to holiness,
To number Ave-Maries on his beads;
His champions are the prophets and apostles,
His weapons holy saws of sacred writ,
His study is his tilt-yard, and his loves
Are brazen images of canonized saints.
I would the college of the cardinals

Would choose him pope, and carry him to Rome,
And set the triple crown upon his head:
That were a state fit for his holiness.
SUFFOLK
Madam, be patient: as I was cause
Your highness came to England, so will I
In England work your grace's full content.
QUEEN MARGARET
Beside the haughty protector, have we Beaufort,
The imperious churchman, Somerset, Buckingham,
And grumbling York: and not the least of these
But can do more in England than the king.
SUFFOLK
And he of these that can do most of all
Cannot do more in England than the Nevils:
Salisbury and Warwick are no simple peers.
QUEEN MARGARET
Not all these lords do vex me half so much
As that proud dame, the lord protector's wife.
She sweeps it through the court with troops of ladies,
More like an empress than Duke Humphrey's wife:
Strangers in court do take her for the queen:
She bears a duke's revenues on her back,
And in her heart she scorns our poverty:
Shall I not live to be avenged on her?
Contemptuous base-born callet as she is,
She vaunted 'mongst her minions t'other day,
The very train of her worst wearing gown
Was better worth than all my father's lands,
Till Suffolk gave two dukedoms for his daughter.
SUFFOLK
Madam, myself have limed a bush for her,
And placed a quire of such enticing birds,
That she will light to listen to the lays,
And never mount to trouble you again.
So, let her rest: and, madam, list to me;
For I am bold to counsel you in this.
Although we fancy not the cardinal,
Yet must we join with him and with the lords,
Till we have brought Duke Humphrey in disgrace.
As for the Duke of York, this late complaint
Will make but little for his benefit.
So, one by one, we'll weed them all at last,
And you yourself shall steer the happy helm.
Sound a sennet. Enter KING HENRY VI, GLOUCESTER, CARDINAL, BUCKINGHAM, YORK, SOMERSET, SALISBURY, WARWICK, and the DUCHESS
KING HENRY VI
For my part, noble lords, I care not which;
Or Somerset or York, all's one to me.
YORK
If York have ill demean'd himself in France,
Then let him be denay'd the regentship.
SOMERSET
If Somerset be unworthy of the place,
Let York be regent; I will yield to him.
WARWICK
Whether your grace be worthy, yea or no,
Dispute not that: York is the worthier.
CARDINAL
Ambitious Warwick, let thy betters speak.
WARWICK
The cardinal's not my better in the field.
BUCKINGHAM

All in this presence are thy betters, Warwick.
WARWICK
Warwick may live to be the best of all.
SALISBURY
Peace, son! and show some reason, Buckingham,
Why Somerset should be preferred in this.
QUEEN MARGARET
Because the king, forsooth, will have it so.
GLOUCESTER
Madam, the king is old enough himself
To give his censure: these are no women's matters.
QUEEN MARGARET
If he be old enough, what needs your grace
To be protector of his excellence?
GLOUCESTER
Madam, I am protector of the realm;
And, at his pleasure, will resign my place.
SUFFOLK
Resign it then and leave thine insolence.
Since thou wert king--as who is king but thou?--
The commonwealth hath daily run to wreck;
The Dauphin hath prevail'd beyond the seas;
And all the peers and nobles of the realm
Have been as bondmen to thy sovereignty.
CARDINAL
The commons hast thou rack'd; the clergy's bags
Are lank and lean with thy extortions.
SOMERSET
Thy sumptuous buildings and thy wife's attire
Have cost a mass of public treasury.
BUCKINGHAM
Thy cruelty in execution
Upon offenders, hath exceeded law,
And left thee to the mercy of the law.
QUEEN MARGARET
They sale of offices and towns in France,
If they were known, as the suspect is great,
Would make thee quickly hop without thy head.
Exit GLOUCESTER. QUEEN MARGARET drops her fan
Give me my fan: what, minion! can ye not?
She gives the DUCHESS a box on the ear
I cry you mercy, madam; was it you?
DUCHESS
Was't I! yea, I it was, proud Frenchwoman:
Could I come near your beauty with my nails,
I'd set my ten commandments in your face.
KING HENRY VI
Sweet aunt, be quiet; 'twas against her will.
DUCHESS
Against her will! good king, look to't in time;
She'll hamper thee, and dandle thee like a baby:
Though in this place most master wear no breeches,
She shall not strike Dame Eleanor unrevenged.
Exit
BUCKINGHAM
Lord cardinal, I will follow Eleanor,
And listen after Humphrey, how he proceeds:
She's tickled now; her fume needs no spurs,
She'll gallop far enough to her destruction.
Exit
Re-enter GLOUCESTER
GLOUCESTER

Now, lords, my choler being over-blown
With walking once about the quadrangle,
I come to talk of commonwealth affairs.
As for your spiteful false objections,
Prove them, and I lie open to the law:
But God in mercy so deal with my soul,
As I in duty love my king and country!
But, to the matter that we have in hand:
I say, my sovereign, York is meetest man
To be your regent in the realm of France.

SUFFOLK
Before we make election, give me leave
To show some reason, of no little force,
That York is most unmeet of any man.

YORK
I'll tell thee, Suffolk, why I am unmeet:
First, for I cannot flatter thee in pride;
Next, if I be appointed for the place,
My Lord of Somerset will keep me here,
Without discharge, money, or furniture,
Till France be won into the Dauphin's hands:
Last time, I danced attendance on his will
Till Paris was besieged, famish'd, and lost.

WARWICK
That can I witness; and a fouler fact
Did never traitor in the land commit.

SUFFOLK
Peace, headstrong Warwick!

WARWICK
Image of pride, why should I hold my peace?

Enter HORNER, the Armourer, and his man PETER, guarded

SUFFOLK
Because here is a man accused of treason:
Pray God the Duke of York excuse himself!

YORK
Doth any one accuse York for a traitor?

KING HENRY VI
What mean'st thou, Suffolk; tell me, what are these?

SUFFOLK
Please it your majesty, this is the man
That doth accuse his master of high treason:
His words were these: that Richard, Duke of York,
Was rightful heir unto the English crown
And that your majesty was a usurper.

KING HENRY VI
Say, man, were these thy words?

HORNER
An't shall please your majesty, I never said nor
thought any such matter: God is my witness, I am
falsely accused by the villain.

PETER
By these ten bones, my lords, he did speak them to
me in the garret one night, as we were scouring my
Lord of York's armour.

YORK
Base dunghill villain and mechanical,
I'll have thy head for this thy traitor's speech.
I do beseech your royal majesty,
Let him have all the rigor of the law.

HORNER
Alas, my lord, hang me, if ever I spake the words.
My accuser is my 'prentice; and when I did correct
him for his fault the other day, he did vow upon his

knees he would be even with me: I have good
witness of this: therefore I beseech your majesty,
do not cast away an honest man for a villain's
accusation.
KING HENRY VI
Uncle, what shall we say to this in law?
GLOUCESTER
This doom, my lord, if I may judge:
Let Somerset be regent over the French,
Because in York this breeds suspicion:
And let these have a day appointed them
For single combat in convenient place,
For he hath witness of his servant's malice:
This is the law, and this Duke Humphrey's doom.
SOMERSET
I humbly thank your royal majesty.
HORNER
And I accept the combat willingly.
PETER
Alas, my lord, I cannot fight; for God's sake, pity
my case. The spite of man prevaileth against me. O
Lord, have mercy upon me! I shall never be able to
fight a blow. O Lord, my heart!
GLOUCESTER
Sirrah, or you must fight, or else be hang'd.
KING HENRY VI
Away with them to prison; and the day of combat
shall be the last of the next month. Come,
Somerset, we'll see thee sent away.
Flourish. Exeunt
SCENE IV. GLOUCESTER's garden.
Enter MARGARET JOURDAIN, HUME, SOUTHWELL, and BOLINGBROKE
HUME
Come, my masters; the duchess, I tell you, expects
performance of your promises.
BOLINGBROKE
Master Hume, we are therefore provided: will her
ladyship behold and hear our exorcisms?
HUME
Ay, what else? fear you not her courage.
BOLINGBROKE
I have heard her reported to be a woman of an
invincible spirit: but it shall be convenient,
Master Hume, that you be by her aloft, while we be
busy below; and so, I pray you, go, in God's name,
and leave us.
Exit HUME
Mother Jourdain, be you
prostrate and grovel on the earth; John Southwell,
read you; and let us to our work.
Enter the DUCHESS aloft, HUME following
DUCHESS
Well said, my masters; and welcome all. To this
gear the sooner the better.
BOLINGBROKE
Patience, good lady; wizards know their times:
Deep night, dark night, the silent of the night,
The time of night when Troy was set on fire;
The time when screech-owls cry and ban-dogs howl,
And spirits walk and ghosts break up their graves,
That time best fits the work we have in hand.
Madam, sit you and fear not: whom we raise,
We will make fast within a hallow'd verge.

Here they do the ceremonies belonging, and make the circle; BOLINGBROKE or SOUTHWELL reads, Conjuro te, & c. It thunders and lightens terribly; then the Spirit riseth
Spirit
Adsum.
MARGARET JOURDAIN
Asmath,
By the eternal God, whose name and power
Thou tremblest at, answer that I shall ask;
For, till thou speak, thou shalt not pass from hence.
Spirit
Ask what thou wilt. That I had said and done!
BOLINGBROKE
'First of the king: what shall of him become?'
Reading out of a paper
Spirit
The duke yet lives that Henry shall depose;
But him outlive, and die a violent death.
As the Spirit speaks, SOUTHWELL writes the answer
BOLINGBROKE
'What fates await the Duke of Suffolk?'
Spirit
By water shall he die, and take his end.
BOLINGBROKE
'What shall befall the Duke of Somerset?'
Spirit
Let him shun castles;
Safer shall he be upon the sandy plains
Than where castles mounted stand.
Have done, for more I hardly can endure.
BOLINGBROKE
Descend to darkness and the burning lake!
False fiend, avoid!
Thunder and lightning. Exit Spirit
Enter YORK and BUCKINGHAM with their Guard and break in
YORK
Lay hands upon these traitors and their trash.
Beldam, I think we watch'd you at an inch.
What, madam, are you there? the king and commonweal
Are deeply indebted for this piece of pains:
My lord protector will, I doubt it not,
See you well guerdon'd for these good deserts.
DUCHESS
Not half so bad as thine to England's king,
Injurious duke, that threatest where's no cause.
BUCKINGHAM
True, madam, none at all: what call you this?
Away with them! let them be clapp'd up close.
And kept asunder. You, madam, shall with us.
Stafford, take her to thee.
Exeunt above DUCHESS and HUME, guarded
We'll see your trinkets here all forthcoming.
All, away!
Exeunt guard with MARGARET JOURDAIN, SOUTHWELL, & c
YORK
Lord Buckingham, methinks, you watch'd her well:
A pretty plot, well chosen to build upon!
Now, pray, my lord, let's see the devil's writ.
What have we here?
Reads
'The duke yet lives, that Henry shall depose;
But him outlive, and die a violent death.'
Why, this is just
'Aio te, AEacida, Romanos vincere posse.'

55

Well, to the rest:
'Tell me what fate awaits the Duke of Suffolk?
By water shall he die, and take his end.
What shall betide the Duke of Somerset?
Let him shun castles;
Safer shall he be upon the sandy plains
Than where castles mounted stand.'
Come, come, my lords;
These oracles are hardly attain'd,
And hardly understood.
The king is now in progress towards Saint Alban's,
With him the husband of this lovely lady:
Thither go these news, as fast as horse can
carry them:
A sorry breakfast for my lord protector.
BUCKINGHAM
Your grace shall give me leave, my Lord of York,
To be the post, in hope of his reward.
YORK
At your pleasure, my good lord. Who's within
there, ho!
Enter a Servingman
Invite my Lords of Salisbury and Warwick
To sup with me to-morrow night. Away!
Exeunt

ACT II

SCENE I. Saint Alban's.

Enter KING HENRY VI, QUEEN MARGARET, GLOUCESTER, CARDINAL, and SUFFOLK, with Falconers halloing

QUEEN MARGARET
Believe me, lords, for flying at the brook,
I saw not better sport these seven years' day:
Yet, by your leave, the wind was very high;
And, ten to one, old Joan had not gone out.
KING HENRY VI
But what a point, my lord, your falcon made,
And what a pitch she flew above the rest!
To see how God in all his creatures works!
Yea, man and birds are fain of climbing high.
SUFFOLK
No marvel, an it like your majesty,
My lord protector's hawks do tower so well;
They know their master loves to be aloft,
And bears his thoughts above his falcon's pitch.
GLOUCESTER
My lord, 'tis but a base ignoble mind
That mounts no higher than a bird can soar.
CARDINAL
I thought as much; he would be above the clouds.
GLOUCESTER
Ay, my lord cardinal? how think you by that?
Were it not good your grace could fly to heaven?
KING HENRY VI
The treasury of everlasting joy.
CARDINAL
Thy heaven is on earth; thine eyes and thoughts
Beat on a crown, the treasure of thy heart;
Pernicious protector, dangerous peer,
That smooth'st it so with king and commonweal!
GLOUCESTER
What, cardinal, is your priesthood grown peremptory?
Tantaene animis coelestibus irae?
Churchmen so hot? good uncle, hide such malice;
With such holiness can you do it?
SUFFOLK
No malice, sir; no more than well becomes
So good a quarrel and so bad a peer.
GLOUCESTER
As who, my lord?
SUFFOLK
Why, as you, my lord,
An't like your lordly lord-protectorship.
GLOUCESTER
Why, Suffolk, England knows thine insolence.
QUEEN MARGARET
And thy ambition, Gloucester.
KING HENRY VI
I prithee, peace, good queen,
And whet not on these furious peers;
For blessed are the peacemakers on earth.
CARDINAL
Let me be blessed for the peace I make,
Against this proud protector, with my sword!
GLOUCESTER
[Aside to CARDINAL] Faith, holy uncle, would
'twere come to that!
CARDINAL
[Aside to GLOUCESTER] Marry, when thou darest.

GLOUCESTER
[Aside to CARDINAL] Make up no factious
numbers for the matter;
In thine own person answer thy abuse.
CARDINAL
[Aside to GLOUCESTER] Ay, where thou darest
not peep: an if thou darest,
This evening, on the east side of the grove.
KING HENRY VI
How now, my lords!
CARDINAL
Believe me, cousin Gloucester,
Had not your man put up the fowl so suddenly,
We had had more sport.
Aside to GLOUCESTER
Come with thy two-hand sword.
GLOUCESTER
True, uncle.
CARDINAL
[Aside to GLOUCESTER] Are ye advised? the
east side of the grove?
GLOUCESTER
[Aside to CARDINAL] Cardinal, I am with you.
KING HENRY VI
Why, how now, uncle Gloucester!
GLOUCESTER
Talking of hawking; nothing else, my lord.
Aside to CARDINAL
Now, by God's mother, priest, I'll shave your crown for this,
Or all my fence shall fail.
CARDINAL
[Aside to GLOUCESTER] Medice, teipsum--
Protector, see to't well, protect yourself.
KING HENRY VI
The winds grow high; so do your stomachs, lords.
How irksome is this music to my heart!
When such strings jar, what hope of harmony?
I pray, my lords, let me compound this strife.
Enter a Townsman of Saint Alban's, crying 'A miracle!'
GLOUCESTER
What means this noise?
Fellow, what miracle dost thou proclaim?
Townsman
A miracle! a miracle!
SUFFOLK
Come to the king and tell him what miracle.
Townsman
Forsooth, a blind man at Saint Alban's shrine,
Within this half-hour, hath received his sight;
A man that ne'er saw in his life before.
KING HENRY VI
Now, God be praised, that to believing souls
Gives light in darkness, comfort in despair!
Enter the Mayor of Saint Alban's and his brethren, bearing SIMPCOX, between two in a chair, SIMPCOX's Wife following
CARDINAL
Here comes the townsmen on procession,
To present your highness with the man.
KING HENRY VI
Great is his comfort in this earthly vale,
Although by his sight his sin be multiplied.
GLOUCESTER
Stand by, my masters: bring him near the king;
His highness' pleasure is to talk with him.

KING HENRY VI
Good fellow, tell us here the circumstance,
That we for thee may glorify the Lord.
What, hast thou been long blind and now restored?
SIMPCOX
Born blind, an't please your grace.
Wife
Ay, indeed, was he.
SUFFOLK
What woman is this?
Wife
His wife, an't like your worship.
GLOUCESTER
Hadst thou been his mother, thou couldst have
better told.
KING HENRY VI
Where wert thou born?
SIMPCOX
At Berwick in the north, an't like your grace.
KING HENRY VI
Poor soul, God's goodness hath been great to thee:
Let never day nor night unhallow'd pass,
But still remember what the Lord hath done.
QUEEN MARGARET
Tell me, good fellow, camest thou here by chance,
Or of devotion, to this holy shrine?
SIMPCOX
God knows, of pure devotion; being call'd
A hundred times and oftener, in my sleep,
By good Saint Alban; who said, 'Simpcox, come,
Come, offer at my shrine, and I will help thee.'
Wife
Most true, forsooth; and many time and oft
Myself have heard a voice to call him so.
CARDINAL
What, art thou lame?
SIMPCOX
Ay, God Almighty help me!
SUFFOLK
How camest thou so?
SIMPCOX
A fall off of a tree.
Wife
A plum-tree, master.
GLOUCESTER
How long hast thou been blind?
SIMPCOX
Born so, master.
GLOUCESTER
What, and wouldst climb a tree?
SIMPCOX
But that in all my life, when I was a youth.
Wife
Too true; and bought his climbing very dear.
GLOUCESTER
Mass, thou lovedst plums well, that wouldst
venture so.
SIMPCOX
Alas, good master, my wife desired some damsons,
And made me climb, with danger of my life.
GLOUCESTER

A subtle knave! but yet it shall not serve.
Let me see thine eyes: wink now: now open them:
In my opinion yet thou seest not well.
SIMPCOX
Yes, master, clear as day, I thank God and
Saint Alban.
GLOUCESTER
Say'st thou me so? What colour is this cloak of?
SIMPCOX
Red, master; red as blood.
GLOUCESTER
Why, that's well said. What colour is my gown of?
SIMPCOX
Black, forsooth: coal-black as jet.
KING HENRY VI
Why, then, thou know'st what colour jet is of?
SUFFOLK
And yet, I think, jet did he never see.
GLOUCESTER
But cloaks and gowns, before this day, a many.
Wife
Never, before this day, in all his life.
GLOUCESTER
Tell me, sirrah, what's my name?
SIMPCOX
Alas, master, I know not.
GLOUCESTER
What's his name?
SIMPCOX
I know not.
GLOUCESTER
Nor his?
SIMPCOX
No, indeed, master.
GLOUCESTER
What's thine own name?
SIMPCOX
Saunder Simpcox, an if it please you, master.
GLOUCESTER
Then, Saunder, sit there, the lyingest knave in
Christendom. If thou hadst been born blind, thou
mightest as well have known all our names as thus to
name the several colours we do wear. Sight may
distinguish of colours, but suddenly to nominate them
all, it is impossible. My lords, Saint Alban here
hath done a miracle; and would ye not think his
cunning to be great, that could restore this cripple
to his legs again?
SIMPCOX
O master, that you could!
GLOUCESTER
My masters of Saint Alban's, have you not beadles in
your town, and things called whips?
Mayor
Yes, my lord, if it please your grace.
GLOUCESTER
Then send for one presently.
Mayor
Sirrah, go fetch the beadle hither straight.
Exit an Attendant
GLOUCESTER

Now fetch me a stool hither by and by. Now, sirrah,
if you mean to save yourself from whipping, leap me
over this stool and run away.
SIMPCOX
Alas, master, I am not able to stand alone:
You go about to torture me in vain.
Enter a Beadle with whips
GLOUCESTER
Well, sir, we must have you find your legs. Sirrah
beadle, whip him till he leap over that same stool.
Beadle
I will, my lord. Come on, sirrah; off with your
doublet quickly.
SIMPCOX
Alas, master, what shall I do? I am not able to stand.
After the Beadle hath hit him once, he leaps over the stool and runs away; and they follow and cry, 'A miracle!'
KING HENRY VI
O God, seest Thou this, and bearest so long?
QUEEN MARGARET
It made me laugh to see the villain run.
GLOUCESTER
Follow the knave; and take this drab away.
Wife
Alas, sir, we did it for pure need.
GLOUCESTER
Let them be whipped through every market-town, till
they come to Berwick, from whence they came.
Exeunt Wife, Beadle, Mayor, & c
CARDINAL
Duke Humphrey has done a miracle to-day.
SUFFOLK
True; made the lame to leap and fly away.
GLOUCESTER
But you have done more miracles than I;
You made in a day, my lord, whole towns to fly.
Enter BUCKINGHAM
KING HENRY VI
What tidings with our cousin Buckingham?
BUCKINGHAM
Such as my heart doth tremble to unfold.
A sort of naughty persons, lewdly bent,
Under the countenance and confederacy
Of Lady Eleanor, the protector's wife,
The ringleader and head of all this rout,
Have practised dangerously against your state,
Dealing with witches and with conjurers:
Whom we have apprehended in the fact;
Raising up wicked spirits from under ground,
Demanding of King Henry's life and death,
And other of your highness' privy-council;
As more at large your grace shall understand.
CARDINAL
[Aside to GLOUCESTER] And so, my lord protector,
by this means
Your lady is forthcoming yet at London.
This news, I think, hath turn'd your weapon's edge;
'Tis like, my lord, you will not keep your hour.
GLOUCESTER
Ambitious churchman, leave to afflict my heart:
Sorrow and grief have vanquish'd all my powers;
And, vanquish'd as I am, I yield to thee,
Or to the meanest groom.
KING HENRY VI

O God, what mischiefs work the wicked ones,
Heaping confusion on their own heads thereby!
QUEEN MARGARET
Gloucester, see here the tainture of thy nest.
And look thyself be faultless, thou wert best.
GLOUCESTER
Madam, for myself, to heaven I do appeal,
How I have loved my king and commonweal:
And, for my wife, I know not how it stands;
Sorry I am to hear what I have heard:
Noble she is, but if she have forgot
Honour and virtue and conversed with such
As, like to pitch, defile nobility,
I banish her my bed and company
And give her as a prey to law and shame,
That hath dishonour'd Gloucester's honest name.
KING HENRY VI
Well, for this night we will repose us here:
To-morrow toward London back again,
To look into this business thoroughly
And call these foul offenders to their answers
And poise the cause in justice' equal scales,
Whose beam stands sure, whose rightful cause prevails.
Flourish. Exeunt
SCENE II. London. YORK'S garden.
Enter YORK, SALISBURY, and WARWICK
YORK
Now, my good Lords of Salisbury and Warwick,
Our simple supper ended, give me leave
In this close walk to satisfy myself,
In craving your opinion of my title,
Which is infallible, to England's crown.
SALISBURY
My lord, I long to hear it at full.
WARWICK
Sweet York, begin: and if thy claim be good,
The Nevils are thy subjects to command.
YORK
Then thus:
Edward the Third, my lords, had seven sons:
The first, Edward the Black Prince, Prince of Wales;
The second, William of Hatfield, and the third,
Lionel Duke of Clarence: next to whom
Was John of Gaunt, the Duke of Lancaster;
The fifth was Edmund Langley, Duke of York;
The sixth was Thomas of Woodstock, Duke of Gloucester;
William of Windsor was the seventh and last.
Edward the Black Prince died before his father
And left behind him Richard, his only son,
Who after Edward the Third's death reign'd as king;
Till Henry Bolingbroke, Duke of Lancaster,
The eldest son and heir of John of Gaunt,
Crown'd by the name of Henry the Fourth,
Seized on the realm, deposed the rightful king,
Sent his poor queen to France, from whence she came,
And him to Pomfret; where, as all you know,
Harmless Richard was murder'd traitorously.
WARWICK
Father, the duke hath told the truth:
Thus got the house of Lancaster the crown.
YORK

Which now they hold by force and not by right;
For Richard, the first son's heir, being dead,
The issue of the next son should have reign'd.
SALISBURY
But William of Hatfield died without an heir.
YORK
The third son, Duke of Clarence, from whose line
I claimed the crown, had issue, Philippe, a daughter,
Who married Edmund Mortimer, Earl of March:
Edmund had issue, Roger Earl of March;
Roger had issue, Edmund, Anne and Eleanor.
SALISBURY
This Edmund, in the reign of Bolingbroke,
As I have read, laid claim unto the crown;
And, but for Owen Glendower, had been king,
Who kept him in captivity till he died.
But to the rest.
YORK
His eldest sister, Anne,
My mother, being heir unto the crown
Married Richard Earl of Cambridge; who was son
To Edmund Langley, Edward the Third's fifth son.
By her I claim the kingdom: she was heir
To Roger Earl of March, who was the son
Of Edmund Mortimer, who married Philippe,
Sole daughter unto Lionel Duke of Clarence:
So, if the issue of the elder son
Succeed before the younger, I am king.
WARWICK
What plain proceeding is more plain than this?
Henry doth claim the crown from John of Gaunt,
The fourth son; York claims it from the third.
Till Lionel's issue fails, his should not reign:
It fails not yet, but flourishes in thee
And in thy sons, fair slips of such a stock.
Then, father Salisbury, kneel we together;
And in this private plot be we the first
That shall salute our rightful sovereign
With honour of his birthright to the crown.
BOTH
Long live our sovereign Richard, England's king!
YORK
We thank you, lords. But I am not your king
Till I be crown'd and that my sword be stain'd
With heart-blood of the house of Lancaster;
And that's not suddenly to be perform'd,
But with advice and silent secrecy.
Do you as I do in these dangerous days:
Wink at the Duke of Suffolk's insolence,
At Beaufort's pride, at Somerset's ambition,
At Buckingham and all the crew of them,
Till they have snared the shepherd of the flock,
That virtuous prince, the good Duke Humphrey:
'Tis that they seek, and they in seeking that
Shall find their deaths, if York can prophesy.
SALISBURY
My lord, break we off; we know your mind at full.
WARWICK
My heart assures me that the Earl of Warwick
Shall one day make the Duke of York a king.
YORK

And, Nevil, this I do assure myself:
Richard shall live to make the Earl of Warwick
The greatest man in England but the king.
Exeunt
SCENE III. A hall of justice.
Sound trumpets. Enter KING HENRY VI, QUEEN MARGARET, GLOUCESTER, YORK, SUFFOLK, and SALISBURY; the DUCHESS, MARGARET JOURDAIN, SOUTHWELL, HUME, and BOLINGBROKE, under guard
KING HENRY VI
Stand forth, Dame Eleanor Cobham, Gloucester's wife:
In sight of God and us, your guilt is great:
Receive the sentence of the law for sins
Such as by God's book are adjudged to death.
You four, from hence to prison back again;
From thence unto the place of execution:
The witch in Smithfield shall be burn'd to ashes,
And you three shall be strangled on the gallows.
You, madam, for you are more nobly born,
Despoiled of your honour in your life,
Shall, after three days' open penance done,
Live in your country here in banishment,
With Sir John Stanley, in the Isle of Man.
DUCHESS
Welcome is banishment; welcome were my death.
GLOUCESTER
Eleanor, the law, thou see'st, hath judged thee:
I cannot justify whom the law condemns.
Exeunt DUCHESS and other prisoners, guarded
Mine eyes are full of tears, my heart of grief.
Ah, Humphrey, this dishonour in thine age
Will bring thy head with sorrow to the ground!
I beseech your majesty, give me leave to go;
Sorrow would solace and mine age would ease.
KING HENRY VI
Stay, Humphrey Duke of Gloucester: ere thou go,
Give up thy staff: Henry will to himself
Protector be; and God shall be my hope,
My stay, my guide and lantern to my feet:
And go in peace, Humphrey, no less beloved
Than when thou wert protector to thy King.
QUEEN MARGARET
I see no reason why a king of years
Should be to be protected like a child.
God and King Henry govern England's realm.
Give up your staff, sir, and the king his realm.
GLOUCESTER
My staff? here, noble Henry, is my staff:
As willingly do I the same resign
As e'er thy father Henry made it mine;
And even as willingly at thy feet I leave it
As others would ambitiously receive it.
Farewell, good king: when I am dead and gone,
May honourable peace attend thy throne!
Exit
QUEEN MARGARET
Why, now is Henry king, and Margaret queen;
And Humphrey Duke of Gloucester scarce himself,
That bears so shrewd a maim; two pulls at once;
His lady banish'd, and a limb lopp'd off.
This staff of honour raught, there let it stand
Where it best fits to be, in Henry's hand.
SUFFOLK

Thus droops this lofty pine and hangs his sprays;
Thus Eleanor's pride dies in her youngest days.
YORK
Lords, let him go. Please it your majesty,
This is the day appointed for the combat;
And ready are the appellant and defendant,
The armourer and his man, to enter the lists,
So please your highness to behold the fight.
QUEEN MARGARET
Ay, good my lord; for purposely therefore
Left I the court, to see this quarrel tried.
KING HENRY VI
O God's name, see the lists and all things fit:
Here let them end it; and God defend the right!
YORK
I never saw a fellow worse bested,
Or more afraid to fight, than is the appellant,
The servant of this armourer, my lords.
Enter at one door, HORNER, the Armourer, and his Neighbours, drinking to him so much that he is drunk; and he enters with a drum before him and his staff with a sand-bag fastened to it; and at the other door PETER, his man, with a drum and sand-bag, and 'Prentices drinking to him
First Neighbour
Here, neighbour Horner, I drink to you in a cup of
sack: and fear not, neighbour, you shall do well enough.
Second Neighbour
And here, neighbour, here's a cup of charneco.
Third Neighbour
And here's a pot of good double beer, neighbour:
drink, and fear not your man.
HORNER
Let it come, i' faith, and I'll pledge you all; and
a fig for Peter!
First 'Prentice Here, Peter, I drink to thee: and be not afraid.
Second 'Prentice Be merry, Peter, and fear not thy master: fight
for credit of the 'prentices.
PETER
I thank you all: drink, and pray for me, I pray
you; for I think I have taken my last draught in
this world. Here, Robin, an if I die, I give thee
my apron: and, Will, thou shalt have my hammer:
and here, Tom, take all the money that I have. O
Lord bless me! I pray God! for I am never able to
deal with my master, he hath learnt me so much fence already.
SALISBURY
Come, leave your drinking, and fall to blows.
Sirrah, what's thy name?
PETER
Peter, forsooth.
SALISBURY
Peter! what more?
PETER
Thump.
SALISBURY
Thump! then see thou thump thy master well.
HORNER
Masters, I am come hither, as it were, upon my man's
instigation, to prove him a knave and myself an
honest man: and touching the Duke of York, I will
take my death, I never meant him any ill, nor the
king, nor the queen: and therefore, Peter, have at
thee with a downright blow!
YORK

Dispatch: this knave's tongue begins to double.
Sound, trumpets, alarum to the combatants!
Alarum. They fight, and PETER strikes him down
HORNER
Hold, Peter, hold! I confess, I confess treason.
Dies
YORK
Take away his weapon. Fellow, thank God, and the
good wine in thy master's way.
PETER
O God, have I overcome mine enemy in this presence?
O Peter, thou hast prevailed in right!
KING HENRY VI
Go, take hence that traitor from our sight;
For his death we do perceive his guilt:
And God in justice hath revealed to us
The truth and innocence of this poor fellow,
Which he had thought to have murder'd wrongfully.
Come, fellow, follow us for thy reward.
Sound a flourish. Exeunt
SCENE IV. A street.
Enter GLOUCESTER and his Servingmen, in mourning cloaks
GLOUCESTER
Thus sometimes hath the brightest day a cloud;
And after summer evermore succeeds
Barren winter, with his wrathful nipping cold:
So cares and joys abound, as seasons fleet.
Sirs, what's o'clock?
Servants
Ten, my lord.
GLOUCESTER
Ten is the hour that was appointed me
To watch the coming of my punish'd duchess:
Uneath may she endure the flinty streets,
To tread them with her tender-feeling feet.
Sweet Nell, ill can thy noble mind abrook
The abject people gazing on thy face,
With envious looks, laughing at thy shame,
That erst did follow thy proud chariot-wheels
When thou didst ride in triumph through the streets.
But, soft! I think she comes; and I'll prepare
My tear-stain'd eyes to see her miseries.
Enter the DUCHESS in a white sheet, and a taper burning in her hand; with STANLEY, the Sheriff, and Officers
Servant
So please your grace, we'll take her from the sheriff.
GLOUCESTER
No, stir not, for your lives; let her pass by.
DUCHESS
Come you, my lord, to see my open shame?
Now thou dost penance too. Look how they gaze!
See how the giddy multitude do point,
And nod their heads, and throw their eyes on thee!
Ah, Gloucester, hide thee from their hateful looks,
And, in thy closet pent up, rue my shame,
And ban thine enemies, both mine and thine!
GLOUCESTER
Be patient, gentle Nell; forget this grief.
DUCHESS
Ah, Gloucester, teach me to forget myself!
For whilst I think I am thy married wife
And thou a prince, protector of this land,
Methinks I should not thus be led along,
Mail'd up in shame, with papers on my back,

And followed with a rabble that rejoice
To see my tears and hear my deep-fet groans.
The ruthless flint doth cut my tender feet,
And when I start, the envious people laugh
And bid me be advised how I tread.
Ah, Humphrey, can I bear this shameful yoke?
Trow'st thou that e'er I'll look upon the world,
Or count them happy that enjoy the sun?
No; dark shall be my light and night my day;
To think upon my pomp shall be my hell.
Sometime I'll say, I am Duke Humphrey's wife,
And he a prince and ruler of the land:
Yet so he ruled and such a prince he was
As he stood by whilst I, his forlorn duchess,
Was made a wonder and a pointing-stock
To every idle rascal follower.
But be thou mild and blush not at my shame,
Nor stir at nothing till the axe of death
Hang over thee, as, sure, it shortly will;
For Suffolk, he that can do all in all
With her that hateth thee and hates us all,
And York and impious Beaufort, that false priest,
Have all limed bushes to betray thy wings,
And, fly thou how thou canst, they'll tangle thee:
But fear not thou, until thy foot be snared,
Nor never seek prevention of thy foes.
GLOUCESTER
Ah, Nell, forbear! thou aimest all awry;
I must offend before I be attainted;
And had I twenty times so many foes,
And each of them had twenty times their power,
All these could not procure me any scathe,
So long as I am loyal, true and crimeless.
Wouldst have me rescue thee from this reproach?
Why, yet thy scandal were not wiped away
But I in danger for the breach of law.
Thy greatest help is quiet, gentle Nell:
I pray thee, sort thy heart to patience;
These few days' wonder will be quickly worn.
Enter a Herald
Herald
I summon your grace to his majesty's parliament,
Holden at Bury the first of this next month.
GLOUCESTER
And my consent ne'er ask'd herein before!
This is close dealing. Well, I will be there.
Exit Herald
My Nell, I take my leave: and, master sheriff,
Let not her penance exceed the king's commission.
Sheriff
An't please your grace, here my commission stays,
And Sir John Stanley is appointed now
To take her with him to the Isle of Man.
GLOUCESTER
Must you, Sir John, protect my lady here?
STANLEY
So am I given in charge, may't please your grace.
GLOUCESTER
Entreat her not the worse in that I pray
You use her well: the world may laugh again;
And I may live to do you kindness if
You do it her: and so, Sir John, farewell!
DUCHESS

What, gone, my lord, and bid me not farewell!
GLOUCESTER
Witness my tears, I cannot stay to speak.
Exeunt GLOUCESTER and Servingmen
DUCHESS
Art thou gone too? all comfort go with thee!
For none abides with me: my joy is death;
Death, at whose name I oft have been afear'd,
Because I wish'd this world's eternity.
Stanley, I prithee, go, and take me hence;
I care not whither, for I beg no favour,
Only convey me where thou art commanded.
STANLEY
Why, madam, that is to the Isle of Man;
There to be used according to your state.
DUCHESS
That's bad enough, for I am but reproach:
And shall I then be used reproachfully?
STANLEY
Like to a duchess, and Duke Humphrey's lady;
According to that state you shall be used.
DUCHESS
Sheriff, farewell, and better than I fare,
Although thou hast been conduct of my shame.
Sheriff
It is my office; and, madam, pardon me.
DUCHESS
Ay, ay, farewell; thy office is discharged.
Come, Stanley, shall we go?
STANLEY
Madam, your penance done, throw off this sheet,
And go we to attire you for our journey.
DUCHESS
My shame will not be shifted with my sheet:
No, it will hang upon my richest robes
And show itself, attire me how I can.
Go, lead the way; I long to see my prison.
Exeunt

ACT III

SCENE I. The Abbey at Bury St. Edmund's.

Sound a sennet. Enter KING HENRY VI, QUEEN MARGARET, CARDINAL, SUFFOLK, YORK, BUCKINGHAM, SALISBURY and WARWICK to the Parliament

KING HENRY VI
I muse my Lord of Gloucester is not come:
'Tis not his wont to be the hindmost man,
Whate'er occasion keeps him from us now.

QUEEN MARGARET
Can you not see? or will ye not observe
The strangeness of his alter'd countenance?
With what a majesty he bears himself,
How insolent of late he is become,
How proud, how peremptory, and unlike himself?
We know the time since he was mild and affable,
And if we did but glance a far-off look,
Immediately he was upon his knee,
That all the court admired him for submission:
But meet him now, and, be it in the morn,
When every one will give the time of day,
He knits his brow and shows an angry eye,
And passeth by with stiff unbowed knee,
Disdaining duty that to us belongs.
Small curs are not regarded when they grin;
But great men tremble when the lion roars;
And Humphrey is no little man in England.
First note that he is near you in descent,
And should you fall, he as the next will mount.
Me seemeth then it is no policy,
Respecting what a rancorous mind he bears
And his advantage following your decease,
That he should come about your royal person
Or be admitted to your highness' council.
By flattery hath he won the commons' hearts,
And when he please to make commotion,
'Tis to be fear'd they all will follow him.
Now 'tis the spring, and weeds are shallow-rooted;
Suffer them now, and they'll o'ergrow the garden
And choke the herbs for want of husbandry.
The reverent care I bear unto my lord
Made me collect these dangers in the duke.
If it be fond, call it a woman's fear;
Which fear if better reasons can supplant,
I will subscribe and say I wrong'd the duke.
My Lord of Suffolk, Buckingham, and York,
Reprove my allegation, if you can;
Or else conclude my words effectual.

SUFFOLK
Well hath your highness seen into this duke;
And, had I first been put to speak my mind,
I think I should have told your grace's tale.
The duchess, by his subornation,
Upon my life, began her devilish practises:
Or, if he were not privy to those faults,
Yet, by reputing of his high descent,
As next the king he was successive heir,
And such high vaunts of his nobility,
Did instigate the bedlam brain-sick duchess
By wicked means to frame our sovereign's fall.
Smooth runs the water where the brook is deep;
And in his simple show he harbours treason.
The fox barks not when he would steal the lamb.

No, no, my sovereign; Gloucester is a man
Unsounded yet and full of deep deceit.
CARDINAL
Did he not, contrary to form of law,
Devise strange deaths for small offences done?
YORK
And did he not, in his protectorship,
Levy great sums of money through the realm
For soldiers' pay in France, and never sent it?
By means whereof the towns each day revolted.
BUCKINGHAM
Tut, these are petty faults to faults unknown,
Which time will bring to light in smooth
Duke Humphrey.
KING HENRY VI
My lords, at once: the care you have of us,
To mow down thorns that would annoy our foot,
Is worthy praise: but, shall I speak my conscience,
Our kinsman Gloucester is as innocent
From meaning treason to our royal person
As is the sucking lamb or harmless dove:
The duke is virtuous, mild and too well given
To dream on evil or to work my downfall.
QUEEN MARGARET
Ah, what's more dangerous than this fond affiance!
Seems he a dove? his feathers are but borrow'd,
For he's disposed as the hateful raven:
Is he a lamb? his skin is surely lent him,
For he's inclined as is the ravenous wolf.
Who cannot steal a shape that means deceit?
Take heed, my lord; the welfare of us all
Hangs on the cutting short that fraudful man.
Enter SOMERSET
SOMERSET
All health unto my gracious sovereign!
KING HENRY VI
Welcome, Lord Somerset. What news from France?
SOMERSET
That all your interest in those territories
Is utterly bereft you; all is lost.
KING HENRY VI
Cold news, Lord Somerset: but God's will be done!
YORK
[Aside] Cold news for me; for I had hope of France
As firmly as I hope for fertile England.
Thus are my blossoms blasted in the bud
And caterpillars eat my leaves away;
But I will remedy this gear ere long,
Or sell my title for a glorious grave.
Enter GLOUCESTER
GLOUCESTER
All happiness unto my lord the king!
Pardon, my liege, that I have stay'd so long.
SUFFOLK
Nay, Gloucester, know that thou art come too soon,
Unless thou wert more loyal than thou art:
I do arrest thee of high treason here.
GLOUCESTER
Well, Suffolk, thou shalt not see me blush
Nor change my countenance for this arrest:
A heart unspotted is not easily daunted.
The purest spring is not so free from mud

As I am clear from treason to my sovereign:
Who can accuse me? wherein am I guilty?
YORK
'Tis thought, my lord, that you took bribes of France,
And, being protector, stayed the soldiers' pay;
By means whereof his highness hath lost France.
GLOUCESTER
Is it but thought so? what are they that think it?
I never robb'd the soldiers of their pay,
Nor ever had one penny bribe from France.
So help me God, as I have watch'd the night,
Ay, night by night, in studying good for England,
That doit that e'er I wrested from the king,
Or any groat I hoarded to my use,
Be brought against me at my trial-day!
No; many a pound of mine own proper store,
Because I would not tax the needy commons,
Have I disbursed to the garrisons,
And never ask'd for restitution.
CARDINAL
It serves you well, my lord, to say so much.
GLOUCESTER
I say no more than truth, so help me God!
YORK
In your protectorship you did devise
Strange tortures for offenders never heard of,
That England was defamed by tyranny.
GLOUCESTER
Why, 'tis well known that, whiles I was protector,
Pity was all the fault that was in me;
For I should melt at an offender's tears,
And lowly words were ransom for their fault.
Unless it were a bloody murderer,
Or foul felonious thief that fleeced poor passengers,
I never gave them condign punishment:
Murder indeed, that bloody sin, I tortured
Above the felon or what trespass else.
SUFFOLK
My lord, these faults are easy, quickly answered:
But mightier crimes are laid unto your charge,
Whereof you cannot easily purge yourself.
I do arrest you in his highness' name;
And here commit you to my lord cardinal
To keep, until your further time of trial.
KING HENRY VI
My lord of Gloucester, 'tis my special hope
That you will clear yourself from all suspect:
My conscience tells me you are innocent.
GLOUCESTER
Ah, gracious lord, these days are dangerous:
Virtue is choked with foul ambition
And charity chased hence by rancour's hand;
Foul subornation is predominant
And equity exiled your highness' land.
I know their complot is to have my life,
And if my death might make this island happy,
And prove the period of their tyranny,
I would expend it with all willingness:
But mine is made the prologue to their play;
For thousands more, that yet suspect no peril,
Will not conclude their plotted tragedy.
Beaufort's red sparkling eyes blab his heart's malice,

And Suffolk's cloudy brow his stormy hate;
Sharp Buckingham unburthens with his tongue
The envious load that lies upon his heart;
And dogged York, that reaches at the moon,
Whose overweening arm I have pluck'd back,
By false accuse doth level at my life:
And you, my sovereign lady, with the rest,
Causeless have laid disgraces on my head,
And with your best endeavour have stirr'd up
My liefest liege to be mine enemy:
Ay, all you have laid your heads together--
Myself had notice of your conventicles--
And all to make away my guiltless life.
I shall not want false witness to condemn me,
Nor store of treasons to augment my guilt;
The ancient proverb will be well effected:
'A staff is quickly found to beat a dog.'

CARDINAL
My liege, his railing is intolerable:
If those that care to keep your royal person
From treason's secret knife and traitors' rage
Be thus upbraided, chid and rated at,
And the offender granted scope of speech,
'Twill make them cool in zeal unto your grace.

SUFFOLK
Hath he not twit our sovereign lady here
With ignominious words, though clerkly couch'd,
As if she had suborned some to swear
False allegations to o'erthrow his state?

QUEEN MARGARET
But I can give the loser leave to chide.

GLOUCESTER
Far truer spoke than meant: I lose, indeed;
Beshrew the winners, for they play'd me false!
And well such losers may have leave to speak.

BUCKINGHAM
He'll wrest the sense and hold us here all day:
Lord cardinal, he is your prisoner.

CARDINAL
Sirs, take away the duke, and guard him sure.

GLOUCESTER
Ah! thus King Henry throws away his crutch
Before his legs be firm to bear his body.
Thus is the shepherd beaten from thy side,
And wolves are gnarling who shall gnaw thee first.
Ah, that my fear were false! ah, that it were!
For, good King Henry, thy decay I fear.
Exit, guarded

KING HENRY VI
My lords, what to your wisdoms seemeth best,
Do or undo, as if ourself were here.

QUEEN MARGARET
What, will your highness leave the parliament?

KING HENRY VI
Ay, Margaret; my heart is drown'd with grief,
Whose flood begins to flow within mine eyes,
My body round engirt with misery,
For what's more miserable than discontent?
Ah, uncle Humphrey! in thy face I see
The map of honour, truth and loyalty:
And yet, good Humphrey, is the hour to come
That e'er I proved thee false or fear'd thy faith.
What louring star now envies thy estate,

That these great lords and Margaret our queen
Do seek subversion of thy harmless life?
Thou never didst them wrong, nor no man wrong;
And as the butcher takes away the calf
And binds the wretch, and beats it when it strays,
Bearing it to the bloody slaughter-house,
Even so remorseless have they borne him hence;
And as the dam runs lowing up and down,
Looking the way her harmless young one went,
And can do nought but wail her darling's loss,
Even so myself bewails good Gloucester's case
With sad unhelpful tears, and with dimm'd eyes
Look after him and cannot do him good,
So mighty are his vowed enemies.
His fortunes I will weep; and, 'twixt each groan
Say 'Who's a traitor? Gloucester he is none.'
Exeunt all but QUEEN MARGARET, CARDINAL, SUFFOLK, and YORK; SOMERSET remains apart
QUEEN MARGARET
Free lords, cold snow melts with the sun's hot beams.
Henry my lord is cold in great affairs,
Too full of foolish pity, and Gloucester's show
Beguiles him as the mournful crocodile
With sorrow snares relenting passengers,
Or as the snake roll'd in a flowering bank,
With shining chequer'd slough, doth sting a child
That for the beauty thinks it excellent.
Believe me, lords, were none more wise than I--
And yet herein I judge mine own wit good--
This Gloucester should be quickly rid the world,
To rid us of the fear we have of him.
CARDINAL
That he should die is worthy policy;
But yet we want a colour for his death:
'Tis meet he be condemn'd by course of law.
SUFFOLK
But, in my mind, that were no policy:
The king will labour still to save his life,
The commons haply rise, to save his life;
And yet we have but trivial argument,
More than mistrust, that shows him worthy death.
YORK
So that, by this, you would not have him die.
SUFFOLK
Ah, York, no man alive so fain as I!
YORK
'Tis York that hath more reason for his death.
But, my lord cardinal, and you, my Lord of Suffolk,
Say as you think, and speak it from your souls,
Were't not all one, an empty eagle were set
To guard the chicken from a hungry kite,
As place Duke Humphrey for the king's protector?
QUEEN MARGARET
So the poor chicken should be sure of death.
SUFFOLK
Madam, 'tis true; and were't not madness, then,
To make the fox surveyor of the fold?
Who being accused a crafty murderer,
His guilt should be but idly posted over,
Because his purpose is not executed.
No; let him die, in that he is a fox,
By nature proved an enemy to the flock,
Before his chaps be stain'd with crimson blood,
As Humphrey, proved by reasons, to my liege.

And do not stand on quillets how to slay him:
Be it by gins, by snares, by subtlety,
Sleeping or waking, 'tis no matter how,
So he be dead; for that is good deceit
Which mates him first that first intends deceit.
QUEEN MARGARET
Thrice-noble Suffolk, 'tis resolutely spoke.
SUFFOLK
Not resolute, except so much were done;
For things are often spoke and seldom meant:
But that my heart accordeth with my tongue,
Seeing the deed is meritorious,
And to preserve my sovereign from his foe,
Say but the word, and I will be his priest.
CARDINAL
But I would have him dead, my Lord of Suffolk,
Ere you can take due orders for a priest:
Say you consent and censure well the deed,
And I'll provide his executioner,
I tender so the safety of my liege.
SUFFOLK
Here is my hand, the deed is worthy doing.
QUEEN MARGARET
And so say I.
YORK
And I and now we three have spoke it,
It skills not greatly who impugns our doom.
Enter a Post
Post
Great lords, from Ireland am I come amain,
To signify that rebels there are up
And put the Englishmen unto the sword:
Send succors, lords, and stop the rage betime,
Before the wound do grow uncurable;
For, being green, there is great hope of help.
CARDINAL
A breach that craves a quick expedient stop!
What counsel give you in this weighty cause?
YORK
That Somerset be sent as regent thither:
'Tis meet that lucky ruler be employ'd;
Witness the fortune he hath had in France.
SOMERSET
If York, with all his far-fet policy,
Had been the regent there instead of me,
He never would have stay'd in France so long.
YORK
No, not to lose it all, as thou hast done:
I rather would have lost my life betimes
Than bring a burthen of dishonour home
By staying there so long till all were lost.
Show me one scar character'd on thy skin:
Men's flesh preserved so whole do seldom win.
QUEEN MARGARET
Nay, then, this spark will prove a raging fire,
If wind and fuel be brought to feed it with:
No more, good York; sweet Somerset, be still:
Thy fortune, York, hadst thou been regent there,
Might happily have proved far worse than his.
YORK
What, worse than nought? nay, then, a shame take all!
SOMERSET
And, in the number, thee that wishest shame!

CARDINAL
My Lord of York, try what your fortune is.
The uncivil kerns of Ireland are in arms
And temper clay with blood of Englishmen:
To Ireland will you lead a band of men,
Collected choicely, from each county some,
And try your hap against the Irishmen?
YORK
I will, my lord, so please his majesty.
SUFFOLK
Why, our authority is his consent,
And what we do establish he confirms:
Then, noble York, take thou this task in hand.
YORK
I am content: provide me soldiers, lords,
Whiles I take order for mine own affairs.
SUFFOLK
A charge, Lord York, that I will see perform'd.
But now return we to the false Duke Humphrey.
CARDINAL
No more of him; for I will deal with him
That henceforth he shall trouble us no more.
And so break off; the day is almost spent:
Lord Suffolk, you and I must talk of that event.
YORK
My Lord of Suffolk, within fourteen days
At Bristol I expect my soldiers;
For there I'll ship them all for Ireland.
SUFFOLK
I'll see it truly done, my Lord of York.
Exeunt all but YORK
YORK
Now, York, or never, steel thy fearful thoughts,
And change misdoubt to resolution:
Be that thou hopest to be, or what thou art
Resign to death; it is not worth the enjoying:
Let pale-faced fear keep with the mean-born man,
And find no harbour in a royal heart.
Faster than spring-time showers comes thought on thought,
And not a thought but thinks on dignity.
My brain more busy than the labouring spider
Weaves tedious snares to trap mine enemies.
Well, nobles, well, 'tis politicly done,
To send me packing with an host of men:
I fear me you but warm the starved snake,
Who, cherish'd in your breasts, will sting your hearts.
'Twas men I lack'd and you will give them me:
I take it kindly; and yet be well assured
You put sharp weapons in a madman's hands.
Whiles I in Ireland nourish a mighty band,
I will stir up in England some black storm
Shall blow ten thousand souls to heaven or hell;
And this fell tempest shall not cease to rage
Until the golden circuit on my head,
Like to the glorious sun's transparent beams,
Do calm the fury of this mad-bred flaw.
And, for a minister of my intent,
I have seduced a headstrong Kentishman,
John Cade of Ashford,
To make commotion, as full well he can,
Under the title of John Mortimer.

In Ireland have I seen this stubborn Cade
Oppose himself against a troop of kerns,
And fought so long, till that his thighs with darts
Were almost like a sharp-quill'd porpentine;
And, in the end being rescued, I have seen
Him caper upright like a wild Morisco,
Shaking the bloody darts as he his bells.
Full often, like a shag-hair'd crafty kern,
Hath he conversed with the enemy,
And undiscover'd come to me again
And given me notice of their villanies.
This devil here shall be my substitute;
For that John Mortimer, which now is dead,
In face, in gait, in speech, he doth resemble:
By this I shall perceive the commons' mind,
How they affect the house and claim of York.
Say he be taken, rack'd and tortured,
I know no pain they can inflict upon him
Will make him say I moved him to those arms.
Say that he thrive, as 'tis great like he will,
Why, then from Ireland come I with my strength
And reap the harvest which that rascal sow'd;
For Humphrey being dead, as he shall be,
And Henry put apart, the next for me.
Exit

SCENE II. Bury St. Edmund's. A room of state.
Enter certain Murderers, hastily
First Murderer
Run to my Lord of Suffolk; let him know
We have dispatch'd the duke, as he commanded.
Second Murderer
O that it were to do! What have we done?
Didst ever hear a man so penitent?
Enter SUFFOLK
First Murder
Here comes my lord.
SUFFOLK
Now, sirs, have you dispatch'd this thing?
First Murderer
Ay, my good lord, he's dead.
SUFFOLK
Why, that's well said. Go, get you to my house;
I will reward you for this venturous deed.
The king and all the peers are here at hand.
Have you laid fair the bed? Is all things well,
According as I gave directions?
First Murderer
'Tis, my good lord.
SUFFOLK
Away! be gone.
Exeunt Murderers
Sound trumpets. Enter KING HENRY VI, QUEEN MARGARET, CARDINAL, SOMERSET, with Attendants
KING HENRY VI
Go, call our uncle to our presence straight;
Say we intend to try his grace to-day.
If he be guilty, as 'tis published.
SUFFOLK
I'll call him presently, my noble lord.
Exit
KING HENRY VI
Lords, take your places; and, I pray you all,
Proceed no straiter 'gainst our uncle Gloucester

Than from true evidence of good esteem
He be approved in practise culpable.
QUEEN MARGARET
God forbid any malice should prevail,
That faultless may condemn a nobleman!
Pray God he may acquit him of suspicion!
KING HENRY VI
I thank thee, Meg; these words content me much.
Re-enter SUFFOLK
How now! why look'st thou pale? why tremblest thou?
Where is our uncle? what's the matter, Suffolk?
SUFFOLK
Dead in his bed, my lord; Gloucester is dead.
QUEEN MARGARET
Marry, God forfend!
CARDINAL
God's secret judgment: I did dream to-night
The duke was dumb and could not speak a word.
KING HENRY VI swoons
QUEEN MARGARET
How fares my lord? Help, lords! the king is dead.
SOMERSET
Rear up his body; wring him by the nose.
QUEEN MARGARET
Run, go, help, help! O Henry, ope thine eyes!
SUFFOLK
He doth revive again: madam, be patient.
KING HENRY VI
O heavenly God!
QUEEN MARGARET
How fares my gracious lord?
SUFFOLK
Comfort, my sovereign! gracious Henry, comfort!
KING HENRY VI
What, doth my Lord of Suffolk comfort me?
Came he right now to sing a raven's note,
Whose dismal tune bereft my vital powers;
And thinks he that the chirping of a wren,
By crying comfort from a hollow breast,
Can chase away the first-conceived sound?
Hide not thy poison with such sugar'd words;
Lay not thy hands on me; forbear, I say;
Their touch affrights me as a serpent's sting.
Thou baleful messenger, out of my sight!
Upon thy eye-balls murderous tyranny
Sits in grim majesty, to fright the world.
Look not upon me, for thine eyes are wounding:
Yet do not go away: come, basilisk,
And kill the innocent gazer with thy sight;
For in the shade of death I shall find joy;
In life but double death, now Gloucester's dead.
QUEEN MARGARET
Why do you rate my Lord of Suffolk thus?
Although the duke was enemy to him,
Yet he most Christian-like laments his death:
And for myself, foe as he was to me,
Might liquid tears or heart-offending groans
Or blood-consuming sighs recall his life,
I would be blind with weeping, sick with groans,
Look pale as primrose with blood-drinking sighs,
And all to have the noble duke alive.
What know I how the world may deem of me?
For it is known we were but hollow friends:

It may be judged I made the duke away;
So shall my name with slander's tongue be wounded,
And princes' courts be fill'd with my reproach.
This get I by his death: ay me, unhappy!
To be a queen, and crown'd with infamy!
KING HENRY VI
Ah, woe is me for Gloucester, wretched man!
QUEEN MARGARET
Be woe for me, more wretched than he is.
What, dost thou turn away and hide thy face?
I am no loathsome leper; look on me.
What! art thou, like the adder, waxen deaf?
Be poisonous too and kill thy forlorn queen.
Is all thy comfort shut in Gloucester's tomb?
Why, then, dame Margaret was ne'er thy joy.
Erect his statue and worship it,
And make my image but an alehouse sign.
Was I for this nigh wreck'd upon the sea
And twice by awkward wind from England's bank
Drove back again unto my native clime?
What boded this, but well forewarning wind
Did seem to say 'Seek not a scorpion's nest,
Nor set no footing on this unkind shore'?
What did I then, but cursed the gentle gusts
And he that loosed them forth their brazen caves:
And bid them blow towards England's blessed shore,
Or turn our stern upon a dreadful rock
Yet AEolus would not be a murderer,
But left that hateful office unto thee:
The pretty-vaulting sea refused to drown me,
Knowing that thou wouldst have me drown'd on shore,
With tears as salt as sea, through thy unkindness:
The splitting rocks cower'd in the sinking sands
And would not dash me with their ragged sides,
Because thy flinty heart, more hard than they,
Might in thy palace perish Margaret.
As far as I could ken thy chalky cliffs,
When from thy shore the tempest beat us back,
I stood upon the hatches in the storm,
And when the dusky sky began to rob
My earnest-gaping sight of thy land's view,
I took a costly jewel from my neck,
A heart it was, bound in with diamonds,
And threw it towards thy land: the sea received it,
And so I wish'd thy body might my heart:
And even with this I lost fair England's view
And bid mine eyes be packing with my heart
And call'd them blind and dusky spectacles,
For losing ken of Albion's wished coast.
How often have I tempted Suffolk's tongue,
The agent of thy foul inconstancy,
To sit and witch me, as Ascanius did
When he to madding Dido would unfold
His father's acts commenced in burning Troy!
Am I not witch'd like her? or thou not false like him?
Ay me, I can no more! die, Margaret!
For Henry weeps that thou dost live so long.
Noise within. Enter WARWICK, SALISBURY, and many Commons
WARWICK
It is reported, mighty sovereign,
That good Duke Humphrey traitorously is murder'd
By Suffolk and the Cardinal Beaufort's means.
The commons, like an angry hive of bees

That want their leader, scatter up and down
And care not who they sting in his revenge.
Myself have calm'd their spleenful mutiny,
Until they hear the order of his death.
KING HENRY VI
That he is dead, good Warwick, 'tis too true;
But how he died God knows, not Henry:
Enter his chamber, view his breathless corpse,
And comment then upon his sudden death.
WARWICK
That shall I do, my liege. Stay, Salisbury,
With the rude multitude till I return.
Exit
KING HENRY VI
O Thou that judgest all things, stay my thoughts,
My thoughts, that labour to persuade my soul
Some violent hands were laid on Humphrey's life!
If my suspect be false, forgive me, God,
For judgment only doth belong to thee.
Fain would I go to chafe his paly lips
With twenty thousand kisses, and to drain
Upon his face an ocean of salt tears,
To tell my love unto his dumb deaf trunk,
And with my fingers feel his hand unfeeling:
But all in vain are these mean obsequies;
And to survey his dead and earthly image,
What were it but to make my sorrow greater?
Re-enter WARWICK and others, bearing GLOUCESTER'S body on a bed
WARWICK
Come hither, gracious sovereign, view this body.
KING HENRY VI
That is to see how deep my grave is made;
For with his soul fled all my worldly solace,
For seeing him I see my life in death.
WARWICK
As surely as my soul intends to live
With that dread King that took our state upon him
To free us from his father's wrathful curse,
I do believe that violent hands were laid
Upon the life of this thrice-famed duke.
SUFFOLK
A dreadful oath, sworn with a solemn tongue!
What instance gives Lord Warwick for his vow?
WARWICK
See how the blood is settled in his face.
Oft have I seen a timely-parted ghost,
Of ashy semblance, meagre, pale and bloodless,
Being all descended to the labouring heart;
Who, in the conflict that it holds with death,
Attracts the same for aidance 'gainst the enemy;
Which with the heart there cools and ne'er returneth
To blush and beautify the cheek again.
But see, his face is black and full of blood,
His eye-balls further out than when he lived,
Staring full ghastly like a strangled man;
His hair uprear'd, his nostrils stretched with struggling;
His hands abroad display'd, as one that grasp'd
And tugg'd for life and was by strength subdued:
Look, on the sheets his hair you see, is sticking;
His well-proportion'd beard made rough and rugged,
Like to the summer's corn by tempest lodged.
It cannot be but he was murder'd here;
The least of all these signs were probable.

SUFFOLK
Why, Warwick, who should do the duke to death?
Myself and Beaufort had him in protection;
And we, I hope, sir, are no murderers.
WARWICK
But both of you were vow'd Duke Humphrey's foes,
And you, forsooth, had the good duke to keep:
'Tis like you would not feast him like a friend;
And 'tis well seen he found an enemy.
QUEEN MARGARET
Then you, belike, suspect these noblemen
As guilty of Duke Humphrey's timeless death.
WARWICK
Who finds the heifer dead and bleeding fresh
And sees fast by a butcher with an axe,
But will suspect 'twas he that made the slaughter?
Who finds the partridge in the puttock's nest,
But may imagine how the bird was dead,
Although the kite soar with unbloodied beak?
Even so suspicious is this tragedy.
QUEEN MARGARET
Are you the butcher, Suffolk? Where's your knife?
Is Beaufort term'd a kite? Where are his talons?
SUFFOLK
I wear no knife to slaughter sleeping men;
But here's a vengeful sword, rusted with ease,
That shall be scoured in his rancorous heart
That slanders me with murder's crimson badge.
Say, if thou darest, proud Lord of Warwick-shire,
That I am faulty in Duke Humphrey's death.
Exeunt CARDINAL, SOMERSET, and others
WARWICK
What dares not Warwick, if false Suffolk dare him?
QUEEN MARGARET
He dares not calm his contumelious spirit
Nor cease to be an arrogant controller,
Though Suffolk dare him twenty thousand times.
WARWICK
Madam, be still; with reverence may I say;
For every word you speak in his behalf
Is slander to your royal dignity.
SUFFOLK
Blunt-witted lord, ignoble in demeanor!
If ever lady wrong'd her lord so much,
Thy mother took into her blameful bed
Some stern untutor'd churl, and noble stock
Was graft with crab-tree slip; whose fruit thou art,
And never of the Nevils' noble race.
WARWICK
But that the guilt of murder bucklers thee
And I should rob the deathsman of his fee,
Quitting thee thereby of ten thousand shames,
And that my sovereign's presence makes me mild,
I would, false murderous coward, on thy knee
Make thee beg pardon for thy passed speech,
And say it was thy mother that thou meant'st
That thou thyself was born in bastardy;
And after all this fearful homage done,
Give thee thy hire and send thy soul to hell,
Pernicious blood-sucker of sleeping men!
SUFFOLK
Thou shall be waking well I shed thy blood,
If from this presence thou darest go with me.

WARWICK
Away even now, or I will drag thee hence:
Unworthy though thou art, I'll cope with thee
And do some service to Duke Humphrey's ghost.
Exeunt SUFFOLK and WARWICK
KING HENRY VI
What stronger breastplate than a heart untainted!
Thrice is he armed that hath his quarrel just,
And he but naked, though lock'd up in steel
Whose conscience with injustice is corrupted.
A noise within
QUEEN MARGARET
What noise is this?
Re-enter SUFFOLK and WARWICK, with their weapons drawn
KING HENRY VI
Why, how now, lords! your wrathful weapons drawn
Here in our presence! dare you be so bold?
Why, what tumultuous clamour have we here?
SUFFOLK
The traitorous Warwick with the men of Bury
Set all upon me, mighty sovereign.
SALISBURY
[To the Commons, entering] Sirs, stand apart;
the king shall know your mind.
Dread lord, the commons send you word by me,
Unless Lord Suffolk straight be done to death,
Or banished fair England's territories,
They will by violence tear him from your palace
And torture him with grievous lingering death.
They say, by him the good Duke Humphrey died;
They say, in him they fear your highness' death;
And mere instinct of love and loyalty,
Free from a stubborn opposite intent,
As being thought to contradict your liking,
Makes them thus forward in his banishment.
They say, in care of your most royal person,
That if your highness should intend to sleep
And charge that no man should disturb your rest
In pain of your dislike or pain of death,
Yet, notwithstanding such a strait edict,
Were there a serpent seen, with forked tongue,
That slily glided towards your majesty,
It were but necessary you were waked,
Lest, being suffer'd in that harmful slumber,
The mortal worm might make the sleep eternal;
And therefore do they cry, though you forbid,
That they will guard you, whether you will or no,
From such fell serpents as false Suffolk is,
With whose envenomed and fatal sting,
Your loving uncle, twenty times his worth,
They say, is shamefully bereft of life.
Commons
[Within] An answer from the king, my
Lord of Salisbury!
SUFFOLK
'Tis like the commons, rude unpolish'd hinds,
Could send such message to their sovereign:
But you, my lord, were glad to be employ'd,
To show how quaint an orator you are:
But all the honour Salisbury hath won
Is, that he was the lord ambassador
Sent from a sort of tinkers to the king.
Commons

[Within] An answer from the king, or we will all break in!
KING HENRY VI
Go, Salisbury, and tell them all from me.
I thank them for their tender loving care;
And had I not been cited so by them,
Yet did I purpose as they do entreat;
For, sure, my thoughts do hourly prophesy
Mischance unto my state by Suffolk's means:
And therefore, by His majesty I swear,
Whose far unworthy deputy I am,
He shall not breathe infection in this air
But three days longer, on the pain of death.
Exit SALISBURY
QUEEN MARGARET
O Henry, let me plead for gentle Suffolk!
KING HENRY VI
Ungentle queen, to call him gentle Suffolk!
No more, I say: if thou dost plead for him,
Thou wilt but add increase unto my wrath.
Had I but said, I would have kept my word,
But when I swear, it is irrevocable.
If, after three days' space, thou here be'st found
On any ground that I am ruler of,
The world shall not be ransom for thy life.
Come, Warwick, come, good Warwick, go with me;
I have great matters to impart to thee.
Exeunt all but QUEEN MARGARET and SUFFOLK
QUEEN MARGARET
Mischance and sorrow go along with you!
Heart's discontent and sour affliction
Be playfellows to keep you company!
There's two of you; the devil make a third!
And threefold vengeance tend upon your steps!
SUFFOLK
Cease, gentle queen, these execrations,
And let thy Suffolk take his heavy leave.
QUEEN MARGARET
Fie, coward woman and soft-hearted wretch!
Hast thou not spirit to curse thine enemy?
SUFFOLK
A plague upon them! wherefore should I curse them?
Would curses kill, as doth the mandrake's groan,
I would invent as bitter-searching terms,
As curst, as harsh and horrible to hear,
Deliver'd strongly through my fixed teeth,
With full as many signs of deadly hate,
As lean-faced Envy in her loathsome cave:
My tongue should stumble in mine earnest words;
Mine eyes should sparkle like the beaten flint;
Mine hair be fixed on end, as one distract;
Ay, every joint should seem to curse and ban:
And even now my burthen'd heart would break,
Should I not curse them. Poison be their drink!
Gall, worse than gall, the daintiest that they taste!
Their sweetest shade a grove of cypress trees!
Their chiefest prospect murdering basilisks!
Their softest touch as smart as lizards' sting!
Their music frightful as the serpent's hiss,
And boding screech-owls make the concert full!
All the foul terrors in dark-seated hell--
QUEEN MARGARET
Enough, sweet Suffolk; thou torment'st thyself;
And these dread curses, like the sun 'gainst glass,

Or like an overcharged gun, recoil,
And turn the force of them upon thyself.
SUFFOLK
You bade me ban, and will you bid me leave?
Now, by the ground that I am banish'd from,
Well could I curse away a winter's night,
Though standing naked on a mountain top,
Where biting cold would never let grass grow,
And think it but a minute spent in sport.
QUEEN MARGARET
O, let me entreat thee cease. Give me thy hand,
That I may dew it with my mournful tears;
Nor let the rain of heaven wet this place,
To wash away my woful monuments.
O, could this kiss be printed in thy hand,
That thou mightst think upon these by the seal,
Through whom a thousand sighs are breathed for thee!
So, get thee gone, that I may know my grief;
'Tis but surmised whiles thou art standing by,
As one that surfeits thinking on a want.
I will repeal thee, or, be well assured,
Adventure to be banished myself:
And banished I am, if but from thee.
Go; speak not to me; even now be gone.
O, go not yet! Even thus two friends condemn'd
Embrace and kiss and take ten thousand leaves,
Loather a hundred times to part than die.
Yet now farewell; and farewell life with thee!
SUFFOLK
Thus is poor Suffolk ten times banished;
Once by the king, and three times thrice by thee.
'Tis not the land I care for, wert thou thence;
A wilderness is populous enough,
So Suffolk had thy heavenly company:
For where thou art, there is the world itself,
With every several pleasure in the world,
And where thou art not, desolation.
I can no more: live thou to joy thy life;
Myself no joy in nought but that thou livest.
Enter VAUX
QUEEN MARGARET
Wither goes Vaux so fast? what news, I prithee?
VAUX
To signify unto his majesty
That Cardinal Beaufort is at point of death;
For suddenly a grievous sickness took him,
That makes him gasp and stare and catch the air,
Blaspheming God and cursing men on earth.
Sometimes he talks as if Duke Humphrey's ghost
Were by his side; sometime he calls the king,
And whispers to his pillow, as to him,
The secrets of his overcharged soul;
And I am sent to tell his majesty
That even now he cries aloud for him.
QUEEN MARGARET
Go tell this heavy message to the king.
Exit VAUX
Ay me! what is this world! what news are these!
But wherefore grieve I at an hour's poor loss,
Omitting Suffolk's exile, my soul's treasure?
Why only, Suffolk, mourn I not for thee,
And with the southern clouds contend in tears,
Theirs for the earth's increase, mine for my sorrows?

Now get thee hence: the king, thou know'st, is coming;
If thou be found by me, thou art but dead.
SUFFOLK
If I depart from thee, I cannot live;
And in thy sight to die, what were it else
But like a pleasant slumber in thy lap?
Here could I breathe my soul into the air,
As mild and gentle as the cradle-babe
Dying with mother's dug between its lips:
Where, from thy sight, I should be raging mad,
And cry out for thee to close up mine eyes,
To have thee with thy lips to stop my mouth;
So shouldst thou either turn my flying soul,
Or I should breathe it so into thy body,
And then it lived in sweet Elysium.
To die by thee were but to die in jest;
From thee to die were torture more than death:
O, let me stay, befall what may befall!
QUEEN MARGARET
Away! though parting be a fretful corrosive,
It is applied to a deathful wound.
To France, sweet Suffolk: let me hear from thee;
For wheresoe'er thou art in this world's globe,
I'll have an Iris that shall find thee out.
SUFFOLK
I go.
QUEEN MARGARET
And take my heart with thee.
SUFFOLK
A jewel, lock'd into the wofull'st cask
That ever did contain a thing of worth.
Even as a splitted bark, so sunder we
This way fall I to death.
QUEEN MARGARET
This way for me.
Exeunt severally
SCENE III. A bedchamber.
Enter the KING, SALISBURY, WARWICK, to the CARDINAL in bed
KING HENRY VI
How fares my lord? speak, Beaufort, to
thy sovereign.
CARDINAL
If thou be'st death, I'll give thee England's treasure,
Enough to purchase such another island,
So thou wilt let me live, and feel no pain.
KING HENRY VI
Ah, what a sign it is of evil life,
Where death's approach is seen so terrible!
WARWICK
Beaufort, it is thy sovereign speaks to thee.
CARDINAL
Bring me unto my trial when you will.
Died he not in his bed? where should he die?
Can I make men live, whether they will or no?
O, torture me no more! I will confess.
Alive again? then show me where he is:
I'll give a thousand pound to look upon him.
He hath no eyes, the dust hath blinded them.
Comb down his hair; look, look! it stands upright,
Like lime-twigs set to catch my winged soul.
Give me some drink; and bid the apothecary
Bring the strong poison that I bought of him.
KING HENRY VI

O thou eternal Mover of the heavens.
Look with a gentle eye upon this wretch!
O, beat away the busy meddling fiend
That lays strong siege unto this wretch's soul.
And from his bosom purge this black despair!
WARWICK
See, how the pangs of death do make him grin!
SALISBURY
Disturb him not; let him pass peaceably.
KING HENRY VI
Peace to his soul, if God's good pleasure be!
Lord cardinal, if thou think'st on heaven's bliss,
Hold up thy hand, make signal of thy hope.
He dies, and makes no sign. O God, forgive him!
WARWICK
So bad a death argues a monstrous life.
KING HENRY VI
Forbear to judge, for we are sinners all.
Close up his eyes and draw the curtain close;
And let us all to meditation.
Exeunt

ACT IV

SCENE I. The coast of Kent.

Alarum. Fight at sea. Ordnance goes off. Enter a Captain, a Master, a Master's-mate, WALTER WHITMORE, and others; with them SUFFOLK, and others, prisoners

Captain
The gaudy, blabbing and remorseful day
Is crept into the bosom of the sea;
And now loud-howling wolves arouse the jades
That drag the tragic melancholy night;
Who, with their drowsy, slow and flagging wings,
Clip dead men's graves and from their misty jaws
Breathe foul contagious darkness in the air.
Therefore bring forth the soldiers of our prize;
For, whilst our pinnace anchors in the Downs,
Here shall they make their ransom on the sand,
Or with their blood stain this discolour'd shore.
Master, this prisoner freely give I thee;
And thou that art his mate, make boot of this;
The other, Walter Whitmore, is thy share.

First Gentleman
What is my ransom, master? let me know.

Master
A thousand crowns, or else lay down your head.
Master's-Mate And so much shall you give, or off goes yours.

Captain
What, think you much to pay two thousand crowns,
And bear the name and port of gentlemen?
Cut both the villains' throats; for die you shall:
The lives of those which we have lost in fight
Be counterpoised with such a petty sum!

First Gentleman
I'll give it, sir; and therefore spare my life.

Second Gentleman
And so will I and write home for it straight.

WHITMORE
I lost mine eye in laying the prize aboard,
And therefore to revenge it, shalt thou die;
To SUFFOLK
And so should these, if I might have my will.

Captain
Be not so rash; take ransom, let him live.

SUFFOLK
Look on my George; I am a gentleman:
Rate me at what thou wilt, thou shalt be paid.

WHITMORE
And so am I; my name is Walter Whitmore.
How now! why start'st thou? what, doth
death affright?

SUFFOLK
Thy name affrights me, in whose sound is death.
A cunning man did calculate my birth
And told me that by water I should die:
Yet let not this make thee be bloody-minded;
Thy name is Gaultier, being rightly sounded.

WHITMORE
Gaultier or Walter, which it is, I care not:
Never yet did base dishonour blur our name,
But with our sword we wiped away the blot;
Therefore, when merchant-like I sell revenge,
Broke be my sword, my arms torn and defaced,
And I proclaim'd a coward through the world!

SUFFOLK

Stay, Whitmore; for thy prisoner is a prince,
The Duke of Suffolk, William de la Pole.
WHITMORE
The Duke of Suffolk muffled up in rags!
SUFFOLK
Ay, but these rags are no part of the duke:
Jove sometimes went disguised, and why not I?
Captain
But Jove was never slain, as thou shalt be.
SUFFOLK
Obscure and lowly swain, King Henry's blood,
The honourable blood of Lancaster,
Must not be shed by such a jaded groom.
Hast thou not kiss'd thy hand and held my stirrup?
Bare-headed plodded by my foot-cloth mule
And thought thee happy when I shook my head?
How often hast thou waited at my cup,
Fed from my trencher, kneel'd down at the board,
When I have feasted with Queen Margaret?
Remember it and let it make thee crest-fall'n,
Ay, and allay this thy abortive pride;
How in our voiding lobby hast thou stood
And duly waited for my coming forth?
This hand of mine hath writ in thy behalf,
And therefore shall it charm thy riotous tongue.
WHITMORE
Speak, captain, shall I stab the forlorn swain?
Captain
First let my words stab him, as he hath me.
SUFFOLK
Base slave, thy words are blunt and so art thou.
Captain
Convey him hence and on our longboat's side
Strike off his head.
SUFFOLK
Thou darest not, for thy own.
Captain
Yes, Pole.
SUFFOLK
Pole!
Captain
Pool! Sir Pool! lord!
Ay, kennel, puddle, sink; whose filth and dirt
Troubles the silver spring where England drinks.
Now will I dam up this thy yawning mouth
For swallowing the treasure of the realm:
Thy lips that kiss'd the queen shall sweep the ground;
And thou that smiledst at good Duke Humphrey's death,
Against the senseless winds shalt grin in vain,
Who in contempt shall hiss at thee again:
And wedded be thou to the hags of hell,
For daring to affy a mighty lord
Unto the daughter of a worthless king,
Having neither subject, wealth, nor diadem.
By devilish policy art thou grown great,
And, like ambitious Sylla, overgorged
With gobbets of thy mother's bleeding heart.
By thee Anjou and Maine were sold to France,
The false revolting Normans thorough thee
Disdain to call us lord, and Picardy
Hath slain their governors, surprised our forts,
And sent the ragged soldiers wounded home.
The princely Warwick, and the Nevils all,

Whose dreadful swords were never drawn in vain,
As hating thee, are rising up in arms:
And now the house of York, thrust from the crown
By shameful murder of a guiltless king
And lofty proud encroaching tyranny,
Burns with revenging fire; whose hopeful colours
Advance our half-faced sun, striving to shine,
Under the which is writ 'Invitis nubibus.'
The commons here in Kent are up in arms:
And, to conclude, reproach and beggary
Is crept into the palace of our king.
And all by thee. Away! convey him hence.
SUFFOLK
O that I were a god, to shoot forth thunder
Upon these paltry, servile, abject drudges!
Small things make base men proud: this villain here,
Being captain of a pinnace, threatens more
Than Bargulus the strong Illyrian pirate.
Drones suck not eagles' blood but rob beehives:
It is impossible that I should die
By such a lowly vassal as thyself.
Thy words move rage and not remorse in me:
I go of message from the queen to France;
I charge thee waft me safely cross the Channel.
Captain
Walter,--
WHITMORE
Come, Suffolk, I must waft thee to thy death.
SUFFOLK
Gelidus timor occupat artus it is thee I fear.
WHITMORE
Thou shalt have cause to fear before I leave thee.
What, are ye daunted now? now will ye stoop?
First Gentleman
My gracious lord, entreat him, speak him fair.
SUFFOLK
Suffolk's imperial tongue is stern and rough,
Used to command, untaught to plead for favour.
Far be it we should honour such as these
With humble suit: no, rather let my head
Stoop to the block than these knees bow to any
Save to the God of heaven and to my king;
And sooner dance upon a bloody pole
Than stand uncover'd to the vulgar groom.
True nobility is exempt from fear:
More can I bear than you dare execute.
Captain
Hale him away, and let him talk no more.
SUFFOLK
Come, soldiers, show what cruelty ye can,
That this my death may never be forgot!
Great men oft die by vile bezonians:
A Roman sworder and banditto slave
Murder'd sweet Tully; Brutus' bastard hand
Stabb'd Julius Caesar; savage islanders
Pompey the Great; and Suffolk dies by pirates.
Exeunt Whitmore and others with Suffolk
Captain
And as for these whose ransom we have set,
It is our pleasure one of them depart;
Therefore come you with us and let him go.
Exeunt all but the First Gentleman
Re-enter WHITMORE with SUFFOLK's body

WHITMORE
There let his head and lifeless body lie,
Until the queen his mistress bury it.
Exit
First Gentleman
O barbarous and bloody spectacle!
His body will I bear unto the king:
If he revenge it not, yet will his friends;
So will the queen, that living held him dear.
Exit with the body
SCENE II. Blackheath.
Enter GEORGE BEVIS and JOHN HOLLAND
BEVIS
Come, and get thee a sword, though made of a lath;
they have been up these two days.
HOLLAND
They have the more need to sleep now, then.
BEVIS
I tell thee, Jack Cade the clothier means to dress
the commonwealth, and turn it, and set a new nap upon it.
HOLLAND
So he had need, for 'tis threadbare. Well, I say it
was never merry world in England since gentlemen came up.
BEVIS
O miserable age! virtue is not regarded in handicrafts-men.
HOLLAND
The nobility think scorn to go in leather aprons.
BEVIS
Nay, more, the king's council are no good workmen.
HOLLAND
True; and yet it is said, labour in thy vocation;
which is as much to say as, let the magistrates be
labouring men; and therefore should we be
magistrates.
BEVIS
Thou hast hit it; for there's no better sign of a
brave mind than a hard hand.
HOLLAND
I see them! I see them! there's Best's son, the
tanner of Wingham,--
BEVIS
He shall have the skin of our enemies, to make
dog's-leather of.
HOLLAND
And Dick the Butcher,--
BEVIS
Then is sin struck down like an ox, and iniquity's
throat cut like a calf.
HOLLAND
And Smith the weaver,--
BEVIS
Argo, their thread of life is spun.
HOLLAND
Come, come, let's fall in with them.
Drum. Enter CADE, DICK the Butcher, SMITH the Weaver, and a Sawyer, with infinite numbers
CADE
We John Cade, so termed of our supposed father,--
DICK
[Aside] Or rather, of stealing a cade of herrings.
CADE
For our enemies shall fall before us, inspired with
the spirit of putting down kings and princes,
--Command silence.

DICK
Silence!
CADE
My father was a Mortimer,--
DICK
[Aside] He was an honest man, and a good bricklayer.
CADE
My mother a Plantagenet,--
DICK
[Aside] I knew her well; she was a midwife.
CADE
My wife descended of the Lacies,--
DICK
[Aside] She was, indeed, a pedler's daughter, and sold many laces.
SMITH
[Aside] But now of late, notable to travel with her furred pack, she washes bucks here at home.
CADE
Therefore am I of an honourable house.
DICK
[Aside] Ay, by my faith, the field is honourable; and there was he borne, under a hedge, for his father had never a house but the cage.
CADE
Valiant I am.
SMITH
[Aside] A' must needs; for beggary is valiant.
CADE
I am able to endure much.
DICK
[Aside] No question of that; for I have seen him whipped three market-days together.
CADE
I fear neither sword nor fire.
SMITH
[Aside] He need not fear the sword; for his coat is of proof.
DICK
[Aside] But methinks he should stand in fear of fire, being burnt i' the hand for stealing of sheep.
CADE
Be brave, then; for your captain is brave, and vows reformation. There shall be in England seven halfpenny loaves sold for a penny: the three-hooped pot; shall have ten hoops and I will make it felony to drink small beer: all the realm shall be in common; and in Cheapside shall my palfrey go to grass: and when I am king, as king I will be,--
ALL
God save your majesty!
CADE
I thank you, good people: there shall be no money; all shall eat and drink on my score; and I will apparel them all in one livery, that they may agree like brothers and worship me their lord.
DICK
The first thing we do, let's kill all the lawyers.
CADE
Nay, that I mean to do. Is not this a lamentable thing, that of the skin of an innocent lamb should be made parchment? that parchment, being scribbled o'er, should undo a man? Some say the bee stings:

but I say, 'tis the bee's wax; for I did but seal
once to a thing, and I was never mine own man
since. How now! who's there?
Enter some, bringing forward the Clerk of Chatham
SMITH
The clerk of Chatham: he can write and read and
cast accompt.
CADE
O monstrous!
SMITH
We took him setting of boys' copies.
CADE
Here's a villain!
SMITH
Has a book in his pocket with red letters in't.
CADE
Nay, then, he is a conjurer.
DICK
Nay, he can make obligations, and write court-hand.
CADE
I am sorry for't: the man is a proper man, of mine
honour; unless I find him guilty, he shall not die.
Come hither, sirrah, I must examine thee: what is thy name?
Clerk
Emmanuel.
DICK
They use to write it on the top of letters: 'twill
go hard with you.
CADE
Let me alone. Dost thou use to write thy name? or
hast thou a mark to thyself, like an honest
plain-dealing man?
CLERK
Sir, I thank God, I have been so well brought up
that I can write my name.
ALL
He hath confessed: away with him! he's a villain
and a traitor.
CADE
Away with him, I say! hang him with his pen and
ink-horn about his neck.
Exit one with the Clerk
Enter MICHAEL
MICHAEL
Where's our general?
CADE
Here I am, thou particular fellow.
MICHAEL
Fly, fly, fly! Sir Humphrey Stafford and his
brother are hard by, with the king's forces.
CADE
Stand, villain, stand, or I'll fell thee down. He
shall be encountered with a man as good as himself:
he is but a knight, is a'?
MICHAEL
No.
CADE
To equal him, I will make myself a knight presently.
Kneels
Rise up Sir John Mortimer.
Rises
Now have at him!
Enter SIR HUMPHREY and WILLIAM STAFFORD, with drum and soldiers

SIR HUMPHREY
Rebellious hinds, the filth and scum of Kent,
Mark'd for the gallows, lay your weapons down;
Home to your cottages, forsake this groom:
The king is merciful, if you revolt.
WILLIAM STAFFORD
But angry, wrathful, and inclined to blood,
If you go forward; therefore yield, or die.
CADE
As for these silken-coated slaves, I pass not:
It is to you, good people, that I speak,
Over whom, in time to come, I hope to reign;
For I am rightful heir unto the crown.
SIR HUMPHREY
Villain, thy father was a plasterer;
And thou thyself a shearman, art thou not?
CADE
And Adam was a gardener.
WILLIAM STAFFORD
And what of that?
CADE
Marry, this: Edmund Mortimer, Earl of March.
Married the Duke of Clarence' daughter, did he not?
SIR HUMPHREY
Ay, sir.
CADE
By her he had two children at one birth.
WILLIAM STAFFORD
That's false.
CADE
Ay, there's the question; but I say, 'tis true:
The elder of them, being put to nurse,
Was by a beggar-woman stolen away;
And, ignorant of his birth and parentage,
Became a bricklayer when he came to age:
His son am I; deny it, if you can.
DICK
Nay, 'tis too true; therefore he shall be king.
SMITH
Sir, he made a chimney in my father's house, and
the bricks are alive at this day to testify it;
therefore deny it not.
SIR HUMPHREY
And will you credit this base drudge's words,
That speaks he knows not what?
ALL
Ay, marry, will we; therefore get ye gone.
WILLIAM STAFFORD
Jack Cade, the Duke of York hath taught you this.
CADE
[Aside] He lies, for I invented it myself.
Go to, sirrah, tell the king from me, that, for his
father's sake, Henry the Fifth, in whose time boys
went to span-counter for French crowns, I am content
he shall reign; but I'll be protector over him.
DICK
And furthermore, well have the Lord Say's head for
selling the dukedom of Maine.
CADE
And good reason; for thereby is England mained, and
fain to go with a staff, but that my puissance holds
it up. Fellow kings, I tell you that that Lord Say
hath gelded the commonwealth, and made it an eunuch:

and more than that, he can speak French; and therefore he is a traitor.
SIR HUMPHREY
O gross and miserable ignorance!
CADE
Nay, answer, if you can: the Frenchmen are our enemies; go to, then, I ask but this: can he that speaks with the tongue of an enemy be a good counsellor, or no?
ALL
No, no; and therefore we'll have his head.
WILLIAM STAFFORD
Well, seeing gentle words will not prevail,
Assail them with the army of the king.
SIR HUMPHREY
Herald, away; and throughout every town
Proclaim them traitors that are up with Cade;
That those which fly before the battle ends
May, even in their wives' and children's sight,
Be hang'd up for example at their doors:
And you that be the king's friends, follow me.
Exeunt WILLIAM STAFFORD and SIR HUMPHREY, and soldiers
CADE
And you that love the commons, follow me.
Now show yourselves men; 'tis for liberty.
We will not leave one lord, one gentleman:
Spare none but such as go in clouted shoon;
For they are thrifty honest men, and such
As would, but that they dare not, take our parts.
DICK
They are all in order and march toward us.
CADE
But then are we in order when we are most out of order. Come, march forward.
Exeunt
SCENE III. Another part of Blackheath.
Alarums to the fight, wherein SIR HUMPHREY and WILLIAM STAFFORD are slain. Enter CADE and the rest
CADE
Where's Dick, the butcher of Ashford?
DICK
Here, sir.
CADE
They fell before thee like sheep and oxen, and thou behavedst thyself as if thou hadst been in thine own slaughter-house: therefore thus will I reward thee, the Lent shall be as long again as it is; and thou shalt have a licence to kill for a hundred lacking one.
DICK
I desire no more.
CADE
And, to speak truth, thou deservest no less. This monument of the victory will I bear;
Putting on SIR HUMPHREY'S brigandine
and the bodies shall be dragged at my horse' heels till I do come to London, where we will have the mayor's sword borne before us.
DICK
If we mean to thrive and do good, break open the gaols and let out the prisoners.
CADE
Fear not that, I warrant thee. Come, let's march towards London.

Exeunt

SCENE IV. London. The palace.

Enter KING HENRY VI with a supplication, and the QUEEN with SUFFOLK'S head, BUCKINGHAM and Lord SAY

QUEEN MARGARET
Oft have I heard that grief softens the mind,
And makes it fearful and degenerate;
Think therefore on revenge and cease to weep.
But who can cease to weep and look on this?
Here may his head lie on my throbbing breast:
But where's the body that I should embrace?

BUCKINGHAM
What answer makes your grace to the rebels'
supplication?

KING HENRY VI
I'll send some holy bishop to entreat;
For God forbid so many simple souls
Should perish by the sword! And I myself,
Rather than bloody war shall cut them short,
Will parley with Jack Cade their general:
But stay, I'll read it over once again.

QUEEN MARGARET
Ah, barbarous villains! hath this lovely face
Ruled, like a wandering planet, over me,
And could it not enforce them to relent,
That were unworthy to behold the same?

KING HENRY VI
Lord Say, Jack Cade hath sworn to have thy head.

SAY
Ay, but I hope your highness shall have his.

KING HENRY VI
How now, madam!
Still lamenting and mourning for Suffolk's death?
I fear me, love, if that I had been dead,
Thou wouldst not have mourn'd so much for me.

QUEEN MARGARET
No, my love, I should not mourn, but die for thee.

Enter a Messenger

KING HENRY VI
How now! what news? why comest thou in such haste?

Messenger
The rebels are in Southwark; fly, my lord!
Jack Cade proclaims himself Lord Mortimer,
Descended from the Duke of Clarence' house,
And calls your grace usurper openly
And vows to crown himself in Westminster.
His army is a ragged multitude
Of hinds and peasants, rude and merciless:
Sir Humphrey Stafford and his brother's death
Hath given them heart and courage to proceed:
All scholars, lawyers, courtiers, gentlemen,
They call false caterpillars, and intend their death.

KING HENRY VI
O graceless men! they know not what they do.

BUCKINGHAM
My gracious lord, return to Killingworth,
Until a power be raised to put them down.

QUEEN MARGARET
Ah, were the Duke of Suffolk now alive,
These Kentish rebels would be soon appeased!

KING HENRY VI
Lord Say, the traitors hate thee;
Therefore away with us to Killingworth.

SAY
So might your grace's person be in danger.
The sight of me is odious in their eyes;
And therefore in this city will I stay
And live alone as secret as I may.
Enter another Messenger
Messenger
Jack Cade hath gotten London bridge:
The citizens fly and forsake their houses:
The rascal people, thirsting after prey,
Join with the traitor, and they jointly swear
To spoil the city and your royal court.
BUCKINGHAM
Then linger not, my lord, away, take horse.
KING HENRY VI
Come, Margaret; God, our hope, will succor us.
QUEEN MARGARET
My hope is gone, now Suffolk is deceased.
KING HENRY VI
Farewell, my lord: trust not the Kentish rebels.
BUCKINGHAM
Trust nobody, for fear you be betray'd.
SAY
The trust I have is in mine innocence,
And therefore am I bold and resolute.
Exeunt

SCENE V. London. The Tower.
Enter SCALES upon the Tower, walking. Then enter two or three Citizens below
SCALES
How now! is Jack Cade slain?
First Citizen
No, my lord, nor likely to be slain; for they have
won the bridge, killing all those that withstand
them: the lord mayor craves aid of your honour from
the Tower, to defend the city from the rebels.
SCALES
Such aid as I can spare you shall command;
But I am troubled here with them myself;
The rebels have assay'd to win the Tower.
But get you to Smithfield, and gather head,
And thither I will send you Matthew Goffe;
Fight for your king, your country and your lives;
And so, farewell, for I must hence again.
Exeunt

SCENE VI. London. Cannon Street.
Enter CADE and the rest, and strikes his staff on London-stone
CADE
Now is Mortimer lord of this city. And here, sitting
upon London-stone, I charge and command that, of the
city's cost, the pissing-conduit run nothing but
claret wine this first year of our reign. And now
henceforward it shall be treason for any that calls
me other than Lord Mortimer.
Enter a Soldier, running
Soldier
Jack Cade! Jack Cade!
CADE
Knock him down there.
They kill him
SMITH
If this fellow be wise, he'll never call ye Jack
Cade more: I think he hath a very fair warning.
DICK

My lord, there's an army gathered together in
Smithfield.
CADE
Come, then, let's go fight with them; but first, go
and set London bridge on fire; and, if you can, burn
down the Tower too. Come, let's away.
Exeunt
SCENE VII. London. Smithfield.
Alarums. MATTHEW GOFFE is slain, and all the rest. Then enter CADE, with his company.
CADE
So, sirs: now go some and pull down the Savoy;
others to the inns of court; down with them all.
DICK
I have a suit unto your lordship.
CADE
Be it a lordship, thou shalt have it for that word.
DICK
Only that the laws of England may come out of your mouth.
HOLLAND
[Aside] Mass, 'twill be sore law, then; for he was
thrust in the mouth with a spear, and 'tis not whole
yet.
SMITH
[Aside] Nay, John, it will be stinking law for his
breath stinks with eating toasted cheese.
CADE
I have thought upon it, it shall be so. Away, burn
all the records of the realm: my mouth shall be
the parliament of England.
HOLLAND
[Aside] Then we are like to have biting statutes,
unless his teeth be pulled out.
CADE
And henceforward all things shall be in common.
Enter a Messenger
Messenger
My lord, a prize, a prize! here's the Lord Say,
which sold the towns in France; he that made us pay
one and twenty fifteens, and one shilling to the
pound, the last subsidy.
Enter BEVIS, with Lord SAY
CADE
Well, he shall be beheaded for it ten times. Ah,
thou say, thou serge, nay, thou buckram lord! now
art thou within point-blank of our jurisdiction
regal. What canst thou answer to my majesty for
giving up of Normandy unto Mounsieur Basimecu, the
dauphin of France? Be it known unto thee by these
presence, even the presence of Lord Mortimer, that I
am the besom that must sweep the court clean of such
filth as thou art. Thou hast most traitorously
corrupted the youth of the realm in erecting a
grammar school; and whereas, before, our forefathers
had no other books but the score and the tally, thou
hast caused printing to be used, and, contrary to
the king, his crown and dignity, thou hast built a
paper-mill. It will be proved to thy face that thou
hast men about thee that usually talk of a noun and
a verb, and such abominable words as no Christian
ear can endure to hear. Thou hast appointed
justices of peace, to call poor men before them
about matters they were not able to answer.
Moreover, thou hast put them in prison; and because

they could not read, thou hast hanged them; when,
indeed, only for that cause they have been most
worthy to live. Thou dost ride in a foot-cloth, dost thou not?
SAY
What of that?
CADE
Marry, thou oughtest not to let thy horse wear a
cloak, when honester men than thou go in their hose
and doublets.
DICK
And work in their shirt too; as myself, for example,
that am a butcher.
SAY
You men of Kent,--
DICK
What say you of Kent?
SAY
Nothing but this; 'tis 'bona terra, mala gens.'
CADE
Away with him, away with him! he speaks Latin.
SAY
Hear me but speak, and bear me where you will.
Kent, in the Commentaries Caesar writ,
Is term'd the civil'st place of this isle:
Sweet is the country, because full of riches;
The people liberal, valiant, active, wealthy;
Which makes me hope you are not void of pity.
I sold not Maine, I lost not Normandy,
Yet, to recover them, would lose my life.
Justice with favour have I always done;
Prayers and tears have moved me, gifts could never.
When have I aught exacted at your hands,
But to maintain the king, the realm and you?
Large gifts have I bestow'd on learned clerks,
Because my book preferr'd me to the king,
And seeing ignorance is the curse of God,
Knowledge the wing wherewith we fly to heaven,
Unless you be possess'd with devilish spirits,
You cannot but forbear to murder me:
This tongue hath parley'd unto foreign kings
For your behoof,--
CADE
Tut, when struck'st thou one blow in the field?
SAY
Great men have reaching hands: oft have I struck
Those that I never saw and struck them dead.
BEVIS
O monstrous coward! what, to come behind folks?
SAY
These cheeks are pale for watching for your good.
CADE
Give him a box o' the ear and that will make 'em red again.
SAY
Long sitting to determine poor men's causes
Hath made me full of sickness and diseases.
CADE
Ye shall have a hempen caudle, then, and the help of hatchet.
DICK
Why dost thou quiver, man?
SAY
The palsy, and not fear, provokes me.
CADE

Nay, he nods at us, as who should say, I'll be even
with you: I'll see if his head will stand steadier
on a pole, or no. Take him away, and behead him.
SAY
Tell me wherein have I offended most?
Have I affected wealth or honour? speak.
Are my chests fill'd up with extorted gold?
Is my apparel sumptuous to behold?
Whom have I injured, that ye seek my death?
These hands are free from guiltless bloodshedding,
This breast from harbouring foul deceitful thoughts.
O, let me live!
CADE
[Aside] I feel remorse in myself with his words;
but I'll bridle it: he shall die, an it be but for
pleading so well for his life. Away with him! he
has a familiar under his tongue; he speaks not o'
God's name. Go, take him away, I say, and strike
off his head presently; and then break into his
son-in-law's house, Sir James Cromer, and strike off
his head, and bring them both upon two poles hither.
ALL
It shall be done.
SAY
Ah, countrymen! if when you make your prayers,
God should be so obdurate as yourselves,
How would it fare with your departed souls?
And therefore yet relent, and save my life.
CADE
Away with him! and do as I command ye.
Exeunt some with Lord SAY
The proudest peer in the realm shall not wear a head
on his shoulders, unless he pay me tribute; there
shall not a maid be married, but she shall pay to me
her maidenhead ere they have it: men shall hold of
me in capite; and we charge and command that their
wives be as free as heart can wish or tongue can tell.
DICK
My lord, when shall we go to Cheapside and take up
commodities upon our bills?
CADE
Marry, presently.
ALL
O, brave!
Re-enter one with the heads
CADE
But is not this braver? Let them kiss one another,
for they loved well when they were alive. Now part
them again, lest they consult about the giving up of
some more towns in France. Soldiers, defer the
spoil of the city until night: for with these borne
before us, instead of maces, will we ride through
the streets, and at every corner have them kiss. Away!
Exeunt
SCENE VIII. Southwark.
Alarum and retreat. Enter CADE and all his rabblement
CADE
Up Fish Street! down Saint Magnus' Corner! Kill
and knock down! throw them into Thames!
Sound a parley
What noise is this I hear? Dare any be so bold to
sound retreat or parley, when I command them kill?
Enter BUCKINGHAM and CLIFFORD, attended

BUCKINGHAM
Ay, here they be that dare and will disturb thee:
Know, Cade, we come ambassadors from the king
Unto the commons whom thou hast misled;
And here pronounce free pardon to them all
That will forsake thee and go home in peace.
CLIFFORD
What say ye, countrymen? will ye relent,
And yield to mercy whilst 'tis offer'd you;
Or let a rebel lead you to your deaths?
Who loves the king and will embrace his pardon,
Fling up his cap, and say 'God save his majesty!'
Who hateth him and honours not his father,
Henry the Fifth, that made all France to quake,
Shake he his weapon at us and pass by.
ALL
God save the king! God save the king!
CADE
What, Buckingham and Clifford, are ye so brave? And
you, base peasants, do ye believe him? will you
needs be hanged with your pardons about your necks?
Hath my sword therefore broke through London gates,
that you should leave me at the White Hart in
Southwark? I thought ye would never have given out
these arms till you had recovered your ancient
freedom: but you are all recreants and dastards,
and delight to live in slavery to the nobility. Let
them break your backs with burthens, take your
houses over your heads, ravish your wives and
daughters before your faces: for me, I will make
shift for one; and so, God's curse light upon you
all!
ALL
We'll follow Cade, we'll follow Cade!
CLIFFORD
Is Cade the son of Henry the Fifth,
That thus you do exclaim you'll go with him?
Will he conduct you through the heart of France,
And make the meanest of you earls and dukes?
Alas, he hath no home, no place to fly to;
Nor knows he how to live but by the spoil,
Unless by robbing of your friends and us.
Were't not a shame, that whilst you live at jar,
The fearful French, whom you late vanquished,
Should make a start o'er seas and vanquish you?
Methinks already in this civil broil
I see them lording it in London streets,
Crying 'Villiago!' unto all they meet.
Better ten thousand base-born Cades miscarry
Than you should stoop unto a Frenchman's mercy.
To France, to France, and get what you have lost;
Spare England, for it is your native coast;
Henry hath money, you are strong and manly;
God on our side, doubt not of victory.
ALL
A Clifford! a Clifford! we'll follow the king and Clifford.
CADE
Was ever feather so lightly blown to and fro as this
multitude? The name of Henry the Fifth hales them
to an hundred mischiefs, and makes them leave me
desolate. I see them lay their heads together to
surprise me. My sword make way for me, for here is
no staying. In despite of the devils and hell, have

through the very middest of you? and heavens and
honour be witness, that no want of resolution in me,
but only my followers' base and ignominious
treasons, makes me betake me to my heels.
Exit
BUCKINGHAM
What, is he fled? Go some, and follow him;
And he that brings his head unto the king
Shall have a thousand crowns for his reward.
Exeunt some of them
Follow me, soldiers: we'll devise a mean
To reconcile you all unto the king.
Exeunt
SCENE IX. Kenilworth Castle.
Sound Trumpets. Enter KING HENRY VI, QUEEN MARGARET, and SOMERSET, on the terrace
KING HENRY VI
Was ever king that joy'd an earthly throne,
And could command no more content than I?
No sooner was I crept out of my cradle
But I was made a king, at nine months old.
Was never subject long'd to be a king
As I do long and wish to be a subject.
Enter BUCKINGHAM and CLIFFORD
BUCKINGHAM
Health and glad tidings to your majesty!
KING HENRY VI
Why, Buckingham, is the traitor Cade surprised?
Or is he but retired to make him strong?
Enter below, multitudes, with halters about their necks
CLIFFORD
He is fled, my lord, and all his powers do yield;
And humbly thus, with halters on their necks,
Expect your highness' doom of life or death.
KING HENRY VI
Then, heaven, set ope thy everlasting gates,
To entertain my vows of thanks and praise!
Soldiers, this day have you redeemed your lives,
And show'd how well you love your prince and country:
Continue still in this so good a mind,
And Henry, though he be infortunate,
Assure yourselves, will never be unkind:
And so, with thanks and pardon to you all,
I do dismiss you to your several countries.
ALL
God save the king! God save the king!
Enter a Messenger
Messenger
Please it your grace to be advertised
The Duke of York is newly come from Ireland,
And with a puissant and a mighty power
Of gallowglasses and stout kerns
Is marching hitherward in proud array,
And still proclaimeth, as he comes along,
His arms are only to remove from thee
The Duke of Somerset, whom he terms traitor.
KING HENRY VI
Thus stands my state, 'twixt Cade and York distress'd.
Like to a ship that, having 'scaped a tempest,
Is straightway calm'd and boarded with a pirate:
But now is Cade driven back, his men dispersed;
And now is York in arms to second him.
I pray thee, Buckingham, go and meet him,
And ask him what's the reason of these arms.

Tell him I'll send Duke Edmund to the Tower;
And, Somerset, we'll commit thee thither,
Until his army be dismiss'd from him.
SOMERSET
My lord,
I'll yield myself to prison willingly,
Or unto death, to do my country good.
KING HENRY VI
In any case, be not too rough in terms;
For he is fierce and cannot brook hard language.
BUCKINGHAM
I will, my lord; and doubt not so to deal
As all things shall redound unto your good.
KING HENRY VI
Come, wife, let's in, and learn to govern better;
For yet may England curse my wretched reign.
Flourish. Exeunt
SCENE X. Kent. IDEN's garden.
Enter CADE
CADE
Fie on ambition! fie on myself, that have a sword,
and yet am ready to famish! These five days have I
hid me in these woods and durst not peep out, for
all the country is laid for me; but now am I so
hungry that if I might have a lease of my life for a
thousand years I could stay no longer. Wherefore,
on a brick wall have I climbed into this garden, to
see if I can eat grass, or pick a sallet another
while, which is not amiss to cool a man's stomach
this hot weather. And I think this word 'sallet'
was born to do me good: for many a time, but for a
sallet, my brainpan had been cleft with a brown
bill; and many a time, when I have been dry and
bravely marching, it hath served me instead of a
quart pot to drink in; and now the word 'sallet'
must serve me to feed on.
Enter IDEN
IDEN
Lord, who would live turmoiled in the court,
And may enjoy such quiet walks as these?
This small inheritance my father left me
Contenteth me, and worth a monarchy.
I seek not to wax great by others' waning,
Or gather wealth, I care not, with what envy:
Sufficeth that I have maintains my state
And sends the poor well pleased from my gate.
CADE
Here's the lord of the soil come to seize me for a
stray, for entering his fee-simple without leave.
Ah, villain, thou wilt betray me, and get a thousand
crowns of the king carrying my head to him: but
I'll make thee eat iron like an ostrich, and swallow
my sword like a great pin, ere thou and I part.
IDEN
Why, rude companion, whatsoe'er thou be,
I know thee not; why, then, should I betray thee?
Is't not enough to break into my garden,
And, like a thief, to come to rob my grounds,
Climbing my walls in spite of me the owner,
But thou wilt brave me with these saucy terms?
CADE
Brave thee! ay, by the best blood that ever was
broached, and beard thee too. Look on me well: I

have eat no meat these five days; yet, come thou and
thy five men, and if I do not leave you all as dead
as a doornail, I pray God I may never eat grass more.
IDEN
Nay, it shall ne'er be said, while England stands,
That Alexander Iden, an esquire of Kent,
Took odds to combat a poor famish'd man.
Oppose thy steadfast-gazing eyes to mine,
See if thou canst outface me with thy looks:
Set limb to limb, and thou art far the lesser;
Thy hand is but a finger to my fist,
Thy leg a stick compared with this truncheon;
My foot shall fight with all the strength thou hast;
And if mine arm be heaved in the air,
Thy grave is digg'd already in the earth.
As for words, whose greatness answers words,
Let this my sword report what speech forbears.
CADE
By my valour, the most complete champion that ever I
heard! Steel, if thou turn the edge, or cut not out
the burly-boned clown in chines of beef ere thou
sleep in thy sheath, I beseech God on my knees thou
mayst be turned to hobnails.
Here they fight. CADE falls
O, I am slain! famine and no other hath slain me:
let ten thousand devils come against me, and give me
but the ten meals I have lost, and I'll defy them
all. Wither, garden; and be henceforth a
burying-place to all that do dwell in this house,
because the unconquered soul of Cade is fled.
IDEN
Is't Cade that I have slain, that monstrous traitor?
Sword, I will hollow thee for this thy deed,
And hang thee o'er my tomb when I am dead:
Ne'er shall this blood be wiped from thy point;
But thou shalt wear it as a herald's coat,
To emblaze the honour that thy master got.
CADE
Iden, farewell, and be proud of thy victory. Tell
Kent from me, she hath lost her best man, and exhort
all the world to be cowards; for I, that never
feared any, am vanquished by famine, not by valour.
Dies
IDEN
How much thou wrong'st me, heaven be my judge.
Die, damned wretch, the curse of her that bare thee;
And as I thrust thy body in with my sword,
So wish I, I might thrust thy soul to hell.
Hence will I drag thee headlong by the heels
Unto a dunghill which shall be thy grave,
And there cut off thy most ungracious head;
Which I will bear in triumph to the king,
Leaving thy trunk for crows to feed upon.
Exit

ACT V

SCENE I. Fields between Dartford and Blackheath.

Enter YORK, and his army of Irish, with drum and colours

YORK
From Ireland thus comes York to claim his right,
And pluck the crown from feeble Henry's head:
Ring, bells, aloud; burn, bonfires, clear and bright,
To entertain great England's lawful king.
Ah! sancta majestas, who would not buy thee dear?
Let them obey that know not how to rule;
This hand was made to handle naught but gold.
I cannot give due action to my words,
Except a sword or sceptre balance it:
A sceptre shall it have, have I a soul,
On which I'll toss the flower-de-luce of France.

Enter BUCKINGHAM

Whom have we here? Buckingham, to disturb me?
The king hath sent him, sure: I must dissemble.

BUCKINGHAM
York, if thou meanest well, I greet thee well.

YORK
Humphrey of Buckingham, I accept thy greeting.
Art thou a messenger, or come of pleasure?

BUCKINGHAM
A messenger from Henry, our dread liege,
To know the reason of these arms in peace;
Or why thou, being a subject as I am,
Against thy oath and true allegiance sworn,
Should raise so great a power without his leave,
Or dare to bring thy force so near the court.

YORK
[Aside] Scarce can I speak, my choler is so great:
O, I could hew up rocks and fight with flint,
I am so angry at these abject terms;
And now, like Ajax Telamonius,
On sheep or oxen could I spend my fury.
I am far better born than is the king,
More like a king, more kingly in my thoughts:
But I must make fair weather yet a while,
Till Henry be more weak and I more strong,--
Buckingham, I prithee, pardon me,
That I have given no answer all this while;
My mind was troubled with deep melancholy.
The cause why I have brought this army hither
Is to remove proud Somerset from the king,
Seditious to his grace and to the state.

BUCKINGHAM
That is too much presumption on thy part:
But if thy arms be to no other end,
The king hath yielded unto thy demand:
The Duke of Somerset is in the Tower.

YORK
Upon thine honour, is he prisoner?

BUCKINGHAM
Upon mine honour, he is prisoner.

YORK
Then, Buckingham, I do dismiss my powers.
Soldiers, I thank you all; disperse yourselves;
Meet me to-morrow in St. George's field,
You shall have pay and every thing you wish.
And let my sovereign, virtuous Henry,
Command my eldest son, nay, all my sons,
As pledges of my fealty and love;

I'll send them all as willing as I live:
Lands, goods, horse, armour, any thing I have,
Is his to use, so Somerset may die.
BUCKINGHAM
York, I commend this kind submission:
We twain will go into his highness' tent.
Enter KING HENRY VI and Attendants
KING HENRY VI
Buckingham, doth York intend no harm to us,
That thus he marcheth with thee arm in arm?
YORK
In all submission and humility
York doth present himself unto your highness.
KING HENRY VI
Then what intends these forces thou dost bring?
YORK
To heave the traitor Somerset from hence,
And fight against that monstrous rebel Cade,
Who since I heard to be discomfited.
Enter IDEN, with CADE'S head
IDEN
If one so rude and of so mean condition
May pass into the presence of a king,
Lo, I present your grace a traitor's head,
The head of Cade, whom I in combat slew.
KING HENRY VI
The head of Cade! Great God, how just art Thou!
O, let me view his visage, being dead,
That living wrought me such exceeding trouble.
Tell me, my friend, art thou the man that slew him?
IDEN
I was, an't like your majesty.
KING HENRY VI
How art thou call'd? and what is thy degree?
IDEN
Alexander Iden, that's my name;
A poor esquire of Kent, that loves his king.
BUCKINGHAM
So please it you, my lord, 'twere not amiss
He were created knight for his good service.
KING HENRY VI
Iden, kneel down.
He kneels
Rise up a knight.
We give thee for reward a thousand marks,
And will that thou henceforth attend on us.
IDEN
May Iden live to merit such a bounty.
And never live but true unto his liege!
Rises
Enter QUEEN MARGARET and SOMERSET
KING HENRY VI
See, Buckingham, Somerset comes with the queen:
Go, bid her hide him quickly from the duke.
QUEEN MARGARET
For thousand Yorks he shall not hide his head,
But boldly stand and front him to his face.
YORK
How now! is Somerset at liberty?
Then, York, unloose thy long-imprison'd thoughts,
And let thy tongue be equal with thy heart.
Shall I endure the sight of Somerset?
False king! why hast thou broken faith with me,

Knowing how hardly I can brook abuse?
King did I call thee? no, thou art not king,
Not fit to govern and rule multitudes,
Which darest not, no, nor canst not rule a traitor.
That head of thine doth not become a crown;
Thy hand is made to grasp a palmer's staff,
And not to grace an awful princely sceptre.
That gold must round engirt these brows of mine,
Whose smile and frown, like to Achilles' spear,
Is able with the change to kill and cure.
Here is a hand to hold a sceptre up
And with the same to act controlling laws.
Give place: by heaven, thou shalt rule no more
O'er him whom heaven created for thy ruler.

SOMERSET
O monstrous traitor! I arrest thee, York,
Of capital treason 'gainst the king and crown;
Obey, audacious traitor; kneel for grace.

YORK
Wouldst have me kneel? first let me ask of these,
If they can brook I bow a knee to man.
Sirrah, call in my sons to be my bail;
Exit Attendant
I know, ere they will have me go to ward,
They'll pawn their swords for my enfranchisement.

QUEEN MARGARET
Call hither Clifford! bid him come amain,
To say if that the bastard boys of York
Shall be the surety for their traitor father.
Exit BUCKINGHAM

YORK
O blood-besotted Neapolitan,
Outcast of Naples, England's bloody scourge!
The sons of York, thy betters in their birth,
Shall be their father's bail; and bane to those
That for my surety will refuse the boys!
Enter EDWARD and RICHARD
See where they come: I'll warrant they'll
make it good.
Enter CLIFFORD and YOUNG CLIFFORD

QUEEN MARGARET
And here comes Clifford to deny their bail.

CLIFFORD
Health and all happiness to my lord the king!
Kneels

YORK
I thank thee, Clifford: say, what news with thee?
Nay, do not fright us with an angry look;
We are thy sovereign, Clifford, kneel again;
For thy mistaking so, we pardon thee.

CLIFFORD
This is my king, York, I do not mistake;
But thou mistakest me much to think I do:
To Bedlam with him! is the man grown mad?

KING HENRY VI
Ay, Clifford; a bedlam and ambitious humour
Makes him oppose himself against his king.

CLIFFORD
He is a traitor; let him to the Tower,
And chop away that factious pate of his.

QUEEN MARGARET
He is arrested, but will not obey;
His sons, he says, shall give their words for him.

YORK
Will you not, sons?
EDWARD
Ay, noble father, if our words will serve.
RICHARD
And if words will not, then our weapons shall.
CLIFFORD
Why, what a brood of traitors have we here!
YORK
Look in a glass, and call thy image so:
I am thy king, and thou a false-heart traitor.
Call hither to the stake my two brave bears,
That with the very shaking of their chains
They may astonish these fell-lurking curs:
Bid Salisbury and Warwick come to me.
Enter the WARWICK and SALISBURY
CLIFFORD
Are these thy bears? we'll bait thy bears to death.
And manacle the bear-ward in their chains,
If thou darest bring them to the baiting place.
RICHARD
Oft have I seen a hot o'erweening cur
Run back and bite, because he was withheld;
Who, being suffer'd with the bear's fell paw,
Hath clapp'd his tail between his legs and cried:
And such a piece of service will you do,
If you oppose yourselves to match Lord Warwick.
CLIFFORD
Hence, heap of wrath, foul indigested lump,
As crooked in thy manners as thy shape!
YORK
Nay, we shall heat you thoroughly anon.
CLIFFORD
Take heed, lest by your heat you burn yourselves.
KING HENRY VI
Why, Warwick, hath thy knee forgot to bow?
Old Salisbury, shame to thy silver hair,
Thou mad misleader of thy brain-sick son!
What, wilt thou on thy death-bed play the ruffian,
And seek for sorrow with thy spectacles?
O, where is faith? O, where is loyalty?
If it be banish'd from the frosty head,
Where shall it find a harbour in the earth?
Wilt thou go dig a grave to find out war,
And shame thine honourable age with blood?
Why art thou old, and want'st experience?
Or wherefore dost abuse it, if thou hast it?
For shame! in duty bend thy knee to me
That bows unto the grave with mickle age.
SALISBURY
My lord, I have consider'd with myself
The title of this most renowned duke;
And in my conscience do repute his grace
The rightful heir to England's royal seat.
KING HENRY VI
Hast thou not sworn allegiance unto me?
SALISBURY
I have.
KING HENRY VI
Canst thou dispense with heaven for such an oath?
SALISBURY
It is great sin to swear unto a sin,
But greater sin to keep a sinful oath.

Who can be bound by any solemn vow
To do a murderous deed, to rob a man,
To force a spotless virgin's chastity,
To reave the orphan of his patrimony,
To wring the widow from her custom'd right,
And have no other reason for this wrong
But that he was bound by a solemn oath?
QUEEN MARGARET
A subtle traitor needs no sophister.
KING HENRY VI
Call Buckingham, and bid him arm himself.
YORK
Call Buckingham, and all the friends thou hast,
I am resolved for death or dignity.
CLIFFORD
The first I warrant thee, if dreams prove true.
WARWICK
You were best to go to bed and dream again,
To keep thee from the tempest of the field.
CLIFFORD
I am resolved to bear a greater storm
Than any thou canst conjure up to-day;
And that I'll write upon thy burgonet,
Might I but know thee by thy household badge.
WARWICK
Now, by my father's badge, old Nevil's crest,
The rampant bear chain'd to the ragged staff,
This day I'll wear aloft my burgonet,
As on a mountain top the cedar shows
That keeps his leaves in spite of any storm,
Even to affright thee with the view thereof.
CLIFFORD
And from thy burgonet I'll rend thy bear
And tread it under foot with all contempt,
Despite the bear-ward that protects the bear.
YOUNG CLIFFORD
And so to arms, victorious father,
To quell the rebels and their complices.
RICHARD
Fie! charity, for shame! speak not in spite,
For you shall sup with Jesu Christ to-night.
YOUNG CLIFFORD
Foul stigmatic, that's more than thou canst tell.
RICHARD
If not in heaven, you'll surely sup in hell.
Exeunt severally
SCENE II. Saint Alban's.
Alarums to the battle. Enter WARWICK
WARWICK
Clifford of Cumberland, 'tis Warwick calls:
And if thou dost not hide thee from the bear,
Now, when the angry trumpet sounds alarum
And dead men's cries do fill the empty air,
Clifford, I say, come forth and fight with me:
Proud northern lord, Clifford of Cumberland,
Warwick is hoarse with calling thee to arms.
Enter YORK
How now, my noble lord? what, all afoot?
YORK
The deadly-handed Clifford slew my steed,
But match to match I have encounter'd him
And made a prey for carrion kites and crows
Even of the bonny beast he loved so well.

Enter CLIFFORD
WARWICK
Of one or both of us the time is come.
YORK
Hold, Warwick, seek thee out some other chase,
For I myself must hunt this deer to death.
WARWICK
Then, nobly, York; 'tis for a crown thou fight'st.
As I intend, Clifford, to thrive to-day,
It grieves my soul to leave thee unassail'd.
Exit
CLIFFORD
What seest thou in me, York? why dost thou pause?
YORK
With thy brave bearing should I be in love,
But that thou art so fast mine enemy.
CLIFFORD
Nor should thy prowess want praise and esteem,
But that 'tis shown ignobly and in treason.
YORK
So let it help me now against thy sword
As I in justice and true right express it.
CLIFFORD
My soul and body on the action both!
YORK
A dreadful lay! Address thee instantly.
They fight, and CLIFFORD falls
CLIFFORD
La fin couronne les oeuvres.
Dies
YORK
Thus war hath given thee peace, for thou art still.
Peace with his soul, heaven, if it be thy will!
Exit
Enter YOUNG CLIFFORD
YOUNG CLIFFORD
Shame and confusion! all is on the rout;
Fear frames disorder, and disorder wounds
Where it should guard. O war, thou son of hell,
Whom angry heavens do make their minister
Throw in the frozen bosoms of our part
Hot coals of vengeance! Let no soldier fly.
He that is truly dedicate to war
Hath no self-love, nor he that loves himself
Hath not essentially but by circumstance
The name of valour.
Seeing his dead father
O, let the vile world end,
And the premised flames of the last day
Knit earth and heaven together!
Now let the general trumpet blow his blast,
Particularities and petty sounds
To cease! Wast thou ordain'd, dear father,
To lose thy youth in peace, and to achieve
The silver livery of advised age,
And, in thy reverence and thy chair-days, thus
To die in ruffian battle? Even at this sight
My heart is turn'd to stone: and while 'tis mine,
It shall be stony. York not our old men spares;
No more will I their babes: tears virginal
Shall be to me even as the dew to fire,
And beauty that the tyrant oft reclaims
Shall to my flaming wrath be oil and flax.

Henceforth I will not have to do with pity:
Meet I an infant of the house of York,
Into as many gobbets will I cut it
As wild Medea young Absyrtus did:
In cruelty will I seek out my fame.
Come, thou new ruin of old Clifford's house:
As did AEneas old Anchises bear,
So bear I thee upon my manly shoulders;
But then AEneas bare a living load,
Nothing so heavy as these woes of mine.
Exit, bearing off his father
Enter RICHARD and SOMERSET to fight. SOMERSET is killed
RICHARD
So, lie thou there;
For underneath an alehouse' paltry sign,
The Castle in Saint Alban's, Somerset
Hath made the wizard famous in his death.
Sword, hold thy temper; heart, be wrathful still:
Priests pray for enemies, but princes kill.
Exit
Fight: excursions. Enter KING HENRY VI, QUEEN MARGARET, and others
QUEEN MARGARET
Away, my lord! you are slow; for shame, away!
KING HENRY VI
Can we outrun the heavens? good Margaret, stay.
QUEEN MARGARET
What are you made of? you'll nor fight nor fly:
Now is it manhood, wisdom and defence,
To give the enemy way, and to secure us
By what we can, which can no more but fly.
Alarum afar off
If you be ta'en, we then should see the bottom
Of all our fortunes: but if we haply scape,
As well we may, if not through your neglect,
We shall to London get, where you are loved
And where this breach now in our fortunes made
May readily be stopp'd.
Re-enter YOUNG CLIFFORD
YOUNG CLIFFORD
But that my heart's on future mischief set,
I would speak blasphemy ere bid you fly:
But fly you must; uncurable discomfit
Reigns in the hearts of all our present parts.
Away, for your relief! and we will live
To see their day and them our fortune give:
Away, my lord, away!
Exeunt
SCENE III. Fields near St. Alban's.
Alarum. Retreat. Enter YORK, RICHARD, WARWICK, and Soldiers, with drum and colours
YORK
Of Salisbury, who can report of him,
That winter lion, who in rage forgets
Aged contusions and all brush of time,
And, like a gallant in the brow of youth,
Repairs him with occasion? This happy day
Is not itself, nor have we won one foot,
If Salisbury be lost.
RICHARD
My noble father,
Three times to-day I holp him to his horse,
Three times bestrid him; thrice I led him off,
Persuaded him from any further act:
But still, where danger was, still there I met him;

And like rich hangings in a homely house,
So was his will in his old feeble body.
But, noble as he is, look where he comes.
Enter SALISBURY
SALISBURY
Now, by my sword, well hast thou fought to-day;
By the mass, so did we all. I thank you, Richard:
God knows how long it is I have to live;
And it hath pleased him that three times to-day
You have defended me from imminent death.
Well, lords, we have not got that which we have:
'Tis not enough our foes are this time fled,
Being opposites of such repairing nature.
YORK
I know our safety is to follow them;
For, as I hear, the king is fled to London,
To call a present court of parliament.
Let us pursue him ere the writs go forth.
What says Lord Warwick? shall we after them?
WARWICK
After them! nay, before them, if we can.
Now, by my faith, lords, 'twas a glorious day:
Saint Alban's battle won by famous York
Shall be eternized in all age to come.
Sound drums and trumpets, and to London all:
And more such days as these to us befall!
Exeunt
END PART 2

DRAMATIS PERSONAE

KING HENRY THE SIXTH
EDWARD, PRINCE OF WALES, his son
LEWIS XI, King of France   DUKE OF SOMERSET
DUKE OF EXETER   EARL OF OXFORD
EARL OF NORTHUMBERLAND   EARL OF WESTMORELAND
LORD CLIFFORD
RICHARD PLANTAGENET, DUKE OF YORK
EDWARD, EARL OF MARCH, afterwards KING EDWARD IV, his son
EDMUND, EARL OF RUTLAND, his son
GEORGE, afterwards DUKE OF CLARENCE, his son
RICHARD, afterwards DUKE OF GLOUCESTER, his son
DUKE OF NORFOLK   MARQUIS OF MONTAGUE
EARL OF WARWICK   EARL OF PEMBROKE
LORD HASTINGS   LORD STAFFORD
SIR JOHN MORTIMER, uncle to the Duke of York
SIR HUGH MORTIMER, uncle to the Duke of York
HENRY, EARL OF RICHMOND, a youth
LORD RIVERS, brother to Lady Grey
SIR WILLIAM STANLEY   SIR JOHN MONTGOMERY
SIR JOHN SOMERVILLE   TUTOR, to Rutland
MAYOR OF YORK   LIEUTENANT OF THE TOWER
A NOBLEMAN   TWO KEEPERS
A HUNTSMAN
A SON that has killed his father
A FATHER that has killed his son

QUEEN MARGARET
LADY GREY, afterwards QUEEN to Edward IV
BONA, sister to the French Queen

Soldiers, Attendants, Messengers, Watchmen, etc.

ACT I

SCENE I. London. The Parliament-house.
Alarum. Enter YORK, EDWARD, RICHARD, NORFOLK, MONTAGUE, WARWICK, and Soldiers
WARWICK
I wonder how the king escaped our hands.
YORK
While we pursued the horsemen of the north,
He slily stole away and left his men:
Whereat the great Lord of Northumberland,
Whose warlike ears could never brook retreat,
Cheer'd up the drooping army; and himself,
Lord Clifford and Lord Stafford, all abreast,
Charged our main battle's front, and breaking in
Were by the swords of common soldiers slain.
EDWARD
Lord Stafford's father, Duke of Buckingham,
Is either slain or wounded dangerously;
I cleft his beaver with a downright blow:
That this is true, father, behold his blood.
MONTAGUE
And, brother, here's the Earl of Wiltshire's blood,
Whom I encounter'd as the battles join'd.
RICHARD
Speak thou for me and tell them what I did.
Throwing down SOMERSET's head
YORK
Richard hath best deserved of all my sons.
But is your grace dead, my Lord of Somerset?
NORFOLK
Such hope have all the line of John of Gaunt!

RICHARD
Thus do I hope to shake King Henry's head.
WARWICK
And so do I. Victorious Prince of York,
Before I see thee seated in that throne
Which now the house of Lancaster usurps,
I vow by heaven these eyes shall never close.
This is the palace of the fearful king,
And this the regal seat: possess it, York;
For this is thine and not King Henry's heirs'
YORK
Assist me, then, sweet Warwick, and I will;
For hither we have broken in by force.
NORFOLK
We'll all assist you; he that flies shall die.
YORK
Thanks, gentle Norfolk: stay by me, my lords;
And, soldiers, stay and lodge by me this night.
They go up
WARWICK
And when the king comes, offer no violence,
Unless he seek to thrust you out perforce.
YORK
The queen this day here holds her parliament,
But little thinks we shall be of her council:
By words or blows here let us win our right.
RICHARD
Arm'd as we are, let's stay within this house.
WARWICK
The bloody parliament shall this be call'd,
Unless Plantagenet, Duke of York, be king,
And bashful Henry deposed, whose cowardice
Hath made us by-words to our enemies.
YORK
Then leave me not, my lords; be resolute;
I mean to take possession of my right.
WARWICK
Neither the king, nor he that loves him best,
The proudest he that holds up Lancaster,
Dares stir a wing, if Warwick shake his bells.
I'll plant Plantagenet, root him up who dares:
Resolve thee, Richard; claim the English crown.
Flourish. Enter KING HENRY VI, CLIFFORD, NORTHUMBERLAND, WESTMORELAND, EXETER, and the rest
KING HENRY VI
My lords, look where the sturdy rebel sits,
Even in the chair of state: belike he means,
Back'd by the power of Warwick, that false peer,
To aspire unto the crown and reign as king.
Earl of Northumberland, he slew thy father.
And thine, Lord Clifford; and you both have vow'd revenge
On him, his sons, his favourites and his friends.
NORTHUMBERLAND
If I be not, heavens be revenged on me!
CLIFFORD
The hope thereof makes Clifford mourn in steel.
WESTMORELAND
What, shall we suffer this? let's pluck him down:
My heart for anger burns; I cannot brook it.
KING HENRY VI
Be patient, gentle Earl of Westmoreland.
CLIFFORD

Patience is for poltroons, such as he:
He durst not sit there, had your father lived.
My gracious lord, here in the parliament
Let us assail the family of York.
NORTHUMBERLAND
Well hast thou spoken, cousin: be it so.
KING HENRY VI
Ah, know you not the city favours them,
And they have troops of soldiers at their beck?
EXETER
But when the duke is slain, they'll quickly fly.
KING HENRY VI
Far be the thought of this from Henry's heart,
To make a shambles of the parliament-house!
Cousin of Exeter, frowns, words and threats
Shall be the war that Henry means to use.
Thou factious Duke of York, descend my throne,
and kneel for grace and mercy at my feet;
I am thy sovereign.
YORK
I am thine.
EXETER
For shame, come down: he made thee Duke of York.
YORK
'Twas my inheritance, as the earldom was.
EXETER
Thy father was a traitor to the crown.
WARWICK
Exeter, thou art a traitor to the crown
In following this usurping Henry.
CLIFFORD
Whom should he follow but his natural king?
WARWICK
True, Clifford; and that's Richard Duke of York.
KING HENRY VI
And shall I stand, and thou sit in my throne?
YORK
It must and shall be so: content thyself.
WARWICK
Be Duke of Lancaster; let him be king.
WESTMORELAND
He is both king and Duke of Lancaster;
And that the Lord of Westmoreland shall maintain.
WARWICK
And Warwick shall disprove it. You forget
That we are those which chased you from the field
And slew your fathers, and with colours spread
March'd through the city to the palace gates.
NORTHUMBERLAND
Yes, Warwick, I remember it to my grief;
And, by his soul, thou and thy house shall rue it.
WESTMORELAND
Plantagenet, of thee and these thy sons,
Thy kinsman and thy friends, I'll have more lives
Than drops of blood were in my father's veins.
CLIFFORD
Urge it no more; lest that, instead of words,
I send thee, Warwick, such a messenger
As shall revenge his death before I stir.
WARWICK
Poor Clifford! how I scorn his worthless threats!
YORK

113

Will you we show our title to the crown?
If not, our swords shall plead it in the field.
KING HENRY VI
What title hast thou, traitor, to the crown?
Thy father was, as thou art, Duke of York;
Thy grandfather, Roger Mortimer, Earl of March:
I am the son of Henry the Fifth,
Who made the Dauphin and the French to stoop
And seized upon their towns and provinces.
WARWICK
Talk not of France, sith thou hast lost it all.
KING HENRY VI
The lord protector lost it, and not I:
When I was crown'd I was but nine months old.
RICHARD
You are old enough now, and yet, methinks, you lose.
Father, tear the crown from the usurper's head.
EDWARD
Sweet father, do so; set it on your head.
MONTAGUE
Good brother, as thou lovest and honourest arms,
Let's fight it out and not stand cavilling thus.
RICHARD
Sound drums and trumpets, and the king will fly.
YORK
Sons, peace!
KING HENRY VI
Peace, thou! and give King Henry leave to speak.
WARWICK
Plantagenet shall speak first: hear him, lords;
And be you silent and attentive too,
For he that interrupts him shall not live.
KING HENRY VI
Think'st thou that I will leave my kingly throne,
Wherein my grandsire and my father sat?
No: first shall war unpeople this my realm;
Ay, and their colours, often borne in France,
And now in England to our heart's great sorrow,
Shall be my winding-sheet. Why faint you, lords?
My title's good, and better far than his.
WARWICK
Prove it, Henry, and thou shalt be king.
KING HENRY VI
Henry the Fourth by conquest got the crown.
YORK
'Twas by rebellion against his king.
KING HENRY VI
[Aside] I know not what to say; my title's weak.--
Tell me, may not a king adopt an heir?
YORK
What then?
KING HENRY VI
An if he may, then am I lawful king;
For Richard, in the view of many lords,
Resign'd the crown to Henry the Fourth,
Whose heir my father was, and I am his.
YORK
He rose against him, being his sovereign,
And made him to resign his crown perforce.
WARWICK
Suppose, my lords, he did it unconstrain'd,
Think you 'twere prejudicial to his crown?
EXETER

No; for he could not so resign his crown
But that the next heir should succeed and reign.
KING HENRY VI
Art thou against us, Duke of Exeter?
EXETER
His is the right, and therefore pardon me.
YORK
Why whisper you, my lords, and answer not?
EXETER
My conscience tells me he is lawful king.
KING HENRY VI
[Aside] All will revolt from me, and turn to him.
NORTHUMBERLAND
Plantagenet, for all the claim thou lay'st,
Think not that Henry shall be so deposed.
WARWICK
Deposed he shall be, in despite of all.
NORTHUMBERLAND
Thou art deceived: 'tis not thy southern power,
Of Essex, Norfolk, Suffolk, nor of Kent,
Which makes thee thus presumptuous and proud,
Can set the duke up in despite of me.
CLIFFORD
King Henry, be thy title right or wrong,
Lord Clifford vows to fight in thy defence:
May that ground gape and swallow me alive,
Where I shall kneel to him that slew my father!
KING HENRY VI
O Clifford, how thy words revive my heart!
YORK
Henry of Lancaster, resign thy crown.
What mutter you, or what conspire you, lords?
WARWICK
Do right unto this princely Duke of York,
Or I will fill the house with armed men,
And over the chair of state, where now he sits,
Write up his title with usurping blood.
He stamps with his foot and the soldiers show themselves
KING HENRY VI
My Lord of Warwick, hear me but one word:
Let me for this my life-time reign as king.
YORK
Confirm the crown to me and to mine heirs,
And thou shalt reign in quiet while thou livest.
KING HENRY VI
I am content: Richard Plantagenet,
Enjoy the kingdom after my decease.
CLIFFORD
What wrong is this unto the prince your son!
WARWICK
What good is this to England and himself!
WESTMORELAND
Base, fearful and despairing Henry!
CLIFFORD
How hast thou injured both thyself and us!
WESTMORELAND
I cannot stay to hear these articles.
NORTHUMBERLAND
Nor I.
CLIFFORD
Come, cousin, let us tell the queen these news.
WESTMORELAND

Farewell, faint-hearted and degenerate king,
In whose cold blood no spark of honour bides.
NORTHUMBERLAND
Be thou a prey unto the house of York,
And die in bands for this unmanly deed!
CLIFFORD
In dreadful war mayst thou be overcome,
Or live in peace abandon'd and despised!
Exeunt NORTHUMBERLAND, CLIFFORD, and WESTMORELAND
WARWICK
Turn this way, Henry, and regard them not.
EXETER
They seek revenge and therefore will not yield.
KING HENRY VI
Ah, Exeter!
WARWICK
Why should you sigh, my lord?
KING HENRY VI
Not for myself, Lord Warwick, but my son,
Whom I unnaturally shall disinherit.
But be it as it may: I here entail
The crown to thee and to thine heirs for ever;
Conditionally, that here thou take an oath
To cease this civil war, and, whilst I live,
To honour me as thy king and sovereign,
And neither by treason nor hostility
To seek to put me down and reign thyself.
YORK
This oath I willingly take and will perform.
WARWICK
Long live King Henry! Plantagenet embrace him.
KING HENRY VI
And long live thou and these thy forward sons!
YORK
Now York and Lancaster are reconciled.
EXETER
Accursed be he that seeks to make them foes!
Sennet. Here they come down
YORK
Farewell, my gracious lord; I'll to my castle.
WARWICK
And I'll keep London with my soldiers.
NORFOLK
And I to Norfolk with my followers.
MONTAGUE
And I unto the sea from whence I came.
Exeunt YORK, EDWARD, EDMUND, GEORGE, RICHARD, WARWICK, NORFOLK, MONTAGUE, their Soldiers, and Attendants
KING HENRY VI
And I, with grief and sorrow, to the court.
Enter QUEEN MARGARET and PRINCE EDWARD
EXETER
Here comes the queen, whose looks bewray her anger:
I'll steal away.
KING HENRY VI
Exeter, so will I.
QUEEN MARGARET
Nay, go not from me; I will follow thee.
KING HENRY VI
Be patient, gentle queen, and I will stay.
QUEEN MARGARET
Who can be patient in such extremes?
Ah, wretched man! would I had died a maid

And never seen thee, never borne thee son,
Seeing thou hast proved so unnatural a father
Hath he deserved to lose his birthright thus?
Hadst thou but loved him half so well as I,
Or felt that pain which I did for him once,
Or nourish'd him as I did with my blood,
Thou wouldst have left thy dearest heart-blood there,
Rather than have that savage duke thine heir
And disinherited thine only son.
PRINCE EDWARD
Father, you cannot disinherit me:
If you be king, why should not I succeed?
KING HENRY VI
Pardon me, Margaret; pardon me, sweet son:
The Earl of Warwick and the duke enforced me.
QUEEN MARGARET
Enforced thee! art thou king, and wilt be forced?
I shame to hear thee speak. Ah, timorous wretch!
Thou hast undone thyself, thy son and me;
And given unto the house of York such head
As thou shalt reign but by their sufferance.
To entail him and his heirs unto the crown,
What is it, but to make thy sepulchre
And creep into it far before thy time?
Warwick is chancellor and the lord of Calais;
Stern Falconbridge commands the narrow seas;
The duke is made protector of the realm;
And yet shalt thou be safe? such safety finds
The trembling lamb environed with wolves.
Had I been there, which am a silly woman,
The soldiers should have toss'd me on their pikes
Before I would have granted to that act.
But thou preferr'st thy life before thine honour:
And seeing thou dost, I here divorce myself
Both from thy table, Henry, and thy bed,
Until that act of parliament be repeal'd
Whereby my son is disinherited.
The northern lords that have forsworn thy colours
Will follow mine, if once they see them spread;
And spread they shall be, to thy foul disgrace
And utter ruin of the house of York.
Thus do I leave thee. Come, son, let's away;
Our army is ready; come, we'll after them.
KING HENRY VI
Stay, gentle Margaret, and hear me speak.
QUEEN MARGARET
Thou hast spoke too much already: get thee gone.
KING HENRY VI
Gentle son Edward, thou wilt stay with me?
QUEEN MARGARET
Ay, to be murder'd by his enemies.
PRINCE EDWARD
When I return with victory from the field
I'll see your grace: till then I'll follow her.
QUEEN MARGARET
Come, son, away; we may not linger thus.
Exeunt QUEEN MARGARET and PRINCE EDWARD
KING HENRY VI
Poor queen! how love to me and to her son
Hath made her break out into terms of rage!
Revenged may she be on that hateful duke,
Whose haughty spirit, winged with desire,
Will cost my crown, and like an empty eagle

Tire on the flesh of me and of my son!
The loss of those three lords torments my heart:
I'll write unto them and entreat them fair.
Come, cousin you shall be the messenger.
EXETER
And I, I hope, shall reconcile them all.
Exeunt
SCENE II. Sandal Castle.
Enter RICHARD, EDWARD, and MONTAGUE
RICHARD
Brother, though I be youngest, give me leave.
EDWARD
No, I can better play the orator.
MONTAGUE
But I have reasons strong and forcible.
Enter YORK
YORK
Why, how now, sons and brother! at a strife?
What is your quarrel? how began it first?
EDWARD
No quarrel, but a slight contention.
YORK
About what?
RICHARD
About that which concerns your grace and us;
The crown of England, father, which is yours.
YORK
Mine boy? not till King Henry be dead.
RICHARD
Your right depends not on his life or death.
EDWARD
Now you are heir, therefore enjoy it now:
By giving the house of Lancaster leave to breathe,
It will outrun you, father, in the end.
YORK
I took an oath that he should quietly reign.
EDWARD
But for a kingdom any oath may be broken:
I would break a thousand oaths to reign one year.
RICHARD
No; God forbid your grace should be forsworn.
YORK
I shall be, if I claim by open war.
RICHARD
I'll prove the contrary, if you'll hear me speak.
YORK
Thou canst not, son; it is impossible.
RICHARD
An oath is of no moment, being not took
Before a true and lawful magistrate,
That hath authority over him that swears:
Henry had none, but did usurp the place;
Then, seeing 'twas he that made you to depose,
Your oath, my lord, is vain and frivolous.
Therefore, to arms! And, father, do but think
How sweet a thing it is to wear a crown;
Within whose circuit is Elysium
And all that poets feign of bliss and joy.
Why do we finger thus? I cannot rest
Until the white rose that I wear be dyed
Even in the lukewarm blood of Henry's heart.
YORK

Richard, enough; I will be king, or die.
Brother, thou shalt to London presently,
And whet on Warwick to this enterprise.
Thou, Richard, shalt to the Duke of Norfolk,
And tell him privily of our intent.
You Edward, shall unto my Lord Cobham,
With whom the Kentishmen will willingly rise:
In them I trust; for they are soldiers,
Witty, courteous, liberal, full of spirit.
While you are thus employ'd, what resteth more,
But that I seek occasion how to rise,
And yet the king not privy to my drift,
Nor any of the house of Lancaster?
Enter a Messenger
But, stay: what news? Why comest thou in such post?
Messenger
The queen with all the northern earls and lords
Intend here to besiege you in your castle:
She is hard by with twenty thousand men;
And therefore fortify your hold, my lord.
YORK
Ay, with my sword. What! think'st thou that we fear them?
Edward and Richard, you shall stay with me;
My brother Montague shall post to London:
Let noble Warwick, Cobham, and the rest,
Whom we have left protectors of the king,
With powerful policy strengthen themselves,
And trust not simple Henry nor his oaths.
MONTAGUE
Brother, I go; I'll win them, fear it not:
And thus most humbly I do take my leave.
Exit
Enter JOHN MORTIMER and HUGH MORTIMER
Sir John and Sir Hugh Mortimer, mine uncles,
You are come to Sandal in a happy hour;
The army of the queen mean to besiege us.
JOHN MORTIMER
She shall not need; we'll meet her in the field.
YORK
What, with five thousand men?
RICHARD
Ay, with five hundred, father, for a need:
A woman's general; what should we fear?
A march afar off
EDWARD
I hear their drums: let's set our men in order,
And issue forth and bid them battle straight.
YORK
Five men to twenty! though the odds be great,
I doubt not, uncle, of our victory.
Many a battle have I won in France,
When as the enemy hath been ten to one:
Why should I not now have the like success?
Alarum. Exeunt
SCENE III. Field of battle betwixt Sandal Castle and Wakefield.
Alarums. Enter RUTLAND and his Tutor
RUTLAND
Ah, whither shall I fly to 'scape their hands?
Ah, tutor, look where bloody Clifford comes!
Enter CLIFFORD and Soldiers
CLIFFORD

Chaplain, away! thy priesthood saves thy life.
As for the brat of this accursed duke,
Whose father slew my father, he shall die.
Tutor
And I, my lord, will bear him company.
CLIFFORD
Soldiers, away with him!
Tutor
Ah, Clifford, murder not this innocent child,
Lest thou be hated both of God and man!
Exit, dragged off by Soldiers
CLIFFORD
How now! is he dead already? or is it fear
That makes him close his eyes? I'll open them.
RUTLAND
So looks the pent-up lion o'er the wretch
That trembles under his devouring paws;
And so he walks, insulting o'er his prey,
And so he comes, to rend his limbs asunder.
Ah, gentle Clifford, kill me with thy sword,
And not with such a cruel threatening look.
Sweet Clifford, hear me speak before I die.
I am too mean a subject for thy wrath:
Be thou revenged on men, and let me live.
CLIFFORD
In vain thou speak'st, poor boy; my father's blood
Hath stopp'd the passage where thy words should enter.
RUTLAND
Then let my father's blood open it again:
He is a man, and, Clifford, cope with him.
CLIFFORD
Had thy brethren here, their lives and thine
Were not revenge sufficient for me;
No, if I digg'd up thy forefathers' graves
And hung their rotten coffins up in chains,
It could not slake mine ire, nor ease my heart.
The sight of any of the house of York
Is as a fury to torment my soul;
And till I root out their accursed line
And leave not one alive, I live in hell.
Therefore--
Lifting his hand
RUTLAND
O, let me pray before I take my death!
To thee I pray; sweet Clifford, pity me!
CLIFFORD
Such pity as my rapier's point affords.
RUTLAND
I never did thee harm: why wilt thou slay me?
CLIFFORD
Thy father hath.
RUTLAND
But 'twas ere I was born.
Thou hast one son; for his sake pity me,
Lest in revenge thereof, sith God is just,
He be as miserably slain as I.
Ah, let me live in prison all my days;
And when I give occasion of offence,
Then let me die, for now thou hast no cause.
CLIFFORD
No cause!
Thy father slew my father; therefore, die.
Stabs him

RUTLAND
Di faciant laudis summa sit ista tuae!
Dies
CLIFFORD
Plantagenet! I come, Plantagenet!
And this thy son's blood cleaving to my blade
Shall rust upon my weapon, till thy blood,
Congeal'd with this, do make me wipe off both.
Exit

SCENE IV. Another part of the field.
Alarum. Enter YORK
YORK
The army of the queen hath got the field:
My uncles both are slain in rescuing me;
And all my followers to the eager foe
Turn back and fly, like ships before the wind
Or lambs pursued by hunger-starved wolves.
My sons, God knows what hath bechanced them:
But this I know, they have demean'd themselves
Like men born to renown by life or death.
Three times did Richard make a lane to me.
And thrice cried 'Courage, father! fight it out!'
And full as oft came Edward to my side,
With purple falchion, painted to the hilt
In blood of those that had encounter'd him:
And when the hardiest warriors did retire,
Richard cried 'Charge! and give no foot of ground!'
And cried 'A crown, or else a glorious tomb!
A sceptre, or an earthly sepulchre!'
With this, we charged again: but, out, alas!
We bodged again; as I have seen a swan
With bootless labour swim against the tide
And spend her strength with over-matching waves.
A short alarum within
Ah, hark! the fatal followers do pursue;
And I am faint and cannot fly their fury:
And were I strong, I would not shun their fury:
The sands are number'd that make up my life;
Here must I stay, and here my life must end.
Enter QUEEN MARGARET, CLIFFORD, NORTHUMBERLAND, PRINCE EDWARD, and Soldiers
Come, bloody Clifford, rough Northumberland,
I dare your quenchless fury to more rage:
I am your butt, and I abide your shot.
NORTHUMBERLAND
Yield to our mercy, proud Plantagenet.
CLIFFORD
Ay, to such mercy as his ruthless arm,
With downright payment, show'd unto my father.
Now Phaethon hath tumbled from his car,
And made an evening at the noontide prick.
YORK
My ashes, as the phoenix, may bring forth
A bird that will revenge upon you all:
And in that hope I throw mine eyes to heaven,
Scorning whate'er you can afflict me with.
Why come you not? what! multitudes, and fear?
CLIFFORD
So cowards fight when they can fly no further;
So doves do peck the falcon's piercing talons;
So desperate thieves, all hopeless of their lives,
Breathe out invectives 'gainst the officers.
YORK

O Clifford, but bethink thee once again,
And in thy thought o'er-run my former time;
And, if though canst for blushing, view this face,
And bite thy tongue, that slanders him with cowardice
Whose frown hath made thee faint and fly ere this!
CLIFFORD
I will not bandy with thee word for word,
But buckle with thee blows, twice two for one.
QUEEN MARGARET
Hold, valiant Clifford! for a thousand causes
I would prolong awhile the traitor's life.
Wrath makes him deaf: speak thou, Northumberland.
NORTHUMBERLAND
Hold, Clifford! do not honour him so much
To prick thy finger, though to wound his heart:
What valour were it, when a cur doth grin,
For one to thrust his hand between his teeth,
When he might spurn him with his foot away?
It is war's prize to take all vantages;
And ten to one is no impeach of valour.
They lay hands on YORK, who struggles
CLIFFORD
Ay, ay, so strives the woodcock with the gin.
NORTHUMBERLAND
So doth the cony struggle in the net.
YORK
So triumph thieves upon their conquer'd booty;
So true men yield, with robbers so o'ermatch'd.
NORTHUMBERLAND
What would your grace have done unto him now?
QUEEN MARGARET
Brave warriors, Clifford and Northumberland,
Come, make him stand upon this molehill here,
That raught at mountains with outstretched arms,
Yet parted but the shadow with his hand.
What! was it you that would be England's king?
Was't you that revell'd in our parliament,
And made a preachment of your high descent?
Where are your mess of sons to back you now?
The wanton Edward, and the lusty George?
And where's that valiant crook-back prodigy,
Dicky your boy, that with his grumbling voice
Was wont to cheer his dad in mutinies?
Or, with the rest, where is your darling Rutland?
Look, York: I stain'd this napkin with the blood
That valiant Clifford, with his rapier's point,
Made issue from the bosom of the boy;
And if thine eyes can water for his death,
I give thee this to dry thy cheeks withal.
Alas poor York! but that I hate thee deadly,
I should lament thy miserable state.
I prithee, grieve, to make me merry, York.
What, hath thy fiery heart so parch'd thine entrails
That not a tear can fall for Rutland's death?
Why art thou patient, man? thou shouldst be mad;
And I, to make thee mad, do mock thee thus.
Stamp, rave, and fret, that I may sing and dance.
Thou wouldst be fee'd, I see, to make me sport:
York cannot speak, unless he wear a crown.
A crown for York! and, lords, bow low to him:
Hold you his hands, whilst I do set it on.
Putting a paper crown on his head

Ay, marry, sir, now looks he like a king!
Ay, this is he that took King Henry's chair,
And this is he was his adopted heir.
But how is it that great Plantagenet
Is crown'd so soon, and broke his solemn oath?
As I bethink me, you should not be king
Till our King Henry had shook hands with death.
And will you pale your head in Henry's glory,
And rob his temples of the diadem,
Now in his life, against your holy oath?
O, 'tis a fault too too unpardonable!
Off with the crown, and with the crown his head;
And, whilst we breathe, take time to do him dead.
CLIFFORD
That is my office, for my father's sake.
QUEEN MARGARET
Nay, stay; lets hear the orisons he makes.
YORK
She-wolf of France, but worse than wolves of France,
Whose tongue more poisons than the adder's tooth!
How ill-beseeming is it in thy sex
To triumph, like an Amazonian trull,
Upon their woes whom fortune captivates!
But that thy face is, vizard-like, unchanging,
Made impudent with use of evil deeds,
I would assay, proud queen, to make thee blush.
To tell thee whence thou camest, of whom derived,
Were shame enough to shame thee, wert thou not shameless.
Thy father bears the type of King of Naples,
Of both the Sicils and Jerusalem,
Yet not so wealthy as an English yeoman.
Hath that poor monarch taught thee to insult?
It needs not, nor it boots thee not, proud queen,
Unless the adage must be verified,
That beggars mounted run their horse to death.
'Tis beauty that doth oft make women proud;
But, God he knows, thy share thereof is small:
'Tis virtue that doth make them most admired;
The contrary doth make thee wonder'd at:
'Tis government that makes them seem divine;
The want thereof makes thee abominable:
Thou art as opposite to every good
As the Antipodes are unto us,
Or as the south to the septentrion.
O tiger's heart wrapt in a woman's hide!
How couldst thou drain the life-blood of the child,
To bid the father wipe his eyes withal,
And yet be seen to bear a woman's face?
Women are soft, mild, pitiful and flexible;
Thou stern, obdurate, flinty, rough, remorseless.
Bids't thou me rage? why, now thou hast thy wish:
Wouldst have me weep? why, now thou hast thy will:
For raging wind blows up incessant showers,
And when the rage allays, the rain begins.
These tears are my sweet Rutland's obsequies:
And every drop cries vengeance for his death,
'Gainst thee, fell Clifford, and thee, false
Frenchwoman.
NORTHUMBERLAND
Beshrew me, but his passion moves me so
That hardly can I cheque my eyes from tears.
YORK

That face of his the hungry cannibals
Would not have touch'd, would not have stain'd with blood:
But you are more inhuman, more inexorable,
O, ten times more, than tigers of Hyrcania.
See, ruthless queen, a hapless father's tears:
This cloth thou dip'dst in blood of my sweet boy,
And I with tears do wash the blood away.
Keep thou the napkin, and go boast of this:
And if thou tell'st the heavy story right,
Upon my soul, the hearers will shed tears;
Yea even my foes will shed fast-falling tears,
And say 'Alas, it was a piteous deed!'
There, take the crown, and, with the crown, my curse;
And in thy need such comfort come to thee
As now I reap at thy too cruel hand!
Hard-hearted Clifford, take me from the world:
My soul to heaven, my blood upon your heads!

NORTHUMBERLAND
Had he been slaughter-man to all my kin,
I should not for my life but weep with him,
To see how inly sorrow gripes his soul.

QUEEN MARGARET
What, weeping-ripe, my Lord Northumberland?
Think but upon the wrong he did us all,
And that will quickly dry thy melting tears.

CLIFFORD
Here's for my oath, here's for my father's death.
Stabbing him

QUEEN MARGARET
And here's to right our gentle-hearted king.
Stabbing him

YORK
Open Thy gate of mercy, gracious God!
My soul flies through these wounds to seek out Thee.
Dies

QUEEN MARGARET
Off with his head, and set it on York gates;
So York may overlook the town of York.
Flourish. Exeunt

ACT II

SCENE I. A plain near Mortimer's Cross in Herefordshire.

A march. Enter EDWARD, RICHARD, and their power

EDWARD
I wonder how our princely father 'scaped,
Or whether he be 'scaped away or no
From Clifford's and Northumberland's pursuit:
Had he been ta'en, we should have heard the news;
Had he been slain, we should have heard the news;
Or had he 'scaped, methinks we should have heard
The happy tidings of his good escape.
How fares my brother? why is he so sad?
RICHARD
I cannot joy, until I be resolved
Where our right valiant father is become.
I saw him in the battle range about;
And watch'd him how he singled Clifford forth.
Methought he bore him in the thickest troop
As doth a lion in a herd of neat;
Or as a bear, encompass'd round with dogs,
Who having pinch'd a few and made them cry,
The rest stand all aloof, and bark at him.
So fared our father with his enemies;
So fled his enemies my warlike father:
Methinks, 'tis prize enough to be his son.
See how the morning opes her golden gates,
And takes her farewell of the glorious sun!
How well resembles it the prime of youth,
Trimm'd like a younker prancing to his love!
EDWARD
Dazzle mine eyes, or do I see three suns?
RICHARD
Three glorious suns, each one a perfect sun;
Not separated with the racking clouds,
But sever'd in a pale clear-shining sky.
See, see! they join, embrace, and seem to kiss,
As if they vow'd some league inviolable:
Now are they but one lamp, one light, one sun.
In this the heaven figures some event.
EDWARD
'Tis wondrous strange, the like yet never heard of.
I think it cites us, brother, to the field,
That we, the sons of brave Plantagenet,
Each one already blazing by our meeds,
Should notwithstanding join our lights together
And over-shine the earth as this the world.
Whate'er it bodes, henceforward will I bear
Upon my target three fair-shining suns.
RICHARD
Nay, bear three daughters: by your leave I speak it,
You love the breeder better than the male.
Enter a Messenger
But what art thou, whose heavy looks foretell
Some dreadful story hanging on thy tongue?
Messenger
Ah, one that was a woful looker-on
When as the noble Duke of York was slain,
Your princely father and my loving lord!
EDWARD
O, speak no more, for I have heard too much.
RICHARD
Say how he died, for I will hear it all.
Messenger

Environed he was with many foes,
And stood against them, as the hope of Troy
Against the Greeks that would have enter'd Troy.
But Hercules himself must yield to odds;
And many strokes, though with a little axe,
Hew down and fell the hardest-timber'd oak.
By many hands your father was subdued;
But only slaughter'd by the ireful arm
Of unrelenting Clifford and the queen,
Who crown'd the gracious duke in high despite,
Laugh'd in his face; and when with grief he wept,
The ruthless queen gave him to dry his cheeks
A napkin steeped in the harmless blood
Of sweet young Rutland, by rough Clifford slain:
And after many scorns, many foul taunts,
They took his head, and on the gates of York
They set the same; and there it doth remain,
The saddest spectacle that e'er I view'd.

EDWARD
Sweet Duke of York, our prop to lean upon,
Now thou art gone, we have no staff, no stay.
O Clifford, boisterous Clifford! thou hast slain
The flower of Europe for his chivalry;
And treacherously hast thou vanquish'd him,
For hand to hand he would have vanquish'd thee.
Now my soul's palace is become a prison:
Ah, would she break from hence, that this my body
Might in the ground be closed up in rest!
For never henceforth shall I joy again,
Never, O never shall I see more joy!

RICHARD
I cannot weep; for all my body's moisture
Scarce serves to quench my furnace-burning heart:
Nor can my tongue unload my heart's great burthen;
For selfsame wind that I should speak withal
Is kindling coals that fires all my breast,
And burns me up with flames that tears would quench.
To weep is to make less the depth of grief:
Tears then for babes; blows and revenge for me
Richard, I bear thy name; I'll venge thy death,
Or die renowned by attempting it.

EDWARD
His name that valiant duke hath left with thee;
His dukedom and his chair with me is left.

RICHARD
Nay, if thou be that princely eagle's bird,
Show thy descent by gazing 'gainst the sun:
For chair and dukedom, throne and kingdom say;
Either that is thine, or else thou wert not his.
March. Enter WARWICK, MONTAGUE, and their army

WARWICK
How now, fair lords! What fare? what news abroad?

RICHARD
Great Lord of Warwick, if we should recount
Our baleful news, and at each word's deliverance
Stab poniards in our flesh till all were told,
The words would add more anguish than the wounds.
O valiant lord, the Duke of York is slain!

EDWARD
O Warwick, Warwick! that Plantagenet,
Which held three dearly as his soul's redemption,
Is by the stern Lord Clifford done to death.

WARWICK

Ten days ago I drown'd these news in tears;
And now, to add more measure to your woes,
I come to tell you things sith then befall'n.
After the bloody fray at Wakefield fought,
Where your brave father breathed his latest gasp,
Tidings, as swiftly as the posts could run,
Were brought me of your loss and his depart.
I, then in London keeper of the king,
Muster'd my soldiers, gather'd flocks of friends,
And very well appointed, as I thought,
March'd toward Saint Alban's to intercept the queen,
Bearing the king in my behalf along;
For by my scouts I was advertised
That she was coming with a full intent
To dash our late decree in parliament
Touching King Henry's oath and your succession.
Short tale to make, we at Saint Alban's met
Our battles join'd, and both sides fiercely fought:
But whether 'twas the coldness of the king,
Who look'd full gently on his warlike queen,
That robb'd my soldiers of their heated spleen;
Or whether 'twas report of her success;
Or more than common fear of Clifford's rigour,
Who thunders to his captives blood and death,
I cannot judge: but to conclude with truth,
Their weapons like to lightning came and went;
Our soldiers', like the night-owl's lazy flight,
Or like an idle thresher with a flail,
Fell gently down, as if they struck their friends.
I cheer'd them up with justice of our cause,
With promise of high pay and great rewards:
But all in vain; they had no heart to fight,
And we in them no hope to win the day;
So that we fled; the king unto the queen;
Lord George your brother, Norfolk and myself,
In haste, post-haste, are come to join with you:
For in the marches here we heard you were,
Making another head to fight again.
EDWARD
Where is the Duke of Norfolk, gentle Warwick?
And when came George from Burgundy to England?
WARWICK
Some six miles off the duke is with the soldiers;
And for your brother, he was lately sent
From your kind aunt, Duchess of Burgundy,
With aid of soldiers to this needful war.
RICHARD
'Twas odds, belike, when valiant Warwick fled:
Oft have I heard his praises in pursuit,
But ne'er till now his scandal of retire.
WARWICK
Nor now my scandal, Richard, dost thou hear;
For thou shalt know this strong right hand of mine
Can pluck the diadem from faint Henry's head,
And wring the awful sceptre from his fist,
Were he as famous and as bold in war
As he is famed for mildness, peace, and prayer.
RICHARD
I know it well, Lord Warwick; blame me not:
'Tis love I bear thy glories makes me speak.
But in this troublous time what's to be done?
Shall we go throw away our coats of steel,
And wrap our bodies in black mourning gowns,

Numbering our Ave-Maries with our beads?
Or shall we on the helmets of our foes
Tell our devotion with revengeful arms?
If for the last, say ay, and to it, lords.
WARWICK
Why, therefore Warwick came to seek you out;
And therefore comes my brother Montague.
Attend me, lords. The proud insulting queen,
With Clifford and the haught Northumberland,
And of their feather many more proud birds,
Have wrought the easy-melting king like wax.
He swore consent to your succession,
His oath enrolled in the parliament;
And now to London all the crew are gone,
To frustrate both his oath and what beside
May make against the house of Lancaster.
Their power, I think, is thirty thousand strong:
Now, if the help of Norfolk and myself,
With all the friends that thou, brave Earl of March,
Amongst the loving Welshmen canst procure,
Will but amount to five and twenty thousand,
Why, Via! to London will we march amain,
And once again bestride our foaming steeds,
And once again cry 'Charge upon our foes!'
But never once again turn back and fly.
RICHARD
Ay, now methinks I hear great Warwick speak:
Ne'er may he live to see a sunshine day,
That cries 'Retire,' if Warwick bid him stay.
EDWARD
Lord Warwick, on thy shoulder will I lean;
And when thou fail'st--as God forbid the hour!--
Must Edward fall, which peril heaven forfend!
WARWICK
No longer Earl of March, but Duke of York:
The next degree is England's royal throne;
For King of England shalt thou be proclaim'd
In every borough as we pass along;
And he that throws not up his cap for joy
Shall for the fault make forfeit of his head.
King Edward, valiant Richard, Montague,
Stay we no longer, dreaming of renown,
But sound the trumpets, and about our task.
RICHARD
Then, Clifford, were thy heart as hard as steel,
As thou hast shown it flinty by thy deeds,
I come to pierce it, or to give thee mine.
EDWARD
Then strike up drums: God and Saint George for us!
Enter a Messenger
WARWICK
How now! what news?
Messenger
The Duke of Norfolk sends you word by me,
The queen is coming with a puissant host;
And craves your company for speedy counsel.
WARWICK
Why then it sorts, brave warriors, let's away.
Exeunt
SCENE II. Before York.
Flourish. Enter KING HENRY VI, QUEEN MARGARET, PRINCE EDWARD, CLIFFORD, and NORTHUMBERLAND, with drum and trumpets
QUEEN MARGARET

Welcome, my lord, to this brave town of York.
Yonder's the head of that arch-enemy
That sought to be encompass'd with your crown:
Doth not the object cheer your heart, my lord?

KING HENRY VI
Ay, as the rocks cheer them that fear their wreck:
To see this sight, it irks my very soul.
Withhold revenge, dear God! 'tis not my fault,
Nor wittingly have I infringed my vow.

CLIFFORD
My gracious liege, this too much lenity
And harmful pity must be laid aside.
To whom do lions cast their gentle looks?
Not to the beast that would usurp their den.
Whose hand is that the forest bear doth lick?
Not his that spoils her young before her face.
Who 'scapes the lurking serpent's mortal sting?
Not he that sets his foot upon her back.
The smallest worm will turn being trodden on,
And doves will peck in safeguard of their brood.
Ambitious York doth level at thy crown,
Thou smiling while he knit his angry brows:
He, but a duke, would have his son a king,
And raise his issue, like a loving sire;
Thou, being a king, blest with a goodly son,
Didst yield consent to disinherit him,
Which argued thee a most unloving father.
Unreasonable creatures feed their young;
And though man's face be fearful to their eyes,
Yet, in protection of their tender ones,
Who hath not seen them, even with those wings
Which sometime they have used with fearful flight,
Make war with him that climb'd unto their nest,
Offer their own lives in their young's defence?
For shame, my liege, make them your precedent!
Were it not pity that this goodly boy
Should lose his birthright by his father's fault,
And long hereafter say unto his child,
'What my great-grandfather and his grandsire got
My careless father fondly gave away'?
Ah, what a shame were this! Look on the boy;
And let his manly face, which promiseth
Successful fortune, steel thy melting heart
To hold thine own and leave thine own with him.

KING HENRY VI
Full well hath Clifford play'd the orator,
Inferring arguments of mighty force.
But, Clifford, tell me, didst thou never hear
That things ill-got had ever bad success?
And happy always was it for that son
Whose father for his hoarding went to hell?
I'll leave my son my virtuous deeds behind;
And would my father had left me no more!
For all the rest is held at such a rate
As brings a thousand-fold more care to keep
Than in possession and jot of pleasure.
Ah, cousin York! would thy best friends did know
How it doth grieve me that thy head is here!

QUEEN MARGARET
My lord, cheer up your spirits: our foes are nigh,
And this soft courage makes your followers faint.
You promised knighthood to our forward son:

Unsheathe your sword, and dub him presently.
Edward, kneel down.
KING HENRY VI
Edward Plantagenet, arise a knight;
And learn this lesson, draw thy sword in right.
PRINCE
My gracious father, by your kingly leave,
I'll draw it as apparent to the crown,
And in that quarrel use it to the death.
CLIFFORD
Why, that is spoken like a toward prince.
Enter a Messenger
Messenger
Royal commanders, be in readiness:
For with a band of thirty thousand men
Comes Warwick, backing of the Duke of York;
And in the towns, as they do march along,
Proclaims him king, and many fly to him:
Darraign your battle, for they are at hand.
CLIFFORD
I would your highness would depart the field:
The queen hath best success when you are absent.
QUEEN MARGARET
Ay, good my lord, and leave us to our fortune.
KING HENRY VI
Why, that's my fortune too; therefore I'll stay.
NORTHUMBERLAND
Be it with resolution then to fight.
PRINCE EDWARD
My royal father, cheer these noble lords
And hearten those that fight in your defence:
Unsheathe your sword, good father; cry 'Saint George!'
March. Enter EDWARD, GEORGE, RICHARD, WARWICK, NORFOLK, MONTAGUE, and Soldiers
EDWARD
Now, perjured Henry! wilt thou kneel for grace,
And set thy diadem upon my head;
Or bide the mortal fortune of the field?
QUEEN MARGARET
Go, rate thy minions, proud insulting boy!
Becomes it thee to be thus bold in terms
Before thy sovereign and thy lawful king?
EDWARD
I am his king, and he should bow his knee;
I was adopted heir by his consent:
Since when, his oath is broke; for, as I hear,
You, that are king, though he do wear the crown,
Have caused him, by new act of parliament,
To blot out me, and put his own son in.
CLIFFORD
And reason too:
Who should succeed the father but the son?
RICHARD
Are you there, butcher? O, I cannot speak!
CLIFFORD
Ay, crook-back, here I stand to answer thee,
Or any he the proudest of thy sort.
RICHARD
'Twas you that kill'd young Rutland, was it not?
CLIFFORD
Ay, and old York, and yet not satisfied.
RICHARD
For God's sake, lords, give signal to the fight.
WARWICK

What say'st thou, Henry, wilt thou yield the crown?
QUEEN MARGARET
Why, how now, long-tongued Warwick! dare you speak?
When you and I met at Saint Alban's last,
Your legs did better service than your hands.
WARWICK
Then 'twas my turn to fly, and now 'tis thine.
CLIFFORD
You said so much before, and yet you fled.
WARWICK
'Twas not your valour, Clifford, drove me thence.
NORTHUMBERLAND
No, nor your manhood that durst make you stay.
RICHARD
Northumberland, I hold thee reverently.
Break off the parley; for scarce I can refrain
The execution of my big-swoln heart
Upon that Clifford, that cruel child-killer.
CLIFFORD
I slew thy father, call'st thou him a child?
RICHARD
Ay, like a dastard and a treacherous coward,
As thou didst kill our tender brother Rutland;
But ere sunset I'll make thee curse the deed.
KING HENRY VI
Have done with words, my lords, and hear me speak.
QUEEN MARGARET
Defy them then, or else hold close thy lips.
KING HENRY VI
I prithee, give no limits to my tongue:
I am a king, and privileged to speak.
CLIFFORD
My liege, the wound that bred this meeting here
Cannot be cured by words; therefore be still.
RICHARD
Then, executioner, unsheathe thy sword:
By him that made us all, I am resolved
that Clifford's manhood lies upon his tongue.
EDWARD
Say, Henry, shall I have my right, or no?
A thousand men have broke their fasts to-day,
That ne'er shall dine unless thou yield the crown.
WARWICK
If thou deny, their blood upon thy head;
For York in justice puts his armour on.
PRINCE EDWARD
If that be right which Warwick says is right,
There is no wrong, but every thing is right.
RICHARD
Whoever got thee, there thy mother stands;
For, well I wot, thou hast thy mother's tongue.
QUEEN MARGARET
But thou art neither like thy sire nor dam;
But like a foul mis-shapen stigmatic,
Mark'd by the destinies to be avoided,
As venom toads, or lizards' dreadful stings.
RICHARD
Iron of Naples hid with English gilt,
Whose father bears the title of a king,--
As if a channel should be call'd the sea,--
Shamest thou not, knowing whence thou art extraught,
To let thy tongue detect thy base-born heart?
EDWARD

A wisp of straw were worth a thousand crowns,
To make this shameless callet know herself.
Helen of Greece was fairer far than thou,
Although thy husband may be Menelaus;
And ne'er was Agamemnon's brother wrong'd
By that false woman, as this king by thee.
His father revell'd in the heart of France,
And tamed the king, and made the dauphin stoop;
And had he match'd according to his state,
He might have kept that glory to this day;
But when he took a beggar to his bed,
And graced thy poor sire with his bridal-day,
Even then that sunshine brew'd a shower for him,
That wash'd his father's fortunes forth of France,
And heap'd sedition on his crown at home.
For what hath broach'd this tumult but thy pride?
Hadst thou been meek, our title still had slept;
And we, in pity of the gentle king,
Had slipp'd our claim until another age.
GEORGE
But when we saw our sunshine made thy spring,
And that thy summer bred us no increase,
We set the axe to thy usurping root;
And though the edge hath something hit ourselves,
Yet, know thou, since we have begun to strike,
We'll never leave till we have hewn thee down,
Or bathed thy growing with our heated bloods.
EDWARD
And, in this resolution, I defy thee;
Not willing any longer conference,
Since thou deniest the gentle king to speak.
Sound trumpets! let our bloody colours wave!
And either victory, or else a grave.
QUEEN MARGARET
Stay, Edward.
EDWARD
No, wrangling woman, we'll no longer stay:
These words will cost ten thousand lives this day.
Exeunt
SCENE III. A field of battle between Towton and Saxton, in Yorkshire.
Alarum. Excursions. Enter WARWICK
WARWICK
Forspent with toil, as runners with a race,
I lay me down a little while to breathe;
For strokes received, and many blows repaid,
Have robb'd my strong-knit sinews of their strength,
And spite of spite needs must I rest awhile.
Enter EDWARD, running
EDWARD
Smile, gentle heaven! or strike, ungentle death!
For this world frowns, and Edward's sun is clouded.
WARWICK
How now, my lord! what hap? what hope of good?
Enter GEORGE
GEORGE
Our hap is loss, our hope but sad despair;
Our ranks are broke, and ruin follows us:
What counsel give you? whither shall we fly?
EDWARD
Bootless is flight, they follow us with wings;
And weak we are and cannot shun pursuit.
Enter RICHARD

RICHARD
Ah, Warwick, why hast thou withdrawn thyself?
Thy brother's blood the thirsty earth hath drunk,
Broach'd with the steely point of Clifford's lance;
And in the very pangs of death he cried,
Like to a dismal clangour heard from far,
'Warwick, revenge! brother, revenge my death!'
So, underneath the belly of their steeds,
That stain'd their fetlocks in his smoking blood,
The noble gentleman gave up the ghost.
WARWICK
Then let the earth be drunken with our blood:
I'll kill my horse, because I will not fly.
Why stand we like soft-hearted women here,
Wailing our losses, whiles the foe doth rage;
And look upon, as if the tragedy
Were play'd in jest by counterfeiting actors?
Here on my knee I vow to God above,
I'll never pause again, never stand still,
Till either death hath closed these eyes of mine
Or fortune given me measure of revenge.
EDWARD
O Warwick, I do bend my knee with thine;
And in this vow do chain my soul to thine!
And, ere my knee rise from the earth's cold face,
I throw my hands, mine eyes, my heart to thee,
Thou setter up and plucker down of kings,
Beseeching thee, if with they will it stands
That to my foes this body must be prey,
Yet that thy brazen gates of heaven may ope,
And give sweet passage to my sinful soul!
Now, lords, take leave until we meet again,
Where'er it be, in heaven or in earth.
RICHARD
Brother, give me thy hand; and, gentle Warwick,
Let me embrace thee in my weary arms:
I, that did never weep, now melt with woe
That winter should cut off our spring-time so.
WARWICK
Away, away! Once more, sweet lords farewell.
GEORGE
Yet let us all together to our troops,
And give them leave to fly that will not stay;
And call them pillars that will stand to us;
And, if we thrive, promise them such rewards
As victors wear at the Olympian games:
This may plant courage in their quailing breasts;
For yet is hope of life and victory.
Forslow no longer, make we hence amain.
Exeunt
SCENE IV. Another part of the field.
Excursions. Enter RICHARD and CLIFFORD
RICHARD
Now, Clifford, I have singled thee alone:
Suppose this arm is for the Duke of York,
And this for Rutland; both bound to revenge,
Wert thou environ'd with a brazen wall.
CLIFFORD
Now, Richard, I am with thee here alone:
This is the hand that stabb'd thy father York;
And this the hand that slew thy brother Rutland;
And here's the heart that triumphs in their death
And cheers these hands that slew thy sire and brother

To execute the like upon thyself;
And so, have at thee!
They fight. WARWICK comes; CLIFFORD flies
RICHARD
Nay Warwick, single out some other chase;
For I myself will hunt this wolf to death.
Exeunt
SCENE V. Another part of the field.
Alarum. Enter KING HENRY VI alone
KING HENRY VI
This battle fares like to the morning's war,
When dying clouds contend with growing light,
What time the shepherd, blowing of his nails,
Can neither call it perfect day nor night.
Now sways it this way, like a mighty sea
Forced by the tide to combat with the wind;
Now sways it that way, like the selfsame sea
Forced to retire by fury of the wind:
Sometime the flood prevails, and then the wind;
Now one the better, then another best;
Both tugging to be victors, breast to breast,
Yet neither conqueror nor conquered:
So is the equal of this fell war.
Here on this molehill will I sit me down.
To whom God will, there be the victory!
For Margaret my queen, and Clifford too,
Have chid me from the battle; swearing both
They prosper best of all when I am thence.
Would I were dead! if God's good will were so;
For what is in this world but grief and woe?
O God! methinks it were a happy life,
To be no better than a homely swain;
To sit upon a hill, as I do now,
To carve out dials quaintly, point by point,
Thereby to see the minutes how they run,
How many make the hour full complete;
How many hours bring about the day;
How many days will finish up the year;
How many years a mortal man may live.
When this is known, then to divide the times:
So many hours must I tend my flock;
So many hours must I take my rest;
So many hours must I contemplate;
So many hours must I sport myself;
So many days my ewes have been with young;
So many weeks ere the poor fools will ean:
So many years ere I shall shear the fleece:
So minutes, hours, days, months, and years,
Pass'd over to the end they were created,
Would bring white hairs unto a quiet grave.
Ah, what a life were this! how sweet! how lovely!
Gives not the hawthorn-bush a sweeter shade
To shepherds looking on their silly sheep,
Than doth a rich embroider'd canopy
To kings that fear their subjects' treachery?
O, yes, it doth; a thousand-fold it doth.
And to conclude, the shepherd's homely curds,
His cold thin drink out of his leather bottle.
His wonted sleep under a fresh tree's shade,
All which secure and sweetly he enjoys,
Is far beyond a prince's delicates,
His viands sparkling in a golden cup,

His body couched in a curious bed,
When care, mistrust, and treason waits on him.
Alarum. Enter a Son that has killed his father, dragging in the dead body
Son
Ill blows the wind that profits nobody.
This man, whom hand to hand I slew in fight,
May be possessed with some store of crowns;
And I, that haply take them from him now,
May yet ere night yield both my life and them
To some man else, as this dead man doth me.
Who's this? O God! it is my father's face,
Whom in this conflict I unwares have kill'd.
O heavy times, begetting such events!
From London by the king was I press'd forth;
My father, being the Earl of Warwick's man,
Came on the part of York, press'd by his master;
And I, who at his hands received my life, him
Have by my hands of life bereaved him.
Pardon me, God, I knew not what I did!
And pardon, father, for I knew not thee!
My tears shall wipe away these bloody marks;
And no more words till they have flow'd their fill.
KING HENRY VI
O piteous spectacle! O bloody times!
Whiles lions war and battle for their dens,
Poor harmless lambs abide their enmity.
Weep, wretched man, I'll aid thee tear for tear;
And let our hearts and eyes, like civil war,
Be blind with tears, and break o'ercharged with grief.
Enter a Father that has killed his son, bringing in the body
Father
Thou that so stoutly hast resisted me,
Give me thy gold, if thou hast any gold:
For I have bought it with an hundred blows.
But let me see: is this our foeman's face?
Ah, no, no, no, it is mine only son!
Ah, boy, if any life be left in thee,
Throw up thine eye! see, see what showers arise,
Blown with the windy tempest of my heart,
Upon thy wounds, that kill mine eye and heart!
O, pity, God, this miserable age!
What stratagems, how fell, how butcherly,
Erroneous, mutinous and unnatural,
This deadly quarrel daily doth beget!
O boy, thy father gave thee life too soon,
And hath bereft thee of thy life too late!
KING HENRY VI
Woe above woe! grief more than common grief!
O that my death would stay these ruthful deeds!
O pity, pity, gentle heaven, pity!
The red rose and the white are on his face,
The fatal colours of our striving houses:
The one his purple blood right well resembles;
The other his pale cheeks, methinks, presenteth:
Wither one rose, and let the other flourish;
If you contend, a thousand lives must wither.
Son
How will my mother for a father's death
Take on with me and ne'er be satisfied!
Father
How will my wife for slaughter of my son
Shed seas of tears and ne'er be satisfied!
KING HENRY VI

How will the country for these woful chances
Misthink the king and not be satisfied!
Son
Was ever son so rued a father's death?
Father
Was ever father so bemoan'd his son?
KING HENRY VI
Was ever king so grieved for subjects' woe?
Much is your sorrow; mine ten times so much.
Son
I'll bear thee hence, where I may weep my fill.
Exit with the body
Father
These arms of mine shall be thy winding-sheet;
My heart, sweet boy, shall be thy sepulchre,
For from my heart thine image ne'er shall go;
My sighing breast shall be thy funeral bell;
And so obsequious will thy father be,
Even for the loss of thee, having no more,
As Priam was for all his valiant sons.
I'll bear thee hence; and let them fight that will,
For I have murdered where I should not kill.
Exit with the body
KING HENRY VI
Sad-hearted men, much overgone with care,
Here sits a king more woful than you are.
Alarums: excursions. Enter QUEEN MARGARET, PRINCE EDWARD, and EXETER
PRINCE EDWARD
Fly, father, fly! for all your friends are fled,
And Warwick rages like a chafed bull:
Away! for death doth hold us in pursuit.
QUEEN MARGARET
Mount you, my lord; towards Berwick post amain:
Edward and Richard, like a brace of greyhounds
Having the fearful flying hare in sight,
With fiery eyes sparkling for very wrath,
And bloody steel grasp'd in their ireful hands,
Are at our backs; and therefore hence amain.
EXETER
Away! for vengeance comes along with them:
Nay, stay not to expostulate, make speed;
Or else come after: I'll away before.
KING HENRY VI
Nay, take me with thee, good sweet Exeter:
Not that I fear to stay, but love to go
Whither the queen intends. Forward; away!
Exeunt
SCENE VI. Another part of the field.
A loud alarum. Enter CLIFFORD, wounded
CLIFFORD
Here burns my candle out; ay, here it dies,
Which, whiles it lasted, gave King Henry light.
O Lancaster, I fear thy overthrow
More than my body's parting with my soul!
My love and fear glued many friends to thee;
And, now I fall, thy tough commixture melts.
Impairing Henry, strengthening misproud York,
The common people swarm like summer flies;
And whither fly the gnats but to the sun?
And who shines now but Henry's enemies?
O Phoebus, hadst thou never given consent
That Phaethon should cheque thy fiery steeds,
Thy burning car never had scorch'd the earth!

And, Henry, hadst thou sway'd as kings should do,
Or as thy father and his father did,
Giving no ground unto the house of York,
They never then had sprung like summer flies;
I and ten thousand in this luckless realm
Had left no mourning widows for our death;
And thou this day hadst kept thy chair in peace.
For what doth cherish weeds but gentle air?
And what makes robbers bold but too much lenity?
Bootless are plaints, and cureless are my wounds;
No way to fly, nor strength to hold out flight:
The foe is merciless, and will not pity;
For at their hands I have deserved no pity.
The air hath got into my deadly wounds,
And much effuse of blood doth make me faint.
Come, York and Richard, Warwick and the rest;
I stabb'd your fathers' bosoms, split my breast.
He faints
Alarum and retreat. Enter EDWARD, GEORGE, RICHARD, MONTAGUE, WARWICK, and Soldiers
EDWARD
Now breathe we, lords: good fortune bids us pause,
And smooth the frowns of war with peaceful looks.
Some troops pursue the bloody-minded queen,
That led calm Henry, though he were a king,
As doth a sail, fill'd with a fretting gust,
Command an argosy to stem the waves.
But think you, lords, that Clifford fled with them?
WARWICK
No, 'tis impossible he should escape,
For, though before his face I speak the words
Your brother Richard mark'd him for the grave:
And wheresoe'er he is, he's surely dead.
CLIFFORD groans, and dies
EDWARD
Whose soul is that which takes her heavy leave?
RICHARD
A deadly groan, like life and death's departing.
EDWARD
See who it is: and, now the battle's ended,
If friend or foe, let him be gently used.
RICHARD
Revoke that doom of mercy, for 'tis Clifford;
Who not contented that he lopp'd the branch
In hewing Rutland when his leaves put forth,
But set his murdering knife unto the root
From whence that tender spray did sweetly spring,
I mean our princely father, Duke of York.
WARWICK
From off the gates of York fetch down the head,
Your father's head, which Clifford placed there;
Instead whereof let this supply the room:
Measure for measure must be answered.
EDWARD
Bring forth that fatal screech-owl to our house,
That nothing sung but death to us and ours:
Now death shall stop his dismal threatening sound,
And his ill-boding tongue no more shall speak.
WARWICK
I think his understanding is bereft.
Speak, Clifford, dost thou know who speaks to thee?
Dark cloudy death o'ershades his beams of life,
And he nor sees nor hears us what we say.
RICHARD

O, would he did! and so perhaps he doth:
'Tis but his policy to counterfeit,
Because he would avoid such bitter taunts
Which in the time of death he gave our father.
GEORGE
If so thou think'st, vex him with eager words.
RICHARD
Clifford, ask mercy and obtain no grace.
EDWARD
Clifford, repent in bootless penitence.
WARWICK
Clifford, devise excuses for thy faults.
GEORGE
While we devise fell tortures for thy faults.
RICHARD
Thou didst love York, and I am son to York.
EDWARD
Thou pitied'st Rutland; I will pity thee.
GEORGE
Where's Captain Margaret, to fence you now?
WARWICK
They mock thee, Clifford: swear as thou wast wont.
RICHARD
What, not an oath? nay, then the world goes hard
When Clifford cannot spare his friends an oath.
I know by that he's dead; and, by my soul,
If this right hand would buy two hour's life,
That I in all despite might rail at him,
This hand should chop it off, and with the
issuing blood
Stifle the villain whose unstanched thirst
York and young Rutland could not satisfy.
WARWICK
Ay, but he's dead: off with the traitor's head,
And rear it in the place your father's stands.
And now to London with triumphant march,
There to be crowned England's royal king:
From whence shall Warwick cut the sea to France,
And ask the Lady Bona for thy queen:
So shalt thou sinew both these lands together;
And, having France thy friend, thou shalt not dread
The scatter'd foe that hopes to rise again;
For though they cannot greatly sting to hurt,
Yet look to have them buzz to offend thine ears.
First will I see the coronation;
And then to Brittany I'll cross the sea,
To effect this marriage, so it please my lord.
EDWARD
Even as thou wilt, sweet Warwick, let it be;
For in thy shoulder do I build my seat,
And never will I undertake the thing
Wherein thy counsel and consent is wanting.
Richard, I will create thee Duke of Gloucester,
And George, of Clarence: Warwick, as ourself,
Shall do and undo as him pleaseth best.
RICHARD
Let me be Duke of Clarence, George of Gloucester;
For Gloucester's dukedom is too ominous.
WARWICK
Tut, that's a foolish observation:
Richard, be Duke of Gloucester. Now to London,
To see these honours in possession.
Exeunt

ACT III

SCENE I. A forest in the north of England.
Enter two Keepers, with cross-bows in their hands
First Keeper
Under this thick-grown brake we'll shroud ourselves;
For through this laund anon the deer will come;
And in this covert will we make our stand,
Culling the principal of all the deer.
Second Keeper
I'll stay above the hill, so both may shoot.
First Keeper
That cannot be; the noise of thy cross-bow
Will scare the herd, and so my shoot is lost.
Here stand we both, and aim we at the best:
And, for the time shall not seem tedious,
I'll tell thee what befell me on a day
In this self-place where now we mean to stand.
Second Keeper
Here comes a man; let's stay till he be past.
Enter KING HENRY VI, disguised, with a prayerbook
KING HENRY VI
From Scotland am I stol'n, even of pure love,
To greet mine own land with my wishful sight.
No, Harry, Harry, 'tis no land of thine;
Thy place is fill'd, thy sceptre wrung from thee,
Thy balm wash'd off wherewith thou wast anointed:
No bending knee will call thee Caesar now,
No humble suitors press to speak for right,
No, not a man comes for redress of thee;
For how can I help them, and not myself?
First Keeper
Ay, here's a deer whose skin's a keeper's fee:
This is the quondam king; let's seize upon him.
KING HENRY VI
Let me embrace thee, sour adversity,
For wise men say it is the wisest course.
Second Keeper
Why linger we? let us lay hands upon him.
First Keeper
Forbear awhile; we'll hear a little more.
KING HENRY VI
My queen and son are gone to France for aid;
And, as I hear, the great commanding Warwick
Is thither gone, to crave the French king's sister
To wife for Edward: if this news be true,
Poor queen and son, your labour is but lost;
For Warwick is a subtle orator,
And Lewis a prince soon won with moving words.
By this account then Margaret may win him;
For she's a woman to be pitied much:
Her sighs will make a battery in his breast;
Her tears will pierce into a marble heart;
The tiger will be mild whiles she doth mourn;
And Nero will be tainted with remorse,
To hear and see her plaints, her brinish tears.
Ay, but she's come to beg, Warwick to give;
She, on his left side, craving aid for Henry,
He, on his right, asking a wife for Edward.
She weeps, and says her Henry is deposed;
He smiles, and says his Edward is install'd;
That she, poor wretch, for grief can speak no more;
Whiles Warwick tells his title, smooths the wrong,

Inferreth arguments of mighty strength,
And in conclusion wins the king from her,
With promise of his sister, and what else,
To strengthen and support King Edward's place.
O Margaret, thus 'twill be; and thou, poor soul,
Art then forsaken, as thou went'st forlorn!
Second Keeper
Say, what art thou that talk'st of kings and queens?
KING HENRY VI
More than I seem, and less than I was born to:
A man at least, for less I should not be;
And men may talk of kings, and why not I?
Second Keeper
Ay, but thou talk'st as if thou wert a king.
KING HENRY VI
Why, so I am, in mind; and that's enough.
Second Keeper
But, if thou be a king, where is thy crown?
KING HENRY VI
My crown is in my heart, not on my head;
Not decked with diamonds and Indian stones,
Nor to be seen: my crown is called content:
A crown it is that seldom kings enjoy.
Second Keeper
Well, if you be a king crown'd with content,
Your crown content and you must be contented
To go along with us; for as we think,
You are the king King Edward hath deposed;
And we his subjects sworn in all allegiance
Will apprehend you as his enemy.
KING HENRY VI
But did you never swear, and break an oath?
Second Keeper
No, never such an oath; nor will not now.
KING HENRY VI
Where did you dwell when I was King of England?
Second Keeper
Here in this country, where we now remain.
KING HENRY VI
I was anointed king at nine months old;
My father and my grandfather were kings,
And you were sworn true subjects unto me:
And tell me, then, have you not broke your oaths?
First Keeper
No;
For we were subjects but while you were king.
KING HENRY VI
Why, am I dead? do I not breathe a man?
Ah, simple men, you know not what you swear!
Look, as I blow this feather from my face,
And as the air blows it to me again,
Obeying with my wind when I do blow,
And yielding to another when it blows,
Commanded always by the greater gust;
Such is the lightness of you common men.
But do not break your oaths; for of that sin
My mild entreaty shall not make you guilty.
Go where you will, the king shall be commanded;
And be you kings, command, and I'll obey.
First Keeper
We are true subjects to the king, King Edward.
KING HENRY VI

So would you be again to Henry,
If he were seated as King Edward is.
First Keeper
We charge you, in God's name, and the king's,
To go with us unto the officers.
KING HENRY VI
In God's name, lead; your king's name be obey'd:
And what God will, that let your king perform;
And what he will, I humbly yield unto.
Exeunt
SCENE II. London. The palace.
Enter KING EDWARD IV, GLOUCESTER, CLARENCE, and LADY GREY
KING EDWARD IV
Brother of Gloucester, at Saint Alban's field
This lady's husband, Sir Richard Grey, was slain,
His lands then seized on by the conqueror:
Her suit is now to repossess those lands;
Which we in justice cannot well deny,
Because in quarrel of the house of York
The worthy gentleman did lose his life.
GLOUCESTER
Your highness shall do well to grant her suit;
It were dishonour to deny it her.
KING EDWARD IV
It were no less; but yet I'll make a pause.
GLOUCESTER
[Aside to CLARENCE] Yea, is it so?
I see the lady hath a thing to grant,
Before the king will grant her humble suit.
CLARENCE
[Aside to GLOUCESTER] He knows the game: how true
he keeps the wind!
GLOUCESTER
[Aside to CLARENCE] Silence!
KING EDWARD IV
Widow, we will consider of your suit;
And come some other time to know our mind.
LADY GREY
Right gracious lord, I cannot brook delay:
May it please your highness to resolve me now;
And what your pleasure is, shall satisfy me.
GLOUCESTER
[Aside to CLARENCE] Ay, widow? then I'll warrant
you all your lands,
An if what pleases him shall pleasure you.
Fight closer, or, good faith, you'll catch a blow.
CLARENCE
[Aside to GLOUCESTER] I fear her not, unless she
chance to fall.
GLOUCESTER
[Aside to CLARENCE] God forbid that! for he'll
take vantages.
KING EDWARD IV
How many children hast thou, widow? tell me.
CLARENCE
[Aside to GLOUCESTER] I think he means to beg a
child of her.
GLOUCESTER
[Aside to CLARENCE] Nay, whip me then: he'll rather
give her two.
LADY GREY
Three, my most gracious lord.
GLOUCESTER

[Aside to CLARENCE] You shall have four, if you'll be ruled by him.
KING EDWARD IV
'Twere pity they should lose their father's lands.
LADY GREY
Be pitiful, dread lord, and grant it then.
KING EDWARD IV
Lords, give us leave: I'll try this widow's wit.
GLOUCESTER
[Aside to CLARENCE] Ay, good leave have you; for you will have leave,
Till youth take leave and leave you to the crutch.
GLOUCESTER and CLARENCE retire
KING EDWARD IV
Now tell me, madam, do you love your children?
LADY GREY
Ay, full as dearly as I love myself.
KING EDWARD IV
And would you not do much to do them good?
LADY GREY
To do them good, I would sustain some harm.
KING EDWARD IV
Then get your husband's lands, to do them good.
LADY GREY
Therefore I came unto your majesty.
KING EDWARD IV
I'll tell you how these lands are to be got.
LADY GREY
So shall you bind me to your highness' service.
KING EDWARD IV
What service wilt thou do me, if I give them?
LADY GREY
What you command, that rests in me to do.
KING EDWARD IV
But you will take exceptions to my boon.
LADY GREY
No, gracious lord, except I cannot do it.
KING EDWARD IV
Ay, but thou canst do what I mean to ask.
LADY GREY
Why, then I will do what your grace commands.
GLOUCESTER
[Aside to CLARENCE] He plies her hard; and much rain wears the marble.
CLARENCE
[Aside to GLOUCESTER] As red as fire! nay, then her wax must melt.
LADY GREY
Why stops my lord, shall I not hear my task?
KING EDWARD IV
An easy task; 'tis but to love a king.
LADY GREY
That's soon perform'd, because I am a subject.
KING EDWARD IV
Why, then, thy husband's lands I freely give thee.
LADY GREY
I take my leave with many thousand thanks.
GLOUCESTER
[Aside to CLARENCE] The match is made; she seals it with a curtsy.
KING EDWARD IV
But stay thee, 'tis the fruits of love I mean.
LADY GREY

The fruits of love I mean, my loving liege.
KING EDWARD IV
Ay, but, I fear me, in another sense.
What love, think'st thou, I sue so much to get?
LADY GREY
My love till death, my humble thanks, my prayers;
That love which virtue begs and virtue grants.
KING EDWARD IV
No, by my troth, I did not mean such love.
LADY GREY
Why, then you mean not as I thought you did.
KING EDWARD IV
But now you partly may perceive my mind.
LADY GREY
My mind will never grant what I perceive
Your highness aims at, if I aim aright.
KING EDWARD IV
To tell thee plain, I aim to lie with thee.
LADY GREY
To tell you plain, I had rather lie in prison.
KING EDWARD IV
Why, then thou shalt not have thy husband's lands.
LADY GREY
Why, then mine honesty shall be my dower;
For by that loss I will not purchase them.
KING EDWARD IV
Therein thou wrong'st thy children mightily.
LADY GREY
Herein your highness wrongs both them and me.
But, mighty lord, this merry inclination
Accords not with the sadness of my suit:
Please you dismiss me either with 'ay' or 'no.'
KING EDWARD IV
Ay, if thou wilt say 'ay' to my request;
No if thou dost say 'no' to my demand.
LADY GREY
Then, no, my lord. My suit is at an end.
GLOUCESTER
[Aside to CLARENCE] The widow likes him not, she knits her brows.
CLARENCE
[Aside to GLOUCESTER] He is the bluntest wooer in Christendom.
KING EDWARD IV
[Aside] Her looks do argue her replete with modesty;
Her words do show her wit incomparable;
All her perfections challenge sovereignty:
One way or other, she is for a king;
And she shall be my love, or else my queen.--
Say that King Edward take thee for his queen?
LADY GREY
'Tis better said than done, my gracious lord:
I am a subject fit to jest withal,
But far unfit to be a sovereign.
KING EDWARD IV
Sweet widow, by my state I swear to thee
I speak no more than what my soul intends;
And that is, to enjoy thee for my love.
LADY GREY
And that is more than I will yield unto:
I know I am too mean to be your queen,
And yet too good to be your concubine.
KING EDWARD IV

You cavil, widow: I did mean, my queen.
LADY GREY
'Twill grieve your grace my sons should call you father.
KING EDWARD IV
No more than when my daughters call thee mother.
Thou art a widow, and thou hast some children;
And, by God's mother, I, being but a bachelor,
Have other some: why, 'tis a happy thing
To be the father unto many sons.
Answer no more, for thou shalt be my queen.
GLOUCESTER
[Aside to CLARENCE] The ghostly father now hath done his shrift.
CLARENCE
[Aside to GLOUCESTER] When he was made a shriver, 'twas for shift.
KING EDWARD IV
Brothers, you muse what chat we two have had.
GLOUCESTER
The widow likes it not, for she looks very sad.
KING EDWARD IV
You'll think it strange if I should marry her.
CLARENCE
To whom, my lord?
KING EDWARD IV
Why, Clarence, to myself.
GLOUCESTER
That would be ten days' wonder at the least.
CLARENCE
That's a day longer than a wonder lasts.
GLOUCESTER
By so much is the wonder in extremes.
KING EDWARD IV
Well, jest on, brothers: I can tell you both
Her suit is granted for her husband's lands.
Enter a Nobleman
Nobleman
My gracious lord, Henry your foe is taken,
And brought your prisoner to your palace gate.
KING EDWARD IV
See that he be convey'd unto the Tower:
And go we, brothers, to the man that took him,
To question of his apprehension.
Widow, go you along. Lords, use her honourably.
Exeunt all but GLOUCESTER
GLOUCESTER
Ay, Edward will use women honourably.
Would he were wasted, marrow, bones and all,
That from his loins no hopeful branch may spring,
To cross me from the golden time I look for!
And yet, between my soul's desire and me--
The lustful Edward's title buried--
Is Clarence, Henry, and his son young Edward,
And all the unlook'd for issue of their bodies,
To take their rooms, ere I can place myself:
A cold premeditation for my purpose!
Why, then, I do but dream on sovereignty;
Like one that stands upon a promontory,
And spies a far-off shore where he would tread,
Wishing his foot were equal with his eye,
And chides the sea that sunders him from thence,
Saying, he'll lade it dry to have his way:
So do I wish the crown, being so far off;

And so I chide the means that keeps me from it;
And so I say, I'll cut the causes off,
Flattering me with impossibilities.
My eye's too quick, my heart o'erweens too much,
Unless my hand and strength could equal them.
Well, say there is no kingdom then for Richard;
What other pleasure can the world afford?
I'll make my heaven in a lady's lap,
And deck my body in gay ornaments,
And witch sweet ladies with my words and looks.
O miserable thought! and more unlikely
Than to accomplish twenty golden crowns!
Why, love forswore me in my mother's womb:
And, for I should not deal in her soft laws,
She did corrupt frail nature with some bribe,
To shrink mine arm up like a wither'd shrub;
To make an envious mountain on my back,
Where sits deformity to mock my body;
To shape my legs of an unequal size;
To disproportion me in every part,
Like to a chaos, or an unlick'd bear-whelp
That carries no impression like the dam.
And am I then a man to be beloved?
O monstrous fault, to harbour such a thought!
Then, since this earth affords no joy to me,
But to command, to cheque, to o'erbear such
As are of better person than myself,
I'll make my heaven to dream upon the crown,
And, whiles I live, to account this world but hell,
Until my mis-shaped trunk that bears this head
Be round impaled with a glorious crown.
And yet I know not how to get the crown,
For many lives stand between me and home:
And I,--like one lost in a thorny wood,
That rends the thorns and is rent with the thorns,
Seeking a way and straying from the way;
Not knowing how to find the open air,
But toiling desperately to find it out,--
Torment myself to catch the English crown:
And from that torment I will free myself,
Or hew my way out with a bloody axe.
Why, I can smile, and murder whiles I smile,
And cry 'Content' to that which grieves my heart,
And wet my cheeks with artificial tears,
And frame my face to all occasions.
I'll drown more sailors than the mermaid shall;
I'll slay more gazers than the basilisk;
I'll play the orator as well as Nestor,
Deceive more slily than Ulysses could,
And, like a Sinon, take another Troy.
I can add colours to the chameleon,
Change shapes with Proteus for advantages,
And set the murderous Machiavel to school.
Can I do this, and cannot get a crown?
Tut, were it farther off, I'll pluck it down.
Exit

SCENE III. France. KING LEWIS XI's palace.
Flourish. Enter KING LEWIS XI, his sister BONA, his Admiral, called BOURBON, PRINCE EDWARD, QUEEN MARGARET, and OXFORD. KING LEWIS XI sits, and riseth up again

KING LEWIS XI
Fair Queen of England, worthy Margaret,
Sit down with us: it ill befits thy state
And birth, that thou shouldst stand while Lewis doth sit.

QUEEN MARGARET
No, mighty King of France: now Margaret
Must strike her sail and learn awhile to serve
Where kings command. I was, I must confess,
Great Albion's queen in former golden days:
But now mischance hath trod my title down,
And with dishonour laid me on the ground;
Where I must take like seat unto my fortune,
And to my humble seat conform myself.
KING LEWIS XI
Why, say, fair queen, whence springs this deep despair?
QUEEN MARGARET
From such a cause as fills mine eyes with tears
And stops my tongue, while heart is drown'd in cares.
KING LEWIS XI
Whate'er it be, be thou still like thyself,
And sit thee by our side:
Seats her by him
Yield not thy neck
To fortune's yoke, but let thy dauntless mind
Still ride in triumph over all mischance.
Be plain, Queen Margaret, and tell thy grief;
It shall be eased, if France can yield relief.
QUEEN MARGARET
Those gracious words revive my drooping thoughts
And give my tongue-tied sorrows leave to speak.
Now, therefore, be it known to noble Lewis,
That Henry, sole possessor of my love,
Is of a king become a banish'd man,
And forced to live in Scotland a forlorn;
While proud ambitious Edward Duke of York
Usurps the regal title and the seat
Of England's true-anointed lawful king.
This is the cause that I, poor Margaret,
With this my son, Prince Edward, Henry's heir,
Am come to crave thy just and lawful aid;
And if thou fail us, all our hope is done:
Scotland hath will to help, but cannot help;
Our people and our peers are both misled,
Our treasures seized, our soldiers put to flight,
And, as thou seest, ourselves in heavy plight.
KING LEWIS XI
Renowned queen, with patience calm the storm,
While we bethink a means to break it off.
QUEEN MARGARET
The more we stay, the stronger grows our foe.
KING LEWIS XI
The more I stay, the more I'll succor thee.
QUEEN MARGARET
O, but impatience waiteth on true sorrow.
And see where comes the breeder of my sorrow!
Enter WARWICK
KING LEWIS XI
What's he approacheth boldly to our presence?
QUEEN MARGARET
Our Earl of Warwick, Edward's greatest friend.
KING LEWIS XI
Welcome, brave Warwick! What brings thee to France?
He descends. She ariseth
QUEEN MARGARET
Ay, now begins a second storm to rise;
For this is he that moves both wind and tide.
WARWICK

From worthy Edward, King of Albion,
My lord and sovereign, and thy vowed friend,
I come, in kindness and unfeigned love,
First, to do greetings to thy royal person;
And then to crave a league of amity;
And lastly, to confirm that amity
With a nuptial knot, if thou vouchsafe to grant
That virtuous Lady Bona, thy fair sister,
To England's king in lawful marriage.
QUEEN MARGARET
[Aside] If that go forward, Henry's hope is done.
WARWICK
[To BONA] And, gracious madam, in our king's behalf,
I am commanded, with your leave and favour,
Humbly to kiss your hand, and with my tongue
To tell the passion of my sovereign's heart;
Where fame, late entering at his heedful ears,
Hath placed thy beauty's image and thy virtue.
QUEEN MARGARET
King Lewis and Lady Bona, hear me speak,
Before you answer Warwick. His demand
Springs not from Edward's well-meant honest love,
But from deceit bred by necessity;
For how can tyrants safely govern home,
Unless abroad they purchase great alliance?
To prove him tyrant this reason may suffice,
That Henry liveth still: but were he dead,
Yet here Prince Edward stands, King Henry's son.
Look, therefore, Lewis, that by this league and marriage
Thou draw not on thy danger and dishonour;
For though usurpers sway the rule awhile,
Yet heavens are just, and time suppresseth wrongs.
WARWICK
Injurious Margaret!
PRINCE EDWARD
And why not queen?
WARWICK
Because thy father Henry did usurp;
And thou no more are prince than she is queen.
OXFORD
Then Warwick disannuls great John of Gaunt,
Which did subdue the greatest part of Spain;
And, after John of Gaunt, Henry the Fourth,
Whose wisdom was a mirror to the wisest;
And, after that wise prince, Henry the Fifth,
Who by his prowess conquered all France:
From these our Henry lineally descends.
WARWICK
Oxford, how haps it, in this smooth discourse,
You told not how Henry the Sixth hath lost
All that which Henry Fifth had gotten?
Methinks these peers of France should smile at that.
But for the rest, you tell a pedigree
Of threescore and two years; a silly time
To make prescription for a kingdom's worth.
OXFORD
Why, Warwick, canst thou speak against thy liege,
Whom thou obeyed'st thirty and six years,
And not bewray thy treason with a blush?
WARWICK
Can Oxford, that did ever fence the right,
Now buckler falsehood with a pedigree?
For shame! leave Henry, and call Edward king.

OXFORD
Call him my king by whose injurious doom
My elder brother, the Lord Aubrey Vere,
Was done to death? and more than so, my father,
Even in the downfall of his mellow'd years,
When nature brought him to the door of death?
No, Warwick, no; while life upholds this arm,
This arm upholds the house of Lancaster.
WARWICK
And I the house of York.
KING LEWIS XI
Queen Margaret, Prince Edward, and Oxford,
Vouchsafe, at our request, to stand aside,
While I use further conference with Warwick.
They stand aloof
QUEEN MARGARET
Heavens grant that Warwick's words bewitch him not!
KING LEWIS XI
Now Warwick, tell me, even upon thy conscience,
Is Edward your true king? for I were loath
To link with him that were not lawful chosen.
WARWICK
Thereon I pawn my credit and mine honour.
KING LEWIS XI
But is he gracious in the people's eye?
WARWICK
The more that Henry was unfortunate.
KING LEWIS XI
Then further, all dissembling set aside,
Tell me for truth the measure of his love
Unto our sister Bona.
WARWICK
Such it seems
As may beseem a monarch like himself.
Myself have often heard him say and swear
That this his love was an eternal plant,
Whereof the root was fix'd in virtue's ground,
The leaves and fruit maintain'd with beauty's sun,
Exempt from envy, but not from disdain,
Unless the Lady Bona quit his pain.
KING LEWIS XI
Now, sister, let us hear your firm resolve.
BONA
Your grant, or your denial, shall be mine:
To WARWICK
Yet I confess that often ere this day,
When I have heard your king's desert recounted,
Mine ear hath tempted judgment to desire.
KING LEWIS XI
Then, Warwick, thus: our sister shall be Edward's;
And now forthwith shall articles be drawn
Touching the jointure that your king must make,
Which with her dowry shall be counterpoised.
Draw near, Queen Margaret, and be a witness
That Bona shall be wife to the English king.
PRINCE EDWARD
To Edward, but not to the English king.
QUEEN MARGARET
Deceitful Warwick! it was thy device
By this alliance to make void my suit:
Before thy coming Lewis was Henry's friend.
KING LEWIS XI

And still is friend to him and Margaret:
But if your title to the crown be weak,
As may appear by Edward's good success,
Then 'tis but reason that I be released
From giving aid which late I promised.
Yet shall you have all kindness at my hand
That your estate requires and mine can yield.

WARWICK
Henry now lives in Scotland at his ease,
Where having nothing, nothing can he lose.
And as for you yourself, our quondam queen,
You have a father able to maintain you;
And better 'twere you troubled him than France.

QUEEN MARGARET
Peace, impudent and shameless Warwick, peace,
Proud setter up and puller down of kings!
I will not hence, till, with my talk and tears,
Both full of truth, I make King Lewis behold
Thy sly conveyance and thy lord's false love;
For both of you are birds of selfsame feather.
Post blows a horn within

KING LEWIS XI
Warwick, this is some post to us or thee.
Enter a Post

Post
[To WARWICK] My lord ambassador, these letters are for you,
Sent from your brother, Marquess Montague:
To KING LEWIS XI
These from our king unto your majesty:
To QUEEN MARGARET
And, madam, these for you; from whom I know not.
They all read their letters

OXFORD
I like it well that our fair queen and mistress
Smiles at her news, while Warwick frowns at his.

PRINCE EDWARD
Nay, mark how Lewis stamps, as he were nettled:
I hope all's for the best.

KING LEWIS XI
Warwick, what are thy news? and yours, fair queen?

QUEEN MARGARET
Mine, such as fill my heart with unhoped joys.

WARWICK
Mine, full of sorrow and heart's discontent.

KING LEWIS XI
What! has your king married the Lady Grey!
And now, to soothe your forgery and his,
Sends me a paper to persuade me patience?
Is this the alliance that he seeks with France?
Dare he presume to scorn us in this manner?

QUEEN MARGARET
I told your majesty as much before:
This proveth Edward's love and Warwick's honesty.

WARWICK
King Lewis, I here protest, in sight of heaven,
And by the hope I have of heavenly bliss,
That I am clear from this misdeed of Edward's,
No more my king, for he dishonours me,
But most himself, if he could see his shame.
Did I forget that by the house of York
My father came untimely to his death?
Did I let pass the abuse done to my niece?
Did I impale him with the regal crown?

Did I put Henry from his native right?
And am I guerdon'd at the last with shame?
Shame on himself! for my desert is honour:
And to repair my honour lost for him,
I here renounce him and return to Henry.
My noble queen, let former grudges pass,
And henceforth I am thy true servitor:
I will revenge his wrong to Lady Bona,
And replant Henry in his former state.
QUEEN MARGARET
Warwick, these words have turn'd my hate to love;
And I forgive and quite forget old faults,
And joy that thou becomest King Henry's friend.
WARWICK
So much his friend, ay, his unfeigned friend,
That, if King Lewis vouchsafe to furnish us
With some few bands of chosen soldiers,
I'll undertake to land them on our coast
And force the tyrant from his seat by war.
'Tis not his new-made bride shall succor him:
And as for Clarence, as my letters tell me,
He's very likely now to fall from him,
For matching more for wanton lust than honour,
Or than for strength and safety of our country.
BONA
Dear brother, how shall Bona be revenged
But by thy help to this distressed queen?
QUEEN MARGARET
Renowned prince, how shall poor Henry live,
Unless thou rescue him from foul despair?
BONA
My quarrel and this English queen's are one.
WARWICK
And mine, fair lady Bona, joins with yours.
KING LEWIS XI
And mine with hers, and thine, and Margaret's.
Therefore at last I firmly am resolved
You shall have aid.
QUEEN MARGARET
Let me give humble thanks for all at once.
KING LEWIS XI
Then, England's messenger, return in post,
And tell false Edward, thy supposed king,
That Lewis of France is sending over masquers
To revel it with him and his new bride:
Thou seest what's past, go fear thy king withal.
BONA
Tell him, in hope he'll prove a widower shortly,
I'll wear the willow garland for his sake.
QUEEN MARGARET
Tell him, my mourning weeds are laid aside,
And I am ready to put armour on.
WARWICK
Tell him from me that he hath done me wrong,
And therefore I'll uncrown him ere't be long.
There's thy reward: be gone.
Exit Post
KING LEWIS XI
But, Warwick,
Thou and Oxford, with five thousand men,
Shall cross the seas, and bid false Edward battle;
And, as occasion serves, this noble queen
And prince shall follow with a fresh supply.

Yet, ere thou go, but answer me one doubt,
What pledge have we of thy firm loyalty?
WARWICK
This shall assure my constant loyalty,
That if our queen and this young prince agree,
I'll join mine eldest daughter and my joy
To him forthwith in holy wedlock bands.
QUEEN MARGARET
Yes, I agree, and thank you for your motion.
Son Edward, she is fair and virtuous,
Therefore delay not, give thy hand to Warwick;
And, with thy hand, thy faith irrevocable,
That only Warwick's daughter shall be thine.
PRINCE EDWARD
Yes, I accept her, for she well deserves it;
And here, to pledge my vow, I give my hand.
He gives his hand to WARWICK
KING LEWIS XI
Why stay we now? These soldiers shall be levied,
And thou, Lord Bourbon, our high admiral,
Shalt waft them over with our royal fleet.
I long till Edward fall by war's mischance,
For mocking marriage with a dame of France.
Exeunt all but WARWICK
WARWICK
I came from Edward as ambassador,
But I return his sworn and mortal foe:
Matter of marriage was the charge he gave me,
But dreadful war shall answer his demand.
Had he none else to make a stale but me?
Then none but I shall turn his jest to sorrow.
I was the chief that raised him to the crown,
And I'll be chief to bring him down again:
Not that I pity Henry's misery,
But seek revenge on Edward's mockery.
Exit

ACT IV

SCENE I. London. The palace.
Enter GLOUCESTER, CLARENCE, SOMERSET, and MONTAGUE
GLOUCESTER
Now tell me, brother Clarence, what think you
Of this new marriage with the Lady Grey?
Hath not our brother made a worthy choice?
CLARENCE
Alas, you know, 'tis far from hence to France;
How could he stay till Warwick made return?
SOMERSET
My lords, forbear this talk; here comes the king.
GLOUCESTER
And his well-chosen bride.
CLARENCE
I mind to tell him plainly what I think.
Flourish. Enter KING EDWARD IV, attended; QUEEN ELIZABETH, PEMBROKE, STAFFORD, HASTINGS, and others
KING EDWARD IV
Now, brother of Clarence, how like you our choice,
That you stand pensive, as half malcontent?
CLARENCE
As well as Lewis of France, or the Earl of Warwick,
Which are so weak of courage and in judgment
That they'll take no offence at our abuse.
KING EDWARD IV
Suppose they take offence without a cause,
They are but Lewis and Warwick: I am Edward,
Your king and Warwick's, and must have my will.
GLOUCESTER
And shall have your will, because our king:
Yet hasty marriage seldom proveth well.
KING EDWARD IV
Yea, brother Richard, are you offended too?
GLOUCESTER
Not I:
No, God forbid that I should wish them sever'd
Whom God hath join'd together; ay, and 'twere pity
To sunder them that yoke so well together.
KING EDWARD IV
Setting your scorns and your mislike aside,
Tell me some reason why the Lady Grey
Should not become my wife and England's queen.
And you too, Somerset and Montague,
Speak freely what you think.
CLARENCE
Then this is mine opinion: that King Lewis
Becomes your enemy, for mocking him
About the marriage of the Lady Bona.
GLOUCESTER
And Warwick, doing what you gave in charge,
Is now dishonoured by this new marriage.
KING EDWARD IV
What if both Lewis and Warwick be appeased
By such invention as I can devise?
MONTAGUE
Yet, to have join'd with France in such alliance
Would more have strengthen'd this our commonwealth
'Gainst foreign storms than any home-bred marriage.
HASTINGS
Why, knows not Montague that of itself
England is safe, if true within itself?
MONTAGUE

But the safer when 'tis back'd with France.
HASTINGS
'Tis better using France than trusting France:
Let us be back'd with God and with the seas
Which He hath given for fence impregnable,
And with their helps only defend ourselves;
In them and in ourselves our safety lies.
CLARENCE
For this one speech Lord Hastings well deserves
To have the heir of the Lord Hungerford.
KING EDWARD IV
Ay, what of that? it was my will and grant;
And for this once my will shall stand for law.
GLOUCESTER
And yet methinks your grace hath not done well,
To give the heir and daughter of Lord Scales
Unto the brother of your loving bride;
She better would have fitted me or Clarence:
But in your bride you bury brotherhood.
CLARENCE
Or else you would not have bestow'd the heir
Of the Lord Bonville on your new wife's son,
And leave your brothers to go speed elsewhere.
KING EDWARD IV
Alas, poor Clarence! is it for a wife
That thou art malcontent? I will provide thee.
CLARENCE
In choosing for yourself, you show'd your judgment,
Which being shallow, you give me leave
To play the broker in mine own behalf;
And to that end I shortly mind to leave you.
KING EDWARD IV
Leave me, or tarry, Edward will be king,
And not be tied unto his brother's will.
QUEEN ELIZABETH
My lords, before it pleased his majesty
To raise my state to title of a queen,
Do me but right, and you must all confess
That I was not ignoble of descent;
And meaner than myself have had like fortune.
But as this title honours me and mine,
So your dislike, to whom I would be pleasing,
Doth cloud my joys with danger and with sorrow.
KING EDWARD IV
My love, forbear to fawn upon their frowns:
What danger or what sorrow can befall thee,
So long as Edward is thy constant friend,
And their true sovereign, whom they must obey?
Nay, whom they shall obey, and love thee too,
Unless they seek for hatred at my hands;
Which if they do, yet will I keep thee safe,
And they shall feel the vengeance of my wrath.
GLOUCESTER
[Aside] I hear, yet say not much, but think the more.
Enter a Post
KING EDWARD IV
Now, messenger, what letters or what news
From France?
Post
My sovereign liege, no letters; and few words,
But such as I, without your special pardon,
Dare not relate.
KING EDWARD IV

Go to, we pardon thee: therefore, in brief,
Tell me their words as near as thou canst guess them.
What answer makes King Lewis unto our letters?
Post
At my depart, these were his very words:
'Go tell false Edward, thy supposed king,
That Lewis of France is sending over masquers
To revel it with him and his new bride.'
KING EDWARD IV
Is Lewis so brave? belike he thinks me Henry.
But what said Lady Bona to my marriage?
Post
These were her words, utter'd with mad disdain:
'Tell him, in hope he'll prove a widower shortly,
I'll wear the willow garland for his sake.'
KING EDWARD IV
I blame not her, she could say little less;
She had the wrong. But what said Henry's queen?
For I have heard that she was there in place.
Post
'Tell him,' quoth she, 'my mourning weeds are done,
And I am ready to put armour on.'
KING EDWARD IV
Belike she minds to play the Amazon.
But what said Warwick to these injuries?
Post
He, more incensed against your majesty
Than all the rest, discharged me with these words:
'Tell him from me that he hath done me wrong,
And therefore I'll uncrown him ere't be long.'
KING EDWARD IV
Ha! durst the traitor breathe out so proud words?
Well I will arm me, being thus forewarn'd:
They shall have wars and pay for their presumption.
But say, is Warwick friends with Margaret?
Post
Ay, gracious sovereign; they are so link'd in friendship
That young Prince Edward marries Warwick's daughter.
CLARENCE
Belike the elder; Clarence will have the younger.
Now, brother king, farewell, and sit you fast,
For I will hence to Warwick's other daughter;
That, though I want a kingdom, yet in marriage
I may not prove inferior to yourself.
You that love me and Warwick, follow me.
Exit CLARENCE, and SOMERSET follows
GLOUCESTER
[Aside] Not I:
My thoughts aim at a further matter; I
Stay not for the love of Edward, but the crown.
KING EDWARD IV
Clarence and Somerset both gone to Warwick!
Yet am I arm'd against the worst can happen;
And haste is needful in this desperate case.
Pembroke and Stafford, you in our behalf
Go levy men, and make prepare for war;
They are already, or quickly will be landed:
Myself in person will straight follow you.
Exeunt PEMBROKE and STAFFORD
But, ere I go, Hastings and Montague,
Resolve my doubt. You twain, of all the rest,
Are near to Warwick by blood and by alliance:

Tell me if you love Warwick more than me?
If it be so, then both depart to him;
I rather wish you foes than hollow friends:
But if you mind to hold your true obedience,
Give me assurance with some friendly vow,
That I may never have you in suspect.
MONTAGUE
So God help Montague as he proves true!
HASTINGS
And Hastings as he favours Edward's cause!
KING EDWARD IV
Now, brother Richard, will you stand by us?
GLOUCESTER
Ay, in despite of all that shall withstand you.
KING EDWARD IV
Why, so! then am I sure of victory.
Now therefore let us hence; and lose no hour,
Till we meet Warwick with his foreign power.
Exeunt
SCENE II. A plain in Warwickshire.
Enter WARWICK and OXFORD, with French soldiers
WARWICK
Trust me, my lord, all hitherto goes well;
The common people by numbers swarm to us.
Enter CLARENCE and SOMERSET
But see where Somerset and Clarence come!
Speak suddenly, my lords, are we all friends?
CLARENCE
Fear not that, my lord.
WARWICK
Then, gentle Clarence, welcome unto Warwick;
And welcome, Somerset: I hold it cowardice
To rest mistrustful where a noble heart
Hath pawn'd an open hand in sign of love;
Else might I think that Clarence, Edward's brother,
Were but a feigned friend to our proceedings:
But welcome, sweet Clarence; my daughter shall be thine.
And now what rests but, in night's coverture,
Thy brother being carelessly encamp'd,
His soldiers lurking in the towns about,
And but attended by a simple guard,
We may surprise and take him at our pleasure?
Our scouts have found the adventure very easy:
That as Ulysses and stout Diomede
With sleight and manhood stole to Rhesus' tents,
And brought from thence the Thracian fatal steeds,
So we, well cover'd with the night's black mantle,
At unawares may beat down Edward's guard
And seize himself; I say not, slaughter him,
For I intend but only to surprise him.
You that will follow me to this attempt,
Applaud the name of Henry with your leader.
They all cry, 'Henry!'
Why, then, let's on our way in silent sort:
For Warwick and his friends, God and Saint George!
Exeunt
SCENE III. Edward's camp, near Warwick.
Enter three Watchmen, to guard KING EDWARD IV's tent
First Watchman
Come on, my masters, each man take his stand:
The king by this is set him down to sleep.
Second Watchman
What, will he not to bed?

First Watchman
Why, no; for he hath made a solemn vow
Never to lie and take his natural rest
Till Warwick or himself be quite suppress'd.
Second Watchman
To-morrow then belike shall be the day,
If Warwick be so near as men report.
Third Watchman
But say, I pray, what nobleman is that
That with the king here resteth in his tent?
First Watchman
'Tis the Lord Hastings, the king's chiefest friend.
Third Watchman
O, is it so? But why commands the king
That his chief followers lodge in towns about him,
While he himself keeps in the cold field?
Second Watchman
'Tis the more honour, because more dangerous.
Third Watchman
Ay, but give me worship and quietness;
I like it better than a dangerous honour.
If Warwick knew in what estate he stands,
'Tis to be doubted he would waken him.
First Watchman
Unless our halberds did shut up his passage.
Second Watchman
Ay, wherefore else guard we his royal tent,
But to defend his person from night-foes?
Enter WARWICK, CLARENCE, OXFORD, SOMERSET, and French soldiers, silent all
WARWICK
This is his tent; and see where stand his guard.
Courage, my masters! honour now or never!
But follow me, and Edward shall be ours.
First Watchman
Who goes there?
Second Watchman
Stay, or thou diest!
WARWICK and the rest cry all, 'Warwick! Warwick!' and set upon the Guard, who fly, crying, 'Arm! arm!' WARWICK and the rest following them
The drum playing and trumpet sounding, reenter WARWICK, SOMERSET, and the rest, bringing KING EDWARD IV out in his gown, sitting in a chair. RICHARD and HASTINGS fly over the stage
SOMERSET
What are they that fly there?
WARWICK
Richard and Hastings: let them go; here is The duke.
KING EDWARD IV
The duke! Why, Warwick, when we parted,
Thou call'dst me king.
WARWICK
Ay, but the case is alter'd:
When you disgraced me in my embassade,
Then I degraded you from being king,
And come now to create you Duke of York.
Alas! how should you govern any kingdom,
That know not how to use ambassadors,
Nor how to be contented with one wife,
Nor how to use your brothers brotherly,
Nor how to study for the people's welfare,
Nor how to shroud yourself from enemies?
KING EDWARD IV
Yea, brother of Clarence, are thou here too?
Nay, then I see that Edward needs must down.
Yet, Warwick, in despite of all mischance,

Of thee thyself and all thy complices,
Edward will always bear himself as king:
Though fortune's malice overthrow my state,
My mind exceeds the compass of her wheel.
WARWICK
Then, for his mind, be Edward England's king:
Takes off his crown
But Henry now shall wear the English crown,
And be true king indeed, thou but the shadow.
My Lord of Somerset, at my request,
See that forthwith Duke Edward be convey'd
Unto my brother, Archbishop of York.
When I have fought with Pembroke and his fellows,
I'll follow you, and tell what answer
Lewis and the Lady Bona send to him.
Now, for a while farewell, good Duke of York.
They lead him out forcibly
KING EDWARD IV
What fates impose, that men must needs abide;
It boots not to resist both wind and tide.
Exit, guarded
OXFORD
What now remains, my lords, for us to do
But march to London with our soldiers?
WARWICK
Ay, that's the first thing that we have to do;
To free King Henry from imprisonment
And see him seated in the regal throne.
Exeunt
SCENE IV. London. The palace.
Enter QUEEN ELIZABETH and RIVERS
RIVERS
Madam, what makes you in this sudden change?
QUEEN ELIZABETH
Why brother Rivers, are you yet to learn
What late misfortune is befall'n King Edward?
RIVERS
What! loss of some pitch'd battle against Warwick?
QUEEN ELIZABETH
No, but the loss of his own royal person.
RIVERS
Then is my sovereign slain?
QUEEN ELIZABETH
Ay, almost slain, for he is taken prisoner,
Either betray'd by falsehood of his guard
Or by his foe surprised at unawares:
And, as I further have to understand,
Is new committed to the Bishop of York,
Fell Warwick's brother and by that our foe.
RIVERS
These news I must confess are full of grief;
Yet, gracious madam, bear it as you may:
Warwick may lose, that now hath won the day.
QUEEN ELIZABETH
Till then fair hope must hinder life's decay.
And I the rather wean me from despair
For love of Edward's offspring in my womb:
This is it that makes me bridle passion
And bear with mildness my misfortune's cross;
Ay, ay, for this I draw in many a tear
And stop the rising of blood-sucking sighs,
Lest with my sighs or tears I blast or drown
King Edward's fruit, true heir to the English crown.

RIVERS
But, madam, where is Warwick then become?
QUEEN ELIZABETH
I am inform'd that he comes towards London,
To set the crown once more on Henry's head:
Guess thou the rest; King Edward's friends must down,
But, to prevent the tyrant's violence,--
For trust not him that hath once broken faith,--
I'll hence forthwith unto the sanctuary,
To save at least the heir of Edward's right:
There shall I rest secure from force and fraud.
Come, therefore, let us fly while we may fly:
If Warwick take us we are sure to die.
Exeunt

SCENE V. A park near Middleham Castle In Yorkshire.
Enter GLOUCESTER, HASTINGS, and STANLEY
GLOUCESTER
Now, my Lord Hastings and Sir William Stanley,
Leave off to wonder why I drew you hither,
Into this chiefest thicket of the park.
Thus stands the case: you know our king, my brother,
Is prisoner to the bishop here, at whose hands
He hath good usage and great liberty,
And, often but attended with weak guard,
Comes hunting this way to disport himself.
I have advertised him by secret means
That if about this hour he make his way
Under the colour of his usual game,
He shall here find his friends with horse and men
To set him free from his captivity.
Enter KING EDWARD IV and a Huntsman with him
Huntsman
This way, my lord; for this way lies the game.
KING EDWARD IV
Nay, this way, man: see where the huntsmen stand.
Now, brother of Gloucester, Lord Hastings, and the rest,
Stand you thus close, to steal the bishop's deer?
GLOUCESTER
Brother, the time and case requireth haste:
Your horse stands ready at the park-corner.
KING EDWARD IV
But whither shall we then?
HASTINGS
To Lynn, my lord,
And ship from thence to Flanders.
GLOUCESTER
Well guess'd, believe me; for that was my meaning.
KING EDWARD IV
Stanley, I will requite thy forwardness.
GLOUCESTER
But wherefore stay we? 'tis no time to talk.
KING EDWARD IV
Huntsman, what say'st thou? wilt thou go along?
Huntsman
Better do so than tarry and be hang'd.
GLOUCESTER
Come then, away; let's ha' no more ado.
KING EDWARD IV
Bishop, farewell: shield thee from Warwick's frown;
And pray that I may repossess the crown.
Exeunt

SCENE VI. London. The Tower.

Flourish. Enter KING HENRY VI, CLARENCE, WARWICK, SOMERSET, HENRY OF RICHMOND, OXFORD, MONTAGUE, *and Lieutenant of the Tower*

KING HENRY VI
Master lieutenant, now that God and friends
Have shaken Edward from the regal seat,
And turn'd my captive state to liberty,
My fear to hope, my sorrows unto joys,
At our enlargement what are thy due fees?
Lieutenant
Subjects may challenge nothing of their sovereigns;
But if an humble prayer may prevail,
I then crave pardon of your majesty.
KING HENRY VI
For what, lieutenant? for well using me?
Nay, be thou sure I'll well requite thy kindness,
For that it made my imprisonment a pleasure;
Ay, such a pleasure as incaged birds
Conceive when after many moody thoughts
At last by notes of household harmony
They quite forget their loss of liberty.
But, Warwick, after God, thou set'st me free,
And chiefly therefore I thank God and thee;
He was the author, thou the instrument.
Therefore, that I may conquer fortune's spite
By living low, where fortune cannot hurt me,
And that the people of this blessed land
May not be punish'd with my thwarting stars,
Warwick, although my head still wear the crown,
I here resign my government to thee,
For thou art fortunate in all thy deeds.
WARWICK
Your grace hath still been famed for virtuous;
And now may seem as wise as virtuous,
By spying and avoiding fortune's malice,
For few men rightly temper with the stars:
Yet in this one thing let me blame your grace,
For choosing me when Clarence is in place.
CLARENCE
No, Warwick, thou art worthy of the sway,
To whom the heavens in thy nativity
Adjudged an olive branch and laurel crown,
As likely to be blest in peace and war;
And therefore I yield thee my free consent.
WARWICK
And I choose Clarence only for protector.
KING HENRY VI
Warwick and Clarence give me both your hands:
Now join your hands, and with your hands your hearts,
That no dissension hinder government:
I make you both protectors of this land,
While I myself will lead a private life
And in devotion spend my latter days,
To sin's rebuke and my Creator's praise.
WARWICK
What answers Clarence to his sovereign's will?
CLARENCE
That he consents, if Warwick yield consent;
For on thy fortune I repose myself.
WARWICK
Why, then, though loath, yet must I be content:
We'll yoke together, like a double shadow
To Henry's body, and supply his place;
I mean, in bearing weight of government,

While he enjoys the honour and his ease.
And, Clarence, now then it is more than needful
Forthwith that Edward be pronounced a traitor,
And all his lands and goods be confiscate.
CLARENCE
What else? and that succession be determined.
WARWICK
Ay, therein Clarence shall not want his part.
KING HENRY VI
But, with the first of all your chief affairs,
Let me entreat, for I command no more,
That Margaret your queen and my son Edward
Be sent for, to return from France with speed;
For, till I see them here, by doubtful fear
My joy of liberty is half eclipsed.
CLARENCE
It shall be done, my sovereign, with all speed.
KING HENRY VI
My Lord of Somerset, what youth is that,
Of whom you seem to have so tender care?
SOMERSET
My liege, it is young Henry, earl of Richmond.
KING HENRY VI
Come hither, England's hope.
Lays his hand on his head
If secret powers
Suggest but truth to my divining thoughts,
This pretty lad will prove our country's bliss.
His looks are full of peaceful majesty,
His head by nature framed to wear a crown,
His hand to wield a sceptre, and himself
Likely in time to bless a regal throne.
Make much of him, my lords, for this is he
Must help you more than you are hurt by me.
Enter a Post
WARWICK
What news, my friend?
Post
That Edward is escaped from your brother,
And fled, as he hears since, to Burgundy.
WARWICK
Unsavoury news! but how made he escape?
Post
He was convey'd by Richard Duke of Gloucester
And the Lord Hastings, who attended him
In secret ambush on the forest side
And from the bishop's huntsmen rescued him;
For hunting was his daily exercise.
WARWICK
My brother was too careless of his charge.
But let us hence, my sovereign, to provide
A salve for any sore that may betide.
Exeunt all but SOMERSET, HENRY OF RICHMOND, and OXFORD
SOMERSET
My lord, I like not of this flight of Edward's;
For doubtless Burgundy will yield him help,
And we shall have more wars before 't be long.
As Henry's late presaging prophecy
Did glad my heart with hope of this young Richmond,
So doth my heart misgive me, in these conflicts
What may befall him, to his harm and ours:
Therefore, Lord Oxford, to prevent the worst,

Forthwith we'll send him hence to Brittany,
Till storms be past of civil enmity.
OXFORD
Ay, for if Edward repossess the crown,
'Tis like that Richmond with the rest shall down.
SOMERSET
It shall be so; he shall to Brittany.
Come, therefore, let's about it speedily.
Exeunt
SCENE VII. Before York.
Flourish. Enter KING EDWARD IV, GLOUCESTER, HASTINGS, and Soldiers
KING EDWARD IV
Now, brother Richard, Lord Hastings, and the rest,
Yet thus far fortune maketh us amends,
And says that once more I shall interchange
My waned state for Henry's regal crown.
Well have we pass'd and now repass'd the seas
And brought desired help from Burgundy:
What then remains, we being thus arrived
From Ravenspurgh haven before the gates of York,
But that we enter, as into our dukedom?
GLOUCESTER
The gates made fast! Brother, I like not this;
For many men that stumble at the threshold
Are well foretold that danger lurks within.
KING EDWARD IV
Tush, man, abodements must not now affright us:
By fair or foul means we must enter in,
For hither will our friends repair to us.
HASTINGS
My liege, I'll knock once more to summon them.
Enter, on the walls, the Mayor of York, and his Brethren
Mayor
My lords, we were forewarned of your coming,
And shut the gates for safety of ourselves;
For now we owe allegiance unto Henry.
KING EDWARD IV
But, master mayor, if Henry be your king,
Yet Edward at the least is Duke of York.
Mayor
True, my good lord; I know you for no less.
KING EDWARD IV
Why, and I challenge nothing but my dukedom,
As being well content with that alone.
GLOUCESTER
[Aside] But when the fox hath once got in his nose,
He'll soon find means to make the body follow.
HASTINGS
Why, master mayor, why stand you in a doubt?
Open the gates; we are King Henry's friends.
Mayor
Ay, say you so? the gates shall then be open'd.
They descend
GLOUCESTER
A wise stout captain, and soon persuaded!
HASTINGS
The good old man would fain that all were well,
So 'twere not 'long of him; but being enter'd,
I doubt not, I, but we shall soon persuade
Both him and all his brothers unto reason.
Enter the Mayor and two Aldermen, below
KING EDWARD IV

So, master mayor: these gates must not be shut
But in the night or in the time of war.
What! fear not, man, but yield me up the keys;
Takes his keys
For Edward will defend the town and thee,
And all those friends that deign to follow me.
March. Enter MONTGOMERY, with drum and soldiers
GLOUCESTER
Brother, this is Sir John Montgomery,
Our trusty friend, unless I be deceived.
KING EDWARD IV
Welcome, Sir John! But why come you in arms?
MONTAGUE
To help King Edward in his time of storm,
As every loyal subject ought to do.
KING EDWARD IV
Thanks, good Montgomery; but we now forget
Our title to the crown and only claim
Our dukedom till God please to send the rest.
MONTAGUE
Then fare you well, for I will hence again:
I came to serve a king and not a duke.
Drummer, strike up, and let us march away.
The drum begins to march
KING EDWARD IV
Nay, stay, Sir John, awhi le, and we'll debate
By what safe means the crown may be recover'd.
MONTAGUE
What talk you of debating? in few words,
If you'll not here proclaim yourself our king,
I'll leave you to your fortune and be gone
To keep them back that come to succor you:
Why shall we fight, if you pretend no title?
GLOUCESTER
Why, brother, wherefore stand you on nice points?
KING EDWARD IV
When we grow stronger, then we'll make our claim:
Till then, 'tis wisdom to conceal our meaning.
HASTINGS
Away with scrupulous wit! now arms must rule.
GLOUCESTER
And fearless minds climb soonest unto crowns.
Brother, we will proclaim you out of hand:
The bruit thereof will bring you many friends.
KING EDWARD IV
Then be it as you will; for 'tis my right,
And Henry but usurps the diadem.
MONTAGUE
Ay, now my sovereign speaketh like himself;
And now will I be Edward's champion.
HASTINGS
Sound trumpet; Edward shall be here proclaim'd:
Come, fellow-soldier, make thou proclamation.
Flourish
Soldier
Edward the Fourth, by the grace of God, king of
England and France, and lord of Ireland, & c.
MONTAGUE
And whosoe'er gainsays King Edward's right,
By this I challenge him to single fight.
Throws down his gauntlet
All
Long live Edward the Fourth!

KING EDWARD IV
Thanks, brave Montgomery; and thanks unto you all:
If fortune serve me, I'll requite this kindness.
Now, for this night, let's harbour here in York;
And when the morning sun shall raise his car
Above the border of this horizon,
We'll forward towards Warwick and his mates;
For well I wot that Henry is no soldier.
Ah, froward Clarence! how evil it beseems thee
To flatter Henry and forsake thy brother!
Yet, as we may, we'll meet both thee and Warwick.
Come on, brave soldiers: doubt not of the day,
And, that once gotten, doubt not of large pay.
Exeunt

SCENE VIII. London. The palace.

Flourish. Enter KING HENRY VI, WARWICK, MONTAGUE, CLARENCE, EXETER, and OXFORD

WARWICK
What counsel, lords? Edward from Belgia,
With hasty Germans and blunt Hollanders,
Hath pass'd in safety through the narrow seas,
And with his troops doth march amain to London;
And many giddy people flock to him.

KING HENRY VI
Let's levy men, and beat him back again.

CLARENCE
A little fire is quickly trodden out;
Which, being suffer'd, rivers cannot quench.

WARWICK
In Warwickshire I have true-hearted friends,
Not mutinous in peace, yet bold in war;
Those will I muster up: and thou, son Clarence,
Shalt stir up in Suffolk, Norfolk, and in Kent,
The knights and gentlemen to come with thee:
Thou, brother Montague, in Buckingham,
Northampton and in Leicestershire, shalt find
Men well inclined to hear what thou command'st:
And thou, brave Oxford, wondrous well beloved,
In Oxfordshire shalt muster up thy friends.
My sovereign, with the loving citizens,
Like to his island girt in with the ocean,
Or modest Dian circled with her nymphs,
Shall rest in London till we come to him.
Fair lords, take leave and stand not to reply.
Farewell, my sovereign.

KING HENRY VI
Farewell, my Hector, and my Troy's true hope.

CLARENCE
In sign of truth, I kiss your highness' hand.

KING HENRY VI
Well-minded Clarence, be thou fortunate!

MONTAGUE
Comfort, my lord; and so I take my leave.

OXFORD
And thus I seal my truth, and bid adieu.

KING HENRY VI
Sweet Oxford, and my loving Montague,
And all at once, once more a happy farewell.

WARWICK
Farewell, sweet lords: let's meet at Coventry.
Exeunt all but KING HENRY VI and EXETER

KING HENRY VI
Here at the palace I will rest awhile.
Cousin of Exeter, what thinks your lordship?

Methinks the power that Edward hath in field
Should not be able to encounter mine.
EXETER
The doubt is that he will seduce the rest.
KING HENRY VI
That's not my fear; my meed hath got me fame:
I have not stopp'd mine ears to their demands,
Nor posted off their suits with slow delays;
My pity hath been balm to heal their wounds,
My mildness hath allay'd their swelling griefs,
My mercy dried their water-flowing tears;
I have not been desirous of their wealth,
Nor much oppress'd them with great subsidies.
Nor forward of revenge, though they much err'd:
Then why should they love Edward more than me?
No, Exeter, these graces challenge grace:
And when the lion fawns upon the lamb,
The lamb will never cease to follow him.
Shout within. 'A Lancaster! A Lancaster!'
EXETER
Hark, hark, my lord! what shouts are these?
Enter KING EDWARD IV, GLOUCESTER, and soldiers
KING EDWARD IV
Seize on the shame-faced Henry, bear him hence;
And once again proclaim us King of England.
You are the fount that makes small brooks to flow:
Now stops thy spring; my sea sha$l suck them dry,
And swell so much the higher by their ebb.
Hence with him to the Tower; let him not speak.
Exeunt some with KING HENRY VI
And, lords, towards Coventry bend we our course
Where peremptory Warwick now remains:
The sun shines hot; and, if we use delay,
Cold biting winter mars our hoped-for hay.
GLOUCESTER
Away betimes, before his forces join,
And take the great-grown traitor unawares:
Brave warriors, march amain towards Coventry.
Exeunt

ACT V

SCENE I. Coventry.
Enter WARWICK, the Mayor of Coventry, two Messengers, and others upon the walls
WARWICK
Where is the post that came from valiant Oxford?
How far hence is thy lord, mine honest fellow?
First Messenger
By this at Dunsmore, marching hitherward.
WARWICK
How far off is our brother Montague?
Where is the post that came from Montague?
Second Messenger
By this at Daintry, with a puissant troop.
Enter SIR JOHN SOMERVILLE
WARWICK
Say, Somerville, what says my loving son?
And, by thy guess, how nigh is Clarence now?
SOMERSET
At Southam I did leave him with his forces,
And do expect him here some two hours hence.
Drum heard
WARWICK
Then Clarence is at hand, I hear his drum.
SOMERSET
It is not his, my lord; here Southam lies:
The drum your honour hears marcheth from Warwick.
WARWICK
Who should that be? belike, unlook'd-for friends.
SOMERSET
They are at hand, and you shall quickly know.
March: flourish. Enter KING EDWARD IV, GLOUCESTER, and soldiers
KING EDWARD IV
Go, trumpet, to the walls, and sound a parle.
GLOUCESTER
See how the surly Warwick mans the wall!
WARWICK
O unbid spite! is sportful Edward come?
Where slept our scouts, or how are they seduced,
That we could hear no news of his repair?
KING EDWARD IV
Now, Warwick, wilt thou ope the city gates,
Speak gentle words and humbly bend thy knee,
Call Edward king and at his hands beg mercy?
And he shall pardon thee these outrages.
WARWICK
Nay, rather, wilt thou draw thy forces hence,
Confess who set thee up and pluck'd thee own,
Call Warwick patron and be penitent?
And thou shalt still remain the Duke of York.
GLOUCESTER
I thought, at least, he would have said the king;
Or did he make the jest against his will?
WARWICK
Is not a dukedom, sir, a goodly gift?
GLOUCESTER
Ay, by my faith, for a poor earl to give:
I'll do thee service for so good a gift.
WARWICK
'Twas I that gave the kingdom to thy brother.
KING EDWARD IV
Why then 'tis mine, if but by Warwick's gift.
WARWICK

Thou art no Atlas for so great a weight:
And weakling, Warwick takes his gift again;
And Henry is my king, Warwick his subject.
KING EDWARD IV
But Warwick's king is Edward's prisoner:
And, gallant Warwick, do but answer this:
What is the body when the head is off?
GLOUCESTER
Alas, that Warwick had no more forecast,
But, whiles he thought to steal the single ten,
The king was slily finger'd from the deck!
You left poor Henry at the Bishop's palace,
And, ten to one, you'll meet him in the Tower.
EDWARD
'Tis even so; yet you are Warwick still.
GLOUCESTER
Come, Warwick, take the time; kneel down, kneel down:
Nay, when? strike now, or else the iron cools.
WARWICK
I had rather chop this hand off at a blow,
And with the other fling it at thy face,
Than bear so low a sail, to strike to thee.
KING EDWARD IV
Sail how thou canst, have wind and tide thy friend,
This hand, fast wound about thy coal-black hair
Shall, whiles thy head is warm and new cut off,
Write in the dust this sentence with thy blood,
'Wind-changing Warwick now can change no more.'
Enter OXFORD, with drum and colours
WARWICK
O cheerful colours! see where Oxford comes!
OXFORD
Oxford, Oxford, for Lancaster!
He and his forces enter the city
GLOUCESTER
The gates are open, let us enter too.
KING EDWARD IV
So other foes may set upon our backs.
Stand we in good array; for they no doubt
Will issue out again and bid us battle:
If not, the city being but of small defence,
We'll quickly rouse the traitors in the same.
WARWICK
O, welcome, Oxford! for we want thy help.
Enter MONTAGUE with drum and colours
MONTAGUE
Montague, Montague, for Lancaster!
He and his forces enter the city
GLOUCESTER
Thou and thy brother both shall buy this treason
Even with the dearest blood your bodies bear.
KING EDWARD IV
The harder match'd, the greater victory:
My mind presageth happy gain and conquest.
Enter SOMERSET, with drum and colours
SOMERSET
Somerset, Somerset, for Lancaster!
He and his forces enter the city
GLOUCESTER
Two of thy name, both Dukes of Somerset,
Have sold their lives unto the house of York;
And thou shalt be the third if this sword hold.
Enter CLARENCE, with drum and colours

WARWICK
And lo, where George of Clarence sweeps along,
Of force enough to bid his brother battle;
With whom an upright zeal to right prevails
More than the nature of a brother's love!
Come, Clarence, come; thou wilt, if Warwick call.
CLARENCE
Father of Warwick, know you what this means?
Taking his red rose out of his hat
Look here, I throw my infamy at thee
I will not ruinate my father's house,
Who gave his blood to lime the stones together,
And set up Lancaster. Why, trow'st thou, Warwick,
That Clarence is so harsh, so blunt, unnatural,
To bend the fatal instruments of war
Against his brother and his lawful king?
Perhaps thou wilt object my holy oath:
To keep that oath were more impiety
Than Jephthah's, when he sacrificed his daughter.
I am so sorry for my trespass made
That, to deserve well at my brother's hands,
I here proclaim myself thy mortal foe,
With resolution, wheresoe'er I meet thee--
As I will meet thee, if thou stir abroad--
To plague thee for thy foul misleading me.
And so, proud-hearted Warwick, I defy thee,
And to my brother turn my blushing cheeks.
Pardon me, Edward, I will make amends:
And, Richard, do not frown upon my faults,
For I will henceforth be no more unconstant.
KING EDWARD IV
Now welcome more, and ten times more beloved,
Than if thou never hadst deserved our hate.
GLOUCESTER
Welcome, good Clarence; this is brotherlike.
WARWICK
O passing traitor, perjured and unjust!
KING EDWARD IV
What, Warwick, wilt thou leave the town and fight?
Or shall we beat the stones about thine ears?
WARWICK
Alas, I am not coop'd here for defence!
I will away towards Barnet presently,
And bid thee battle, Edward, if thou darest.
KING EDWARD IV
Yes, Warwick, Edward dares, and leads the way.
Lords, to the field; Saint George and victory!
Exeunt King Edward and his company. March. Warwick and his company follow
SCENE II. A field of battle near Barnet.
Alarum and excursions. Enter KING EDWARD IV, bringing forth WARWICK wounded
KING EDWARD IV
So, lie thou there: die thou, and die our fear;
For Warwick was a bug that fear'd us all.
Now, Montague, sit fast; I seek for thee,
That Warwick's bones may keep thine company.
Exit
WARWICK
Ah, who is nigh? come to me, friend or foe,
And tell me who is victor, York or Warwick?
Why ask I that? my mangled body shows,
My blood, my want of strength, my sick heart shows.
That I must yield my body to the earth
And, by my fall, the conquest to my foe.

Thus yields the cedar to the axe's edge,
Whose arms gave shelter to the princely eagle,
Under whose shade the ramping lion slept,
Whose top-branch overpeer'd Jove's spreading tree
And kept low shrubs from winter's powerful wind.
These eyes, that now are dimm'd with death's black veil,
Have been as piercing as the mid-day sun,
To search the secret treasons of the world:
The wrinkles in my brows, now filled with blood,
Were liken'd oft to kingly sepulchres;
For who lived king, but I could dig his grave?
And who durst mine when Warwick bent his brow?
Lo, now my glory smear'd in dust and blood!
My parks, my walks, my manors that I had.
Even now forsake me, and of all my lands
Is nothing left me but my body's length.
Why, what is pomp, rule, reign, but earth and dust?
And, live we how we can, yet die we must.
Enter OXFORD and SOMERSET
SOMERSET
Ah, Warwick, Warwick! wert thou as we are.
We might recover all our loss again;
The queen from France hath brought a puissant power:
Even now we heard the news: ah, could'st thou fly!
WARWICK
Why, then I would not fly. Ah, Montague,
If thou be there, sweet brother, take my hand.
And with thy lips keep in my soul awhile!
Thou lovest me not; for, brother, if thou didst,
Thy tears would wash this cold congealed blood
That glues my lips and will not let me speak.
Come quickly, Montague, or I am dead.
SOMERSET
Ah, Warwick! Montague hath breathed his last;
And to the latest gasp cried out for Warwick,
And said 'Commend me to my valiant brother.'
And more he would have said, and more he spoke,
Which sounded like a clamour in a vault,
That mought not be distinguished; but at last
I well might hear, delivered with a groan,
'O, farewell, Warwick!'
WARWICK
Sweet rest his soul! Fly, lords, and save yourselves;
For Warwick bids you all farewell to meet in heaven.
Dies
OXFORD
Away, away, to meet the queen's great power!
Here they bear away his body. Exeunt
SCENE III. Another part of the field.
Flourish. Enter KING EDWARD IV in triumph; with GLOUCESTER, CLARENCE, and the rest
KING EDWARD IV
Thus far our fortune keeps an upward course,
And we are graced with wreaths of victory.
But, in the midst of this bright-shining day,
I spy a black, suspicious, threatening cloud,
That will encounter with our glorious sun,
Ere he attain his easeful western bed:
I mean, my lords, those powers that the queen
Hath raised in Gallia have arrived our coast
And, as we hear, march on to fight with us.
CLARENCE
A little gale will soon disperse that cloud
And blow it to the source from whence it came:

The very beams will dry those vapours up,
For every cloud engenders not a storm.
GLOUCESTER
The queen is valued thirty thousand strong,
And Somerset, with Oxford fled to her:
If she have time to breathe be well assured
Her faction will be full as strong as ours.
KING EDWARD IV
We are advertised by our loving friends
That they do hold their course toward Tewksbury:
We, having now the best at Barnet field,
Will thither straight, for willingness rids way;
And, as we march, our strength will be augmented
In every county as we go along.
Strike up the drum; cry 'Courage!' and away.
Exeunt

SCENE IV. Plains near Tewksbury.
March. Enter QUEEN MARGARET, PRINCE EDWARD, SOMERSET, OXFORD, and soldiers
QUEEN MARGARET
Great lords, wise men ne'er sit and wail their loss,
But cheerly seek how to redress their harms.
What though the mast be now blown overboard,
The cable broke, the holding-anchor lost,
And half our sailors swallow'd in the flood?
Yet lives our pilot still. Is't meet that he
Should leave the helm and like a fearful lad
With tearful eyes add water to the sea
And give more strength to that which hath too much,
Whiles, in his moan, the ship splits on the rock,
Which industry and courage might have saved?
Ah, what a shame! ah, what a fault were this!
Say Warwick was our anchor; what of that?
And Montague our topmost; what of him?
Our slaughter'd friends the tackles; what of these?
Why, is not Oxford here another anchor?
And Somerset another goodly mast?
The friends of France our shrouds and tacklings?
And, though unskilful, why not Ned and I
For once allow'd the skilful pilot's charge?
We will not from the helm to sit and weep,
But keep our course, though the rough wind say no,
From shelves and rocks that threaten us with wreck.
As good to chide the waves as speak them fair.
And what is Edward but ruthless sea?
What Clarence but a quicksand of deceit?
And Richard but a ragged fatal rock?
All these the enemies to our poor bark.
Say you can swim; alas, 'tis but a while!
Tread on the sand; why, there you quickly sink:
Bestride the rock; the tide will wash you off,
Or else you famish; that's a threefold death.
This speak I, lords, to let you understand,
If case some one of you would fly from us,
That there's no hoped-for mercy with the brothers
More than with ruthless waves, with sands and rocks.
Why, courage then! what cannot be avoided
'Twere childish weakness to lament or fear.
PRINCE EDWARD
Methinks a woman of this valiant spirit
Should, if a coward heard her speak these words,
Infuse his breast with magnanimity
And make him, naked, foil a man at arms.
I speak not this as doubting any here

For did I but suspect a fearful man
He should have leave to go away betimes,
Lest in our need he might infect another
And make him of like spirit to himself.
If any such be here--as God forbid!--
Let him depart before we need his help.
OXFORD
Women and children of so high a courage,
And warriors faint! why, 'twere perpetual shame.
O brave young prince! thy famous grandfather
Doth live again in thee: long mayst thou live
To bear his image and renew his glories!
SOMERSET
And he that will not fight for such a hope.
Go home to bed, and like the owl by day,
If he arise, be mock'd and wonder'd at.
QUEEN MARGARET
Thanks, gentle Somerset; sweet Oxford, thanks.
PRINCE EDWARD
And take his thanks that yet hath nothing else.
Enter a Messenger
Messenger
Prepare you, lords, for Edward is at hand.
Ready to fight; therefore be resolute.
OXFORD
I thought no less: it is his policy
To haste thus fast, to find us unprovided.
SOMERSET
But he's deceived; we are in readiness.
QUEEN MARGARET
This cheers my heart, to see your forwardness.
OXFORD
Here pitch our battle; hence we will not budge.
Flourish and march. Enter KING EDWARD IV, GLOUCESTER, CLARENCE, and soldiers
KING EDWARD IV
Brave followers, yonder stands the thorny wood,
Which, by the heavens' assistance and your strength,
Must by the roots be hewn up yet ere night.
I need not add more fuel to your fire,
For well I wot ye blaze to burn them out
Give signal to the fight, and to it, lords!
QUEEN MARGARET
Lords, knights, and gentlemen, what I should say
My tears gainsay; for every word I speak,
Ye see, I drink the water of mine eyes.
Therefore, no more but this: Henry, your sovereign,
Is prisoner to the foe; his state usurp'd,
His realm a slaughter-house, his subjects slain,
His statutes cancell'd and his treasure spent;
And yonder is the wolf that makes this spoil.
You fight in justice: then, in God's name, lords,
Be valiant and give signal to the fight.
Alarum. Retreat. Excursions. Exeunt
SCENE V. Another part of the field.
Flourish. Enter KING EDWARD IV, GLOUCESTER, CLARENCE, and soldiers; with QUEEN MARGARET, OXFORD, and SOMERSET, prisoners
KING EDWARD IV
Now here a period of tumultuous broils.
Away with Oxford to Hames Castle straight:
For Somerset, off with his guilty head.
Go, bear them hence; I will not hear them speak.
OXFORD
For my part, I'll not trouble thee with words.

SOMERSET
Nor I, but stoop with patience to my fortune.
Exeunt Oxford and Somerset, guarded
QUEEN MARGARET
So part we sadly in this troublous world,
To meet with joy in sweet Jerusalem.
KING EDWARD IV
Is proclamation made, that who finds Edward
Shall have a high reward, and he his life?
GLOUCESTER
It is: and lo, where youthful Edward comes!
Enter soldiers, with PRINCE EDWARD
KING EDWARD IV
Bring forth the gallant, let us hear him speak.
What! can so young a thorn begin to prick?
Edward, what satisfaction canst thou make
For bearing arms, for stirring up my subjects,
And all the trouble thou hast turn'd me to?
PRINCE EDWARD
Speak like a subject, proud ambitious York!
Suppose that I am now my father's mouth;
Resign thy chair, and where I stand kneel thou,
Whilst I propose the selfsame words to thee,
Which traitor, thou wouldst have me answer to.
QUEEN MARGARET
Ah, that thy father had been so resolved!
GLOUCESTER
That you might still have worn the petticoat,
And ne'er have stol'n the breech from Lancaster.
PRINCE EDWARD
Let AEsop fable in a winter's night;
His currish riddles sort not with this place.
GLOUCESTER
By heaven, brat, I'll plague ye for that word.
QUEEN MARGARET
Ay, thou wast born to be a plague to men.
GLOUCESTER
For God's sake, take away this captive scold.
PRINCE EDWARD
Nay, take away this scolding crookback rather.
KING EDWARD IV
Peace, wilful boy, or I will charm your tongue.
CLARENCE
Untutor'd lad, thou art too malapert.
PRINCE EDWARD
I know my duty; you are all undutiful:
Lascivious Edward, and thou perjured George,
And thou mis-shapen Dick, I tell ye all
I am your better, traitors as ye are:
And thou usurp'st my father's right and mine.
KING EDWARD IV
Take that, thou likeness of this railer here.
Stabs him
GLOUCESTER
Sprawl'st thou? take that, to end thy agony.
Stabs him
CLARENCE
And there's for twitting me with perjury.
Stabs him
QUEEN MARGARET
O, kill me too!
GLOUCESTER
Marry, and shall.

Offers to kill her
KING EDWARD IV
Hold, Richard, hold; for we have done too much.
GLOUCESTER
Why should she live, to fill the world with words?
KING EDWARD IV
What, doth she swoon? use means for her recovery.
GLOUCESTER
Clarence, excuse me to the king my brother;
I'll hence to London on a serious matter:
Ere ye come there, be sure to hear some news.
CLARENCE
What? what?
GLOUCESTER
The Tower, the Tower.
Exit
QUEEN MARGARET
O Ned, sweet Ned! speak to thy mother, boy!
Canst thou not speak? O traitors! murderers!
They that stabb'd Caesar shed no blood at all,
Did not offend, nor were not worthy blame,
If this foul deed were by to equal it:
He was a man; this, in respect, a child:
And men ne'er spend their fury on a child.
What's worse than murderer, that I may name it?
No, no, my heart will burst, and if I speak:
And I will speak, that so my heart may burst.
Butchers and villains! bloody cannibals!
How sweet a plant have you untimely cropp'd!
You have no children, butchers! if you had,
The thought of them would have stirr'd up remorse:
But if you ever chance to have a child,
Look in his youth to have him so cut off
As, deathmen, you have rid this sweet young prince!
KING EDWARD IV
Away with her; go, bear her hence perforce.
QUEEN MARGARET
Nay, never bear me hence, dispatch me here,
Here sheathe thy sword, I'll pardon thee my death:
What, wilt thou not? then, Clarence, do it thou.
CLARENCE
By heaven, I will not do thee so much ease.
QUEEN MARGARET
Good Clarence, do; sweet Clarence, do thou do it.
CLARENCE
Didst thou not hear me swear I would not do it?
QUEEN MARGARET
Ay, but thou usest to forswear thyself:
'Twas sin before, but now 'tis charity.
What, wilt thou not? Where is that devil's butcher,
Hard-favour'd Richard? Richard, where art thou?
Thou art not here: murder is thy alms-deed;
Petitioners for blood thou ne'er put'st back.
KING EDWARD IV
Away, I say; I charge ye, bear her hence.
QUEEN MARGARET
So come to you and yours, as to this Prince!
Exit, led out forcibly
KING EDWARD IV
Where's Richard gone?
CLARENCE
To London, all in post; and, as I guess,
To make a bloody supper in the Tower.

KING EDWARD IV
He's sudden, if a thing comes in his head.
Now march we hence: discharge the common sort
With pay and thanks, and let's away to London
And see our gentle queen how well she fares:
By this, I hope, she hath a son for me.
Exeunt

SCENE VI. London. The Tower.

Enter KING HENRY VI and GLOUCESTER, with the Lieutenant, on the walls

GLOUCESTER
Good day, my lord. What, at your book so hard?

KING HENRY VI
Ay, my good lord:--my lord, I should say rather;
'Tis sin to flatter; 'good' was little better:
'Good Gloucester' and 'good devil' were alike,
And both preposterous; therefore, not 'good lord.'

GLOUCESTER
Sirrah, leave us to ourselves: we must confer.
Exit Lieutenant

KING HENRY VI
So flies the reckless shepherd from the wolf;
So first the harmless sheep doth yield his fleece
And next his throat unto the butcher's knife.
What scene of death hath Roscius now to act?

GLOUCESTER
Suspicion always haunts the guilty mind;
The thief doth fear each bush an officer.

KING HENRY VI
The bird that hath been limed in a bush,
With trembling wings misdoubteth every bush;
And I, the hapless male to one sweet bird,
Have now the fatal object in my eye
Where my poor young was limed, was caught and kill'd.

GLOUCESTER
Why, what a peevish fool was that of Crete,
That taught his son the office of a fowl!
An yet, for all his wings, the fool was drown'd.

KING HENRY VI
I, Daedalus; my poor boy, Icarus;
Thy father, Minos, that denied our course;
The sun that sear'd the wings of my sweet boy
Thy brother Edward, and thyself the sea
Whose envious gulf did swallow up his life.
Ah, kill me with thy weapon, not with words!
My breast can better brook thy dagger's point
Than can my ears that tragic history.
But wherefore dost thou come? is't for my life?

GLOUCESTER
Think'st thou I am an executioner?

KING HENRY VI
A persecutor, I am sure, thou art:
If murdering innocents be executing,
Why, then thou art an executioner.

GLOUCESTER
Thy son I kill'd for his presumption.

KING HENRY VI
Hadst thou been kill'd when first thou didst presume,
Thou hadst not lived to kill a son of mine.
And thus I prophesy, that many a thousand,
Which now mistrust no parcel of my fear,
And many an old man's sigh and many a widow's,
And many an orphan's water-standing eye--
Men for their sons, wives for their husbands,

And orphans for their parents timeless death--
Shall rue the hour that ever thou wast born.
The owl shriek'd at thy birth,--an evil sign;
The night-crow cried, aboding luckless time;
Dogs howl'd, and hideous tempest shook down trees;
The raven rook'd her on the chimney's top,
And chattering pies in dismal discords sung.
Thy mother felt more than a mother's pain,
And, yet brought forth less than a mother's hope,
To wit, an indigested and deformed lump,
Not like the fruit of such a goodly tree.
Teeth hadst thou in thy head when thou wast born,
To signify thou camest to bite the world:
And, if the rest be true which I have heard,
Thou camest--
GLOUCESTER
I'll hear no more: die, prophet in thy speech:
Stabs him
For this amongst the rest, was I ordain'd.
KING HENRY VI
Ay, and for much more slaughter after this.
God forgive my sins, and pardon thee!
Dies
GLOUCESTER
What, will the aspiring blood of Lancaster
Sink in the ground? I thought it would have mounted.
See how my sword weeps for the poor king's death!
O, may such purple tears be alway shed
From those that wish the downfall of our house!
If any spark of life be yet remaining,
Down, down to hell; and say I sent thee thither:
Stabs him again
I, that have neither pity, love, nor fear.
Indeed, 'tis true that Henry told me of;
For I have often heard my mother say
I came into the world with my legs forward:
Had I not reason, think ye, to make haste,
And seek their ruin that usurp'd our right?
The midwife wonder'd and the women cried
'O, Jesus bless us, he is born with teeth!'
And so I was; which plainly signified
That I should snarl and bite and play the dog.
Then, since the heavens have shaped my body so,
Let hell make crook'd my mind to answer it.
I have no brother, I am like no brother;
And this word 'love,' which graybeards call divine,
Be resident in men like one another
And not in me: I am myself alone.
Clarence, beware; thou keep'st me from the light:
But I will sort a pitchy day for thee;
For I will buz abroad such prophecies
That Edward shall be fearful of his life,
And then, to purge his fear, I'll be thy death.
King Henry and the prince his son are gone:
Clarence, thy turn is next, and then the rest,
Counting myself but bad till I be best.
I'll throw thy body in another room
And triumph, Henry, in thy day of doom.
Exit, with the body
SCENE VII. London. The palace.
Flourish. Enter KING EDWARD IV, QUEEN ELIZABETH, CLARENCE, GLOUCESTER, HASTINGS, a Nurse with the young Prince, and Attendants
KING EDWARD IV

Once more we sit in England's royal throne,
Re-purchased with the blood of enemies.
What valiant foemen, like to autumn's corn,
Have we mow'd down, in tops of all their pride!
Three Dukes of Somerset, threefold renown'd
For hardy and undoubted champions;
Two Cliffords, as the father and the son,
And two Northumberlands; two braver men
Ne'er spurr'd their coursers at the trumpet's sound;
With them, the two brave bears, Warwick and Montague,
That in their chains fetter'd the kingly lion
And made the forest tremble when they roar'd.
Thus have we swept suspicion from our seat
And made our footstool of security.
Come hither, Bess, and let me kiss my boy.
Young Ned, for thee, thine uncles and myself
Have in our armours watch'd the winter's night,
Went all afoot in summer's scalding heat,
That thou mightst repossess the crown in peace;
And of our labours thou shalt reap the gain.
GLOUCESTER
[Aside] I'll blast his harvest, if your head were laid;
For yet I am not look'd on in the world.
This shoulder was ordain'd so thick to heave;
And heave it shall some weight, or break my back:
Work thou the way,--and thou shalt execute.
KING EDWARD IV
Clarence and Gloucester, love my lovely queen;
And kiss your princely nephew, brothers both.
CLARENCE
The duty that I owe unto your majesty
I seal upon the lips of this sweet babe.
QUEEN ELIZABETH
Thanks, noble Clarence; worthy brother, thanks.
GLOUCESTER
And, that I love the tree from whence thou sprang'st,
Witness the loving kiss I give the fruit.
Aside
And cried 'all hail!' when as he meant all harm.
KING EDWARD IV
Now am I seated as my soul delights,
Having my country's peace and brothers' loves.
CLARENCE
What will your grace have done with Margaret?
Reignier, her father, to the king of France
Hath pawn'd the Sicils and Jerusalem,
And hither have they sent it for her ransom.
KING EDWARD IV
Away with her, and waft her hence to France.
And now what rests but that we spend the time
With stately triumphs, mirthful comic shows,
Such as befits the pleasure of the court?
Sound drums and trumpets! farewell sour annoy!
For here, I hope, begins our lasting joy.
Exeunt

Printed in Great Britain
by Amazon